Getting What She Wants

OTHER ELLORA'S CAVE ANTHOLOGIES
AVAILABLE FROM POCKET BOOKS

Insatiable
By Sherri L. King, Elizabeth Jewell, & S. L. Carpenter

His Fantasies, Her Dreams
By Sherri L. King, S. L. Carpenter, & Trista Ann Michaels

Master Of Secret Desires
By S. L. Carpenter, Elizabeth Jewell, & Tawny Taylor

Bedtime, Playtime
By Jaid Black, Sherri L. King, & Ruth D. Kerce

Hurts So Good
By Gail Faulkner, Lisa Renee Jones, & Sahara Kelly

Lover From Another World
By Rachel Carrington, Elizabeth Jewell, & Shiloh Walker

Fever-Hot Dreams
By Sherri L. King, Jaci Burton, & Samantha Winston

Taming Him
By Kimberly Dean, Summer Devon, & Michelle M. Pillow

All She Wants
By Jaid Black, Dominique Adair, & Shiloh Walker

Getting What She Wants

Diana Hunter
S. L. Carpenter
Chris Tanglen

POCKET BOOKS
New York London Toronto Sydney

Pocket Books
A Division of Simon & Schuster, Inc.
1230 Avenue of the Americas
New York, NY 10020

This book is a work of fiction. Names, characters, places, and incidents either are products of the authors' imagination or are used fictitiously. Any resemblance to actual events or locales or persons, living or dead, is entirely coincidental.

Published by arrangement with Ellora's Cave Publishing, Inc.

First Pocket Books trade paperback edition September 2007

For information about special discounts for bulk purchases, please contact Simon & Schuster Special Sales at 1-800-456-6798 or business@simonandschuster.com

Manufactured in the United States of America

10 9 8 7 6 5 4 3 2 1

Library of Congress Cataloging-in-Publication Data

Getting What She Wants / Diana Hunter, S. L. Carpenter, Chris Tanglen. —1st Pocket Books trade pbk. ed.
p. cm.
1. Erotic stories, American. 2. American fiction—21st century. 1. Hunter, Diana. Hooked. II. Carpenter, S. L. In the end. III. Tanglen, Chris. Mistress Charlotte.
PS648.E7N68 2007
813.'60803538—dc22

2007005489

ISBN-13: 978-1-4165-3618-5

Getting What She Wants

Contents

Hooked

Diana Hunter

For my editor, Pam Campbell, whose polishing cloth is
responsible for making this story into a true gem.

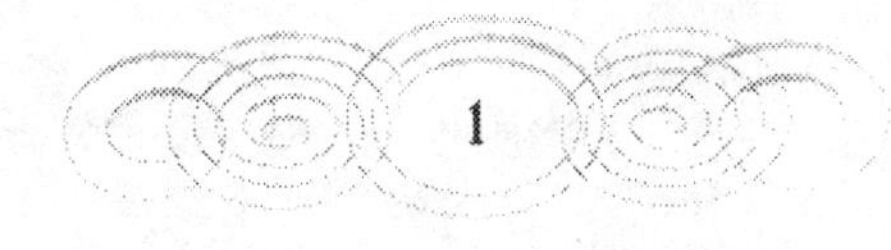

1

Strolling down the busy downtown street, Tania Pelligrini swayed her hips in their tight leather pants. Her stiletto sandals clicked along the sidewalk, their laces tied in neat little bows just above her heels. Bright red nail polish gleamed from her toes in the same shade that shone on her perfectly manicured fingernails. Long tawny hair, swept up into an untidy ponytail, curled tendrils of silk around the sharp features of her face. Her ample bosom, barely contained in the short-sleeved stretch top, bounced enticingly with every step.

Keeping her chin tilted down, she looked up through long lashes and smiled coyly at every man she passed. Whistles filled the air as she passed a construction zone and she waved and grinned at the men leaning from the beams to look their fill. A woman pulled a little girl from her path and scorn crossed Tania's face. She had no disease the child would catch. Except joy in her own sexuality. And that, Tania wished for the little girl with all her heart.

During business hours, Tania dressed with the decorum expected of one who worked in a prestigious law firm, even if she was a lowly research assistant. The pay was good, the hours predictable and at the age of thirty-five, Tania had no aspirations to change her career. The lawyers in the firm treated her well and she got along with them all. From the custodian to the head lawyer affectionately known as the Old Man, all knew her name and she knew theirs.

Except today was Saturday and Tania was horny. With no one special in her life, she hadn't had sex in almost a year. Long ago she had decided that dating coworkers was too messy when things didn't work out—and sometimes even when they did. She enjoyed her independence. No one's sensitive ego to tiptoe around, no one's schedule to have to match. No one she had to prod into action when she was in the mood.

What had happened to all the "take charge" kind of guys? Had the women's movement succeeded in bleeding all the life out of men?

No, she was better off alone even if it meant taking her pleasure by herself. She'd lost count of the late-night sessions she had with the variety of toys she had purchased to keep herself occupied. For a long time, the toys had satisfied her. They didn't talk back or walk out on you, even though she did need to clean up after them and feed them batteries every once in a while. She grinned at the thought and added a lilt to her step.

Unfortunately, the motor had burned out of her favorite toy two weeks ago. And while she knew she could go buy another one, Tania just didn't have the urge. She wanted more than what her toys could offer.

And so this morning, after dressing for fun, Tania had headed out her apartment door and aimed for downtown. The malls provided better shopping for the masses, but tucked away in the corners of the city were shops infinitely more interesting than the mass-market offerings of the suburban malls. With no agenda in mind other than doing a little shopping and striking up a conversation with the first handsome man she found, Tania sauntered along the street.

Jim Delaney had no idea what was about to hit him. His fortieth birthday loomed not too far away and he'd been waking up feeling his age more and more every day. He ate right, visited the gym three times a week and biked to work in addition to his daily regimen of exercise and a three-mile walk. In spite of all this, his body still protested when he forced it out of bed each morning.

He changed his walking route every day, as much for variety as for other reasons. Although his old girlfriend had finally stopped stalking him, threatening retribution for her own guilty interest in kinky sex, Jim still chose not to settle into a routine she could count on. Currently dressed in khaki walking shorts and a white T-shirt, Jim's physique made him the envy of his friends and turned the heads of many women on the street. No paunch hung over his belt, no flab gathered under his chin. Trim and fit with just a touch of gray at the temples in his otherwise black hair, Jim's sexy appearance called to mind the predator of the boardroom, a place he thrived.

The fact that he had inherited his company from his father didn't take away from his accomplishments since taking the helm. He'd expanded their market while keeping both the products' and the company's integrity. For that, his male employees admired him. His female employees adored him. He knew that women primped and preened when he walked by, but his attention was never more than polite. How could he ever explain to a modern-day woman that his sexual interests were politically incorrect? His last foray had proven disastrous.

This Saturday, Jim chose a route that would take him through a quiet section of downtown rather than the more residential areas. With no one special in his life right now, he found himself in need of some company, even though he had adopted a scruffy appearance for the day. He hadn't shaved and he had let the summer wind dry his hair any way it wanted to. His purposeful walk led him along the secondary streets preferred by the city's native pedestrians and into some of the busier neighborhoods.

A sociable man by nature, he didn't subscribe to the attitude held by so many city people. He looked people in the eye as he passed them, knowing only a few would meet his gaze to make a small connection in the sea of people surrounding them. Men more than women returned his glance, which did not surprise him. Over the years he discovered women tended to shield themselves, cloak their bodies in invisible armor to keep strange men at bay. Not that he blamed them. Too many lunatics out there on the street. Playing it safe was totally understandable. But there was no reason he couldn't look and appreciate the beauty of the women he passed.

The smile in his eyes remained as he passed a woman and her little girl. The woman stared straight ahead, as if her eyes could bore a hole that would tunnel the two of them straight to their destination. The little girl's manner was still innocent and untrained, however. She looked around her with the curiosity given to the very young. Her eyes met Jim's and she smiled up at him, revealing a pretty smile that was all the better for the missing two front teeth.

Jim winked at her as they passed and his heart lightened. As long as there were children in the world, there was hope. A sappy thought, but one that sustained him when the mother gave him a dirty look and sniffed. He wished happiness on the child as he continued his brisk walk.

A small café, its four tiny tables nestled under an oversized awning, beckoned to Tania's thirst. Surrounded by a low wrought iron railing, the café would give her respite from her heels, yet still allow her to watch the passersby. It was just too charming to pass up.

Entering the outside enclave, she took the last available table. Using one painted wrought iron chair for her packages, she sank into the other, leaning back with a grateful sigh. Smiling cheerfully at the older but still handsome waiter, she gave him the once-over and accompanying nod of approval before ordering water with lemon.

Her morning had been productive. One small shop, run by a woman from India, produced a beautiful sleeveless silk dress that would go wonderfully with the flat sandals she found in a Moroccan shop. Just two shops down from the café, she'd found a lingerie shop but, after considerable window shopping, did not go in. She had no one to buy sexy things for.

The thought distressed her only a little. Her sister married early and soon gave Tania nieces to dote on. Perhaps someday she would like a family of her own, but for right now, she found being the favorite aunt was actually a role she very much enjoyed. It let her play the heroine when she offered to take the kids for the weekend so Sarah and Rob could have some time together. And on Sunday night, she could give the kids back.

Leaning back with a contented sigh, she took in the view. Tourists and businessmen in their professional attitudes would never find this little out-of-the-way side street. Just the locals knew and populated it with their diversity. Across the street, an older, established Greek market vied for customers with the new Korean market just moved in next door. Shouts in Greek and Korean mingled with the languages of Mexico and Indonesia. Somehow a French café seemed to fit right in with the polyglot cacophony.

And into the mix walked a tiger. Jim Delaney's unshaven appearance did not hide his controlled demeanor, nor his obvious enjoyment of the life that teemed around him. His step, almost cocky in nature, bounced him into Tania's line of sight, and her breath caught in a way it hadn't in quite some time. So when Jim's gaze roved over the patrons of the café, Tania made sure their eyes met.

The striking woman's eyes did not fall or look away. Instead they held a challenge and Jim paused on the sidewalk to smile back at her. His mind filtered through his acquaintances and came up empty. Besides, that smile was a come-hither look if ever he'd seen one. And he was a sucker for those tendrils of dark golden hair that curled around her face.

A waiter approached her table, being sure to lean in to get the full effect of the woman's low-cut top. She rewarded him with a smile and a straightening of her shoulders, flicking her glance back toward him to see if he might also like a closer look.

Jim grinned at the woman's obvious flirtation and it appealed to his ego. Giving her a once-over of his own, he noted the stilettos and the tight pants. The table blocked his view of her waist, but it didn't matter. Her other attributes were presented for display and he liked a woman with ample breasts.

By the time his gaze returned to her face, lust had settled in his groin. Probably a hooker, he decided, then shrugged. He wasn't one to turn down an afternoon's delight just because he would have to pay for it. And his libido could use a good workout, even if it came from a professional. It had been far too long since he had gotten what he wanted from a woman. Another glance around the tables showed only one empty chair, fortuitously the one that held the sexy woman's packages.

The sexy beast sauntered into the shade of the café, casting an inquiring glance in her direction. She nodded and sat up, removing the bags from the chair beside her. Tania watched, intrigued by the bulge in his pants as the tall, handsome stranger pulled the chair closer to hers as he sat.

Tania liked the way his look covered her entire body and she tilted her head to smile at him, almost demure in her own appreciation of his appearance. No beard to tickle her when he kissed her, she noted... only a little weekend scruff. Cunning dimples that played hide-and-seek in his cheeks. Dark hair long enough to tousle and hold on to in passion, and deep blue eyes that twinkled even in the shade of the café awning.

The breeze tossed his scent in her direction—she inhaled deeply, trying him out. A light cologne greeted her, mixed with the perspiration of a walk in the sun. Leaning forward to give him a close-up view of what he'd ogled from the street, she put her hand out in introduction.

"Hi, I'm Tania. Looks like you could use a glass of water."

"Jim Delaney." Decorum dictated that he simply shake her hand and then release her. But her fingers were cool as they wrapped around his and he held it for a moment longer than he would have in polite society. His eyes were again drawn to her breasts, their rounded hills glimmering with a slight sheen in the heat of the day.

"May I take your order, sir?"

Jim barely glanced up at the waiter's abrupt tone. "Water with a lime twist. And then a menu, please."

"Two menus." Tania looked up at the waiter through her lashes and smiled at him. "Please."

Almost tripping over himself, the waiter hurried off to comply.

Oh, she was good, Jim thought to himself as he watched the old man turn into a puddle of jelly. There was another who would willingly pay for the privilege of seeing more of the sexy woman who now turned her attention back to him and smiled.

"Glorious day, isn't it?"

"It is." Now that he sat beside her, he noted the tight leather and tall heels. Weren't those the kind called "fuck me" shoes?

Jim considered the direct approach, but then shied away from it when a uniformed patrol officer strolled by on the sidewalk outside the small fence that separated the café from the passing traffic. Narrowing his eyes, he considered whether she might be setting him up.

"So tell me, Tania. What's a nice girl like you doing in a place like this?" He smiled after delivering the corny line and Tania laughed. It was a pleasant sound, he decided. And he liked the way her eyes crinkled at the corners when she found something funny.

"Just resting my feet. Shade and a seat are a necessity after an exhausting morning of shopping." With an exaggerated motion toward her packages and an overacted sigh, she met his levity, then raised the stakes. "And what's a handsome man like you doing in a neighborhood like this?"

Tania leaned forward on the table, resting her chin in her hand and giving him a full view of her cleavage.

Jim's eyes fell toward her breasts before he glanced up at her again. No blush painted her cheeks, only a coy smile and an invitation in her eyes. For a moment he was discomfited. While women often flirted with him, they were never quite so transparent. And Jim's tastes in sexual activity weren't every woman's cup of tea. Was she truly up to what he thought she was up to? His cock, semihard and beginning to be a bit uncomfortable, certainly voted in her favor.

While Jim still considered his answer, the waiter returned with water and menus, and the question was forgotten as they spent the next several minutes perusing the choices, exchanging small talk about what might be good and discovering neither of them had ever visited this café before. "Fate" Tania called it. "Fortuitous" Jim thought.

The waiter took their orders and disappeared again into the cool recesses of the small restaurant, leaving them to find the threads of their mutual flirtation. Tania reclined in her chair, once more leaning against the heart-shaped back, stretching her legs under the table at an angle to his.

Jim turned to face her, leaning his arm on the back of his chair, ignoring the way the hard, thin metal bit into his skin. Easing his hips, he allowed his cock more room, noting Tania's eyes taking him in. Even though still constrained by the material of his walking shorts, Jim was not a small man. When his college roommate had given him the nickname "Big Jim", it hadn't been because of the width of his muscular shoulders.

Stretched before him, Tania's body was a feast for his eyes and Jim ate up the sight. Her long, slender legs, cased in skintight black leather, led to full hips accentuated by a narrow waist, tightly belted. As his gaze lingered on the curves of her blouse, lust bloomed in his cock and he gave it full rein. This hooker was certainly a looker, as the guys in college used to say. And a hooker would accept his need to dominate her in the bedroom without all the feminist angst that other women seemed to have. The thought of stripping the tight clothes from her and pinning her under him as he ravaged her body with his touch brought his cock to full and uncomfortable hardness in the confines of his walking shorts.

Tania saw him growing, and grinned openly. She loved having that effect on men. This one was hooked. Now all she had to do was decide whether to keep him or throw him back. If he recognized she was more than just a great body, she would play the line a little longer before deciding whether to land him or not. And she did like that little touch of gray at his temples. Very sexy.

"So do you walk this way often?" Tania almost winced at the banality of the question that popped out of her mouth, but the idiotic question was already between them. Instead she grinned, letting him know she knew the question was lame.

"No, rarely, in fact. I take a different route each day." Toasting her with his water glass, he downed the entire contents in one long, thirsty pull.

Tania sat, mesmerized by the way his Adam's apple bobbed up and down as he drank the entire glass of ice-cold water. The perspiration that had clung to his brow when he first sat down was rapidly evaporating in the shade. Tania glanced down at his cock. Still as hard as ever. She resisted the urge to reach over and feel if it was real.

The waiter brought the salads they'd ordered and Tania did not miss the dirty look he gave to Jim as he set the plate in front of her new acquaintance. All smiles for her, the waiter gave one last venomous glance at Jim before disappearing into the cool interior of the café.

Tania laughed out loud. "You might want to switch salads with me. I think the waiter has it in for you."

Jim's grin, rueful and dimpled, played about his lips as he answered her. "Something tells me I can take him on. Or would you rather I not provoke a brawl in the name of your beauty?"

"Oh, it's getting deep in here!" Tania laughed and a woman from the table beside her flicked an envious glance in her direction. "But keep it coming, I like your compliments."

Over their salads, the two talked of nothing of consequence and everything of importance. She discovered his favorite color was light blue and she told him hers was deep purple. She liked seafood, he liked steak. He preferred the arcade and she preferred the roller coaster.

Jim decided Tania couldn't be more opposite to his own tastes, yet was still drawn to her overt sexiness. All through lunch, Tania's eyes remained focused on him as if he were the most important man she had ever met. Only the waiter ever got her attention, and in increasingly smaller increments. The salads were done, the check would come soon. If he wanted her for the rest of the afternoon, it was time to make his move.

"Tania, I would like to spend more time with you. Do you have any plans for today?"

Her smile deepened into a lopsided grin and she gave him her best Mae West imitation. "What did you have in mind, big boy?" Leaning forward, she rested her hand on his bare thigh, caressing the soft, dark hairs with the backs of her fingers.

Jim reached up and played idly with one of her loose strands of hair, curling it around his finger and pulling her face closer to his. Deliberately, he kissed those teasing lips, inhaling the scent of her perfume. And when he was done, he released her almost casually, leaning back in his chair to sip from the water the waiter had replenished. "That's what I had in mind, sexy."

"Oh, I like your style. I do, very much." Tania almost purred. That kiss had left her almost breathless. Playing with her toys would never be the same again.

The waiter came with the bill on a small tray and pointedly placed it beside Jim's plate. Without even glancing at it, Jim pulled a credit card from his wallet and placed it on top of the bill. As Tania started to protest, Jim held up his hand and motioned to the waiter to take care of the matter. With a small look of triumph, the waiter stalked off, bill and card in hand.

"Jim, you shouldn't pay for my lunch."

"Why not? Meeting you and sharing your table was an unexpected pleasure today. And I'm hoping to have more of your company this afternoon." The last time Jim had been in the company of a hooker had been over a decade ago and he couldn't remember if he had bought her dinner first or not. Whatever the etiquette, he was about to get laid and he was sure it was worth far more than the price of a lunch salad.

Tania smiled. "I'd like to have more of your company, too. But that's beside the point."

"What *is* the point?"

That stopped her. For the life of her, Tania could not think of a single reason why he shouldn't offer to pay for her lunch. And this guy had been pretty quick with the card the waiter now returned. Was he rich?

Not that it mattered. She had no illusions about what Jim wanted. The man wanted sex and that was fine with her. The feeling was mutual. Her foray into the city looked like it was about to pay off.

"Walk me home?" Tania reached for the bags she had accumulated in her morning's foray through some of the neighborhood's more interesting shops, but Jim beat her to them. With a gallant flourish, he lifted them and extended his hand to her as if she were the Queen of England. Grinning, she accepted his hand, slipping into a royal pose and smoothly weaving her way through the café's occupied tables.

Tania kept her eyes down and the coy smile on her lips as she sashayed down the crowded street, a man at her side to carry her packages. What was that old film where the man took the packages from the woman and showed her how to walk and get men's attention? *Easter Parade*, that was it. Tilting her chin up and putting on her best Judy Garland face, she enjoyed every glance, stare and ogle.

Continuing to flirt with Jim as they made their way back to her apartment, Tania found herself more and more intrigued by the tall man beside her. With each passing step, her attention became less and less focused on those they passed and more and more focused on the man beside her. This one had the makings of a real keeper.

All too soon they came to the brick building that was home for her. While they'd walked, Tania debated how to play this one. Invite him up now and she might never see him again. Play him out too long and he would disappear forever. She paused at the door of the building, giving him a long look, starting at his sneakers and working all the way up as if considering just what she was going to do with him.

Jim let her look. Turnabout was fair play after all, and he had certainly looked at her long enough. There was no way she could miss his cock, hard and becoming painfully so, in the tightness of his walking shorts.

"Well, thank you for lunch and for the escort home, Mr. Delaney." Tania's voice purred with invitation.

"It was my honor, Miss Tania. I had a very pleasant time." He took a step toward her, his voice dropping to a murmur. "And I would love to continue that pleasant time."

"Mmm...you would, would you? And how would you like to continue that?" Ostensibly retrieving her bags, her hand closed over his.

"Oh, I'm sure we could think of something." He nuzzled her hair, inhaling the scent of her perfume. Her hand brushed against his cock and he gasped.

His cock was larger than she expected and Tania's knees grew weak. Praying that he knew how to use it, she brushed her fingers over his cock again, deciding she didn't want to wait. She wanted him now. Tipping her face up toward him, she invited his kiss.

He obliged her, brushing his fingers over her breast as he raised his hand to her face. The feel of a very hard nipple was a temptation he did not wish to miss. Mentally going through the cash in his wallet, he wondered if he had enough for more than a quickie. Just what did hookers charge these days?

"So what's your fee?" he murmured into her hair.

"What?" He missed the sharpness in her tone that should have warned him.

"I don't want to shortchange you." The apricot scent of her hair filled his senses as he nuzzled along the back of her ear.

The woman in his arms froze. Standing very still, her voice was sweet and deadly.

"Tell me, Jim. What do you think I charge for?"

Still befuddled by the nearness, his cock throbbing with need, he blindly stepped into the abyss. "Sex, of course."

"So you think I'm a hooker?" Her smile of steel did not waver.

The question threw him off guard and he stepped back, confusion clouding his thoughts. The set of her jaw and the flash of controlled anger in her eyes further confused him and he stammered an answer. "Well, you are, aren't you? I mean..." His gaze took in her tight blouse and the twin delights barely hidden there. He didn't need to gesture to the tight leather pants. Who else would dress this way on a Saturday afternoon but a hooker looking for a john?

"Thank you for a nice lunch, Mr. Delaney. Go away."

Tania turned on her stiletto heel and slid her card through the magnetic lock on the outside of the apartment building. Tears stung her eyes, but she would not let them fall in front of him. How could he think that? Just because a girl liked to look sexy didn't mean she did it for a living.

"Tania, wait, I didn't mean, well, that is..." He fumbled, trying to understand what had just happened.

"Yes, you did, Mr. Delaney. Goodbye." She let the door shut in his face. So she liked to show off her figure and she liked it when men appreciated it. What right did that give him to jump to conclusions? Anger at his assumption warred with the hurt caused by his question.

Walking quickly, she made it up the inside stairs to her apartment and just inside before she broke into heartbroken sobs.

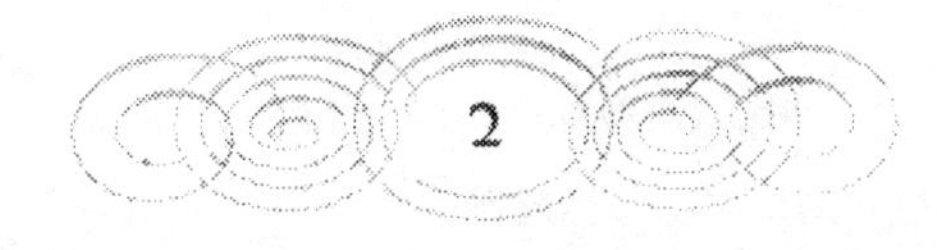

2

Jim stood on the sidewalk, blinking in the sun. His mind raced through the lunch conversation, over her movements and the come-on she had given him. Had he missed something? All the signals of a woman looking for an afternoon of sex were there.

And then it dawned. She wasn't a hooker. She was a witty, intelligent woman who dressed in sexy clothes and who was looking for physical companionship. A woman with whom he had just spent one of the most enjoyable hours of his life. And he'd asked her how much she charged.

"Oh, my God. I can't believe I just did that."

Slapping himself on the head, he paced outside the door. Apologize. That's what he needed to do. His cock, hard as malachite moments before, now hung limp as overcooked pasta as he thought of and discarded several approaches. Another slap on the head as he realized he didn't even know her last name. Searching through the mailboxes brought two choices, "T. Sweet" and "T. Pelligrini".

"Some choices," he muttered to himself. "One makes her sound like a porn star and the other like..." He shrugged. "Like a beautiful Italian." Deciding a fifty-fifty choice was better than nothing, he pushed the button for "T. Pelligrini".

And waited. A bus roared by and still he waited. He pushed the button again. Nothing.

Grimacing, he tried the other button. "Come on, T. Sweet. Let's see if I can apologize for thinking you're a hooker."

A man's voice boomed out of the callbox. "Yeah?"

Startled, Jim stared at the box as if it had come alive.

"Who's there? Whaddya want? This better not be no kid playin' games down there."

"Um, no, it's not. I'm looking for Tania." Jim swallowed hard at the thought of the massive body that must belong to that rumbling and grouchy voice.

"Wrong apartment. Try again, buddy."

"Sorry to have disturbed you."

Jim examined the listings again. "T. Pelligrini" had to be the right one and obviously she didn't want to talk to him. Not that he could blame her. Shaking his head and deciding to chalk this one up to experience, he turned away from the building and retraced his steps to the café. From there, home was only a few short blocks away.

With the lunch hour dwindling, the tables before the café sat empty and accusing. Jim paused, glancing at the table that held such pleasant recent memories. The old waiter, cloth in hand, wiping down a table, stopped to stare at him.

"What?" Jim felt defensive.

For answer the waiter only shook his head and Jim understood the man knew he'd blown it. A perfect opportunity to have a glorious afternoon, gone with one stupid sentence.

Stalking past the café, Jim took his anger out in physical activity. As soon as he cleared the busy street and turned into the quieter neighborhood that was his own, he quickened his pace into a jog, running along a street he didn't really see. His thoughts consumed him. Okay, so he had met and shared a table at lunch with a beautiful woman. So he had mistaken her come-on as a hooker looking for work. So she hadn't been, and she had gone off in a huff. What was the big deal? She didn't mean anything to him. He barely knew her. He ran faster. Running always cleared his mind and helped him forget his troubles.

At least, it had in the past. But today the memory of hurt in a woman's eyes would not leave him. He ran past his own apartment in an attempt to outrun her reproach, running until his anger at himself finally abated and turned to shame. Only then did he turn and jog back home. For whatever reason, T. Pelligrini had gotten under his skin. He would have no rest until he had set things right.

An hour later, freshly showered and shaved, dressed in a blue Oxford short-sleeve shirt that he knew set off the blue of his eyes, a pair of khaki pants and his docksiders with no socks, he left his apartment and headed out once more with a vague plan in his head. A present. Something nice that said, "I'm sorry for what I did, but I'm not looking for strings right now. Let's be friends." Sexual friends, he hoped, but wasn't sure there was a present in the world that would say that. A woman to go to the ballgame with, to take to the movies and to bed. That was all the commitment he wanted.

Of course, he wanted it on his terms. In the shower, he had fantasized about how he wanted Tania—on her knees, begging for her orgasm. Her come-on demeanor at lunch led him to believe that she was the type who always got what she wanted from men. He also suspected she liked to lead in the bedroom, letting her passions rule the dance.

But Jim preferred a different approach and as he had showered, he'd imagined what he would do to her if she would let him. He had rubbed the soap over his cock, feeling it lengthen as the image took shape before his closed eyes. The warm water had relaxed his shoulders, allowing him to concentrate on his fantasy...

Tania knelt before him, her brown eyes wide with eagerness and desire. He stood naked, his legs slightly apart, as his fingers lightly touched her blushing cheeks...

No, that wasn't right. Tania wouldn't blush. He repositioned his hand around his cock, dropping the soap into the dish as he adjusted the fantasy to bring it closer to what he imagined was reality.

His fingers lightly touched her face as color rose in her cheeks, flushing them with the heat of her arousal. His touch explored the softness of her skin, the curve of her cheekbone...then slid into her hair to enjoy its soft caress. He watched her lips part and he stepped closer to guide her open mouth to his cock. With her hands tied behind her back, she could do nothing to stop him from using her mouth as he saw fit. As his long cock entered her mouth, he imagined her hands clenching and opening, wanting to wrap themselves around his length. But the ropes he'd tied around her body, transforming her from an independent woman into the sex toy she wanted to be, prevented her from being anything but his to use.

Pushing deep, Jim felt and heard her gag reflex kick in, but he stayed there a moment longer before pulling back and letting her breathe. She looked up at him, tears in her eyes from the rough usage, but she didn't protest when he plundered her mouth again, his large cock filling her throat.

Her tawny hair made an easy handle and he grabbed it with both hands, guiding her pace faster and faster. The tears flowed freely now, but still she made no sound of protest. He rubbed the tip of his cock against the back of her throat and savored the strangled sound she made as the first spurts of his seed filled her mouth.

In his mind, Tania looked up at him with lust in her eyes as she swallowed hard around his cock and Jim came loudly in the shower, his come squirting into the tub to run down the drain.

He had dressed quickly, knowing he needed to see her again. With no real plan of action, Jim had retraced his route, his steps taking him past the small café where he had met the girl of his dreams.

The veteran waiter was wiping down a table when Jim walked by. He looked up and raised an eyebrow in question. A kinship rose between them that exists between all men who have ever done something stupid when it came to a woman. Jim knew the old man would know what to do. Clearing his throat, he called out to him, "So, then, what do I do to make it up to her?"

With a wise nod that showed he understood perfectly, the waiter indicated the side of the café. Jim's eye followed the nod. A riot of flowers spilled out onto the sidewalk from the florist's shop next door. Perfect.

With gritted teeth and narrowed eyes, he focused on the plan. Marching straight over to the array of blossoms nestled in their plastic bag cones, he surveyed his choices. A spray of large Shasta daisies caught his eye and he reached for them. Another throat-clearing from the waiter made him pause.

The old man shook his head. No good.

Jim stepped back and thought about his situation for a moment. The waiter was right...not just any bunch of flowers would do to smooth the way for his apology. Tania was intelligent and sexy...he needed a flower to match.

Red roses stood in pails of water. Those said "romance". Not quite what he needed. Carnations were beautiful, but too cheap. These flowers had to be something expensive to make up for a blunder of this magnitude.

And there they were, along the top row of the display. Hidden in the shadow of a small awning, Jim almost missed the long stalks of the calla lilies. Smooth white blossoms curved in graceful waves around the long yellow stamen, an age-old symbol of the beauty of woman's sensuousness enfolding man's rigidity. A fitting metaphor for his own blindness. He didn't need to look at the waiter to know he had the older man's approval.

Twelve elegant lilies, carefully boxed and tied with a silk ribbon of sky blue, held Jim's hope for making amends with the woman he had wronged. Now all he needed were the words.

Wondering if he should have gone home and changed into something more formal, Jim turned up the walk toward Tania's apartment. She would just have to take him in his plain pants and Oxford shirt. To go home without seeing her first was risking never seeing her again. Under his breath, he practiced his speech one last time.

Breathing deeply, Jim pushed the button. The quiet, seductive voice he remembered from lunch sounded tinny over the little speaker.

"Yes?"

"Delivery for Ms. Pelligrini." Jim was not stupid.

"What is it?"

"Flowers, ma'am." He screwed up his face in the hopes that this would work.

"Wait there."

Tania paused on the bottom step. From here she could see the "delivery man" with the telltale rectangular box in his arms. He'd rung her bell over and over a half-hour before and she'd not answered him because she didn't know how. What did one say to a man who jumped right from "sexy, independent woman" to "hooker"? And did she want to waste any more of her time with one who did?

With a resigned sigh, she stepped into the short hall and crossed to open the door. Tania gazed at Jim, reproach and hurt clouding her eyes as she listened to his apology.

"The assumption I made was out of line and I apologize. You are a beautiful, sexy woman who deserved much better from me. I do not excuse my behavior because, up until the moment I put my foot in my mouth, I enjoyed our playing. You're intelligent, witty...all the things I like in a woman. I don't know if you'll ever be able to forgive me, but please accept these along with my apology."

Tania wanted to be angry with him and the conclusion he had jumped to. The insult he had given her was not easy to forgive. But he looked so cute standing there with a stray lock of his dark hair curling over his forehead, his head hanging down and hardly able to meet her eyes at the end of his speech. Like a little boy making an apology after his mouth had just gotten washed out with soap. And he had shaved and changed his clothes. His cheeks, now free of the earlier stubble, and the fresh shirt and pants were a testament to the fact that he really was trying to make up to her. She watched his fingers fumble with the ribbon on the box, waiting patiently as he pulled the top off to reveal the sensuous flowers within.

Tania's carefully controlled demeanor slipped at the sight of the calla lilies, their pure white chalice-shaped trumpets gracefully surrounding their golden stamens. Determined as she was to be angry with him, her heart melted at such a wonderful apology bouquet.

"They're beautiful." Her shoulders relaxed, even though she wasn't quite ready to let him off the hook. Tania chose not to reach out for the flowers, waiting instead, quiet and composed, still standing in the doorway but smiling a little in her thaw.

Tania had not changed out of her tight clothes, yet Jim now saw past the external view she presented to the world and glimpsed the woman of breeding and class underneath. Tania was far more complex than he had seen before and worth much more than the casual afternoon he had originally intended to spend with her. This was a woman to taste in small sips, like savoring a fine wine. A woman to spend hours with, consuming every nuance, appreciating and relishing every inch.

Bowing, he lifted the lilies from their carton and stepped forward to place them in her arms. Wisps of hair blew across her eyes as the summer breeze wafted past and Jim took the liberty of brushing them back from her face.

"I would very much like to get to know you, Tania Pelligrini. Will you forgive me?"

The touch of Jim's fingers across her cheek, warm and intoxicating, dissipated her anger, leaving a much more pleasant feeling in its place. Letting her cheek follow his fingers, she turned her head, inviting his hand to linger. He complied, and she looked up through long lashes at his honest face. While making him beg for her forgiveness had a tantalizing, revengeful taste, she did not have the heart to resist his sweet, seductive apology.

"I forgive you, Mr. Delaney."

She wove her charms on him and hoped he would let himself be ensnared. Fascinating men did not often come into her life, and she did not want to let this one go, in spite of his bad beginning. As Jim bent forward, she allowed their breaths to entwine, brushing his lips softly with her own.

Tania was unsure just who was wooing whom. Her lips, full and soft and sensuous, teased him, made him lean forward to capture them with his own. But it was he who pulled her lip in to taste and leave her breathless when he released her.

She almost swayed. Heat flared from her pussy straight up through her stomach, which tightened with anticipation, and continued on up, bursting into twinkles in her eyes. Smiling demurely, she stepped back and gestured with the bouquet she still held. "These will need water. Would you carry the box upstairs, Mr. Delaney, since my hands are full?"

Jim grinned in return. "It would be my pleasure, Ms Pelligrini. Shall I get the door for you?" He caught the door so she could turn and enter, bending and retrieving the discarded box and blue silk ribbon.

Tania made sure she gave him an eyeful as she sauntered along the short corridor and up the single flight of stairs to her apartment. Handing him her key, she stepped back and appreciated the long, slender fingers that manipulated the thin metal against the stubborn lock. Fingers like a musician's, supple and full of grace in such a simple act. Opening the door, he bowed her in and Tania inclined her head almost regally as she passed him. Once inside, she paused to watch his reaction to her small apartment.

Decorated with her rather eclectic tastes, the apartment's many styles should have clashed. What would he think of her mixing an Oriental rug, with its multicolored swirls, and a bright orange vinyl-covered chair of modern design? Yet she knew the chair's brightness brought out the oranges that hid in the pattern of the rug. Peach sheers hung at the windows to pool beneath in puddles of color. The windows were open and the warm, summer breeze wafted the curtains in the afternoon sunlight.

A loveseat rather than a couch sat against the far wall, more traditional in design and covered in another bizarre, yet effective color and pattern choice. Bright yellow brocaded sunflowers danced across the back and seat, producing a riot of summer color against the soft celery green walls, making guests feel as if they stood in the center of a meadow on a lazy summer's day.

Tania let the effect sink in, then tilted her head toward a small kitchenette off to the left of the front door. "There's a vase on the top of the fridge."

Jim took the hint. The serviceable kitchen, neat and clean, gave testament to Tania's ordered lifestyle. Leaving the box on the counter, he lifted the green glass vase carefully from its perch and carried it out to her.

She stood expectantly beside a small table next to the loveseat, the lilies still resting in her folded arms and a smile dancing across her lips. Jim crossed the short distance in slow, powerful strides, taking his time until he was certain he had her total attention. Keeping the vase in one hand, he held out the other and waited for her to put the long stems into his palm. His long fingers closed around the entire bundle and Jim lifted them to enjoy their light fragrance.

But instead of putting them into the vase, he turned and gestured to the floor. "Lie down on the rug."

She hesitated and Jim waited patiently as she considered his command. Apparently deciding to let him lead her in this game, Tania slid to her knees before reclining on her side on the Oriental rug. By the smile playing on her lips, he knew she was making sure that he noticed her sensuous curves covered in black leather. Already her nipples had hardened under her blouse, showing her response to his predatory gaze.

He waited until she was reclined on her side, her hand holding up her head, gazing at him with slightly narrowed eyes as she puzzled his intent. With a smile toying at his lips and a single sweep of his arm, Jim let the flowers fall to cascade over the resplendent curves of her hips. Only one lily remained in his hand and he bent to hold it before her mouth.

Tania leaned forward and closed her lips over the green stem in an open kiss. Jim turned and sat on the loveseat, holding the green vase between his knees, indicating with a gesture what he wanted her do to.

Rising, catlike, onto her knees, Tania crawled with slow, languorous movements toward the vase, the thick stem of the flower still held lightly between her lips. On all fours before him, she rose, tilted the flower and guided the long green stem into the vase. Her eyes flared with mischief and sensuality as she bent down to pick up another flower in her teeth, making sure he saw how she wrapped her lips around the thick stem. With her eyes, she told him how she would wrap her lips around him.

Jim's cock grew as she played his game not only without protest but with relish. His grip on the vase tightened as she placed the second flower, brushing her nose on his knee before twisting down, fluidly retrieving a third flower. Taking a deep breath, Jim relaxed his grip on the vase as he watched how she curved her body around, sensuously turning the tables. He might have started this game, but it was obvious that she intended to win it.

She needed to slither a few steps farther for the next few flowers and the space gave her the opportunity to bend low, leaving her ass high in the air for him to admire. Weaving her body around to face him again, she carefully set each stem with the others between his hands. As the vase filled, he needed to hold the flowers out of her way to give her room and he felt her breath warm his fingers as he held the cool stems from her face.

One last flower remained on the rug. Tania retrieved it, but Jim moved the vase, setting it on the floor beside him. Taking Tania by the elbows, he pulled her up on her knees. Tendrils of hair still fell from the ponytail to frame her face, accenting her fine, thin nose and high cheekbones. Jim studied her beauty, letting his fingers meander over the soft skin of her arms and shoulders, the graceful curve of her neck.

Tania felt his fingers leaving trails of fire in their wake. Feeling as if he had tightened a valve inside her, her breath caught and she closed her eyes to savor the explorations of his hands as they passed over her lips holding the flower, continuing on to brush along her cheeks, her ears. And when he pulled out the tie that held her hair, releasing the soft waves to fall around her face, she tossed her head and smiled at him.

Jim's fingers cupped her chin, pulling her toward him to claim the lips surrounding the sensuous flower. Tania felt his lips envelop hers, caress her, want her. The flower tumbled to the floor and she plunged into the kiss, her passion ignited, needing him to fuel the flames that shot through her. Her arms came up to encircle him, to draw him down onto the floor to lie on the rug, but Jim resisted.

His refusal to do as she wanted forced out a whimper of frustration that surprised her. For answer, Jim pulled her toward him, holding her tightly, crushing her body into his as his mouth plundered hers, his tongue swirling her thoughts as he explored, tasted, drank in her essence. Squirming in his arms, her need threatened to overtake her devoured senses.

But their mutual seduction was complete and they were caught in the net they had woven. The fire in her belly would not be put out as Jim took the lead in their dance. Not releasing her soft, pliable lips, his hands sought hers, bringing them down to her sides and holding them there. He slid off the couch to kneel in front of her, his fingers entwining with hers as he drew back slightly from the kiss.

"Don't move your arms. Let me explore you."

Her breath caught and she nodded once as his fingers brushed up her arms and around the low neckline of her top. The heat of his breath warmed her skin as he moved to kiss the shoulder he'd exposed, pulling the stretchy fabric down to further pin her arms to her sides.

Remaining still tormented her when he scooped her breasts out for his inspection, his tongue leaving a trail of wet heat from her collarbone to her nipple. Taking his time, his hands explored her ample breasts, weighing them as if considering which one to taste first. Like many women, one breast was slightly larger than the other and its pink nipple, roused and aching for his touch, invited his tongue.

What was he doing to her? Why couldn't she focus? The sight of his tongue darting out to softly caress her nipple made her head swim and her muscles ached to move her arms and press him to her.

She could not remain still. A needy whimper fell from her before she could prevent it. Swaying as his lips worked up to nibble at her earlobe, his breath hot on her skin, Tania leaned into him, her loosened hair running through his fingers to cascade like a tawny waterfall of color around her face.

Jim pulled back and smiled at his willing partner. He felt her trembling and knew she wanted him. But he would take her slowly, making her beg for him before he was done. She might not be the hooker he had first thought her to be, but she was still an incredibly sexy, wanton woman...a woman whom he had insulted. Now he would make amends by giving her an experience she would not forget. Recalling his shower fantasy, he entwined his fingers in her hair, the memory of her mouth around his cock making him smile. There might be time for that later. Right now, he was much too intrigued by the hollow of her throat. Drawing her head back, he exposed her neck to his explorations. She smelled of honeysuckle and fresh air and he breathed her scent deep into his lungs before brushing his lips over her vulnerable skin, nipping and kissing and tasting.

To his immense satisfaction, she swayed. Her eyes had closed, and Jim knew she was losing focus. Already she hovered right where he wanted her. Still, he didn't want her moving too fast. If this was to be a memorable afternoon, then he needed to shape the time with a slow and sensuous arc. She deserved the royal treatment. Steadying her by the shoulders, he waited until she had her balance and could open her eyes and focus on him.

"I can take you to heights you've only dreamed of, Tania." He cupped her cheeks in his hands and kissed her lightly on her slightly bruised lips. Willingly, she opened for him, inviting him deeper, but he waited. He could be a very patient man.

"Is that what you want? Will you let me show you?"

Tania's head swam with the passions he'd awakened in her. With previous partners, the excitement had always run hot and quick, the coupling fast, furious and violent. What Jim offered seemed to be something very different and Tania found she wanted to explore it even as it frustrated her.

"I don't know if I have the patience."

"I will teach you patience." As Jim's lips brushed over hers, Tania tried to reach up to turn the touch into a full-blown kiss. But Jim's fingers tightened ever so slightly in her hair and prevented her from moving. His voice, still soft and sensuous, took on an undertone of command. "We do this at my pace—my way. Understood?"

Her temper flared. What was she thinking? And who was he to make demands? She was no cavewoman to be bossed around and dominated by the male of the species. She was a creation of the twenty-first century—an independent, proud and self-reliant woman.

She would have told him so, too...but Jim took that precise moment to close the kiss, his lips pressing against hers, his tongue gently, yet insistently demanding entrance again. Her knees weakened first and her arms came up to encircle his shoulders of their own volition. She gave way, feeling his tongue dance over hers, encircling and capturing her soul.

His lips did not leave hers, nor did his tongue stop its mesmerizing dance against her teeth and tongue, yet she felt him reach up and remove her arms from around his shoulders, placing them back at her sides as he explored. Tania fully understood his meaning—she was to remain still and let him explore as he saw fit.

Did he understand how hard this was for her? How could she remain still when she wanted to explore him, too? She felt his warm hands slide along her back, his fingers finding every hollow from her neck to her waist. Arching, she invited him to explore further, but his fingers stopped just short of the waistband of her leather pants.

"Tell me you like this, Tania. Tell me you want more."

His cologne filled her swimming senses as his fingers skimmed along the edge of her waistband. No doubt remained, and she whispered into his ear, "Yes, please. I want this."

He drew back and smiled, his nose barely touching hers. "I like your manners. Beg me, Tania. Beg me to take you to places you've only dreamed of."

His hands pulled her face up toward him and she stretched upward on her knees, forcing her hands to remain at her sides. Inside, a battle raged as her desire warred with her independence. Jim's thumbs caressed her cheeks as his lips placed warm kisses along her brow, exacerbating her need to return his caress. Why was she doing as he asked? What prevented her from throwing her arms around him and stroking him back?

Even as her mind asked the question, Jim nuzzled her ear, his tongue flicking out to lick the inner rim and drive her insane. She moaned as her knees turned to jelly and independence flew from her mind. All that mattered was his touch. All that mattered were the words that sprang from the depths of her need. He wanted her to beg? Well, if it got them to the part where they were rolling around on the carpet like two animals in heat faster than they were moving now, she'd be happy to beg. In fact, she'd beg to beg. "Oh, yes, Jim. Please...please take me there. Take me to places I've read about but never gone. Oh, Jim, please, yes."

Her voice cracked as she pleaded, humiliation and need mingling to nudge her deeper into his control. Never before had anyone even offered to tame her wild passions. Was it possible Jim Delaney could be that man? Suddenly and very definitely, Tania hoped he would be as the flame inside her ignited again. Reaching toward him, she leaned in to kiss those wonderful lips of his.

But once more, Jim leaned back on his heels, his hands still holding her head, forcing her to stretch upward to look into his eyes. Tania knew he would see the wildcat in her eyes, the animal that lived deep in her psyche, feral and untamed in the ways of love. She understood his intent was to slow her down, to bank her fires, allowing them to roar into a blaze only when he commanded them to and not before. The understanding almost drove her to the edge.

Abruptly Jim rose, pulling her to her feet. He left her blouse half on and half off, placing her in the middle of the room before returning to sit on the loveseat, reclining much as he had earlier. Only this time, he rested his arms along the back and stretched his long legs comfortably into the room, making himself quite at home.

"Undress for me."

Suddenly being deprived of his touch disoriented her for a moment. She took a deep breath and refocused her eyes even as her spirit responded to the command in his voice. She'd done stripteases before for lovers, but always in fun and passion. What this man wanted, however, was something different and she knew it. In spite of herself and the game she had started, she blushed.

Her arms, still confined by the blouse, floundered a moment as she fought free of the garment, finally maneuvering it into a position where she could just rip it off over her head in one quick pull. But when she looked at him and saw the hunger of the predator in his deep blue eyes, it dangled loosely from her fingers.

He would devour her, she realized. Those passionate kisses earlier, and now the removal of her clothes, baring her body to him, layer by layer, were just the first steps. To vamp for time and gather her wits, Tania righted her top and folded it neatly, setting it carefully on the bright orange chair. She turned from him a bit, trying to hide her blush as her heart leapt.

Jim nodded and gave her a small smile before indicating she should continue. With each item she removed, she bared more and more of her psyche as well as her body. Beneath his pants, Tania saw his cock stir at her conflicting emotions of willingness and humiliation.

Reaching behind, she unzipped the tight pants, pushing the leather slowly down over her hips. She could not take her eyes from him, her cheeks burned as she removed another layer of civility. But too late, she remembered her shoes. The pants would never fit over them. And they needed to be unlaced before they would come off.

Biting her lip and bending in embarrassment to have her "dance" turn so clumsy, Tania quickly unlaced the shoes and flung the laces around her ankles, slapping the thin lines against her skin in her hurry. She didn't even feel their sting as she finished and stepped down off the height the heels had given her.

With the shoes off, the pants went quickly so all that remained was her thong. Her lip still caught between her teeth, she hesitated a moment, her thumbs hooked into the sides as she threw a glance in his direction.

He sat with his arms still thrown out along the back of the couch, the very picture of a man taking his ease and enjoying the view. How easy it had been for him to unnerve her. At his nod, she understood he wanted the thong off as well.

Tania wanted to fling it at him. Who did he think he was...calling her a hooker and then bringing her flowers...and what was she doing melting all over him like milk chocolate on a hot afternoon? Where was her dignity? Her pride? Her chin came out and her jaw set as she stood, naked in the sunlight.

"Tania, you are one heck of a sexy woman, do you know that?"

She opened her mouth to protest, then closed it without saying a word. Hadn't she planned to yell at him for something? What was it?

Jim stood up, unbuttoning his shirt as he rose. His smooth chest shone with a thin shimmer of sweat from the warm apartment and the woman who heated it up. Muscular, but not muscle-bound, the ripples of his abdomen made a double row of corded strength.

But he did not give Tania time to stare, advancing on her with the same catlike grace she had used earlier. "Stay still," he commanded her as he circled her, examining her naked body and debating which part he would consume first.

He noticed the tears of humiliation in Tania's eyes and how her hands balled into fists at her sides, doubting she had ever been treated this way before. He noticed that she held her breath, anxiety and arousal building in her as he continued to circle.

The knotted shoulders and clenched fists told him he was pushing her into places she had never been. If he commanded her to spread her legs, she would do so eagerly and he knew she would be wet. He did not give the command. To do so would push her too fast. There would be time for that later.

Quickly he stripped off his pants, letting his cock loose. The shaft stretched long and hard, and ached to sink into the warmth hidden under that tuft of dark hair on her mound. A part of him demanded he hurry things along and give the tensions coiling in his belly the release they needed.

But waiting would make the experience all the sweeter. Reaching down, he pulled a clean white handkerchief from the pocket of his pants. Such a simple thing, really…and yet such a wonderful instrument of torture. Stepping behind her, he pressed his chest to her back, enjoying the warmth of her naked body in the heat of the summer afternoon. His cock brushed the smooth skin of her ass and Jim relished the sweet agony.

"Let me blindfold you, Tania, and I will take you to heights you didn't even know existed."

Tania knew from past experience that by this point, she and whoever her partner was would already be rolling on the floor, yanking clothes off and throwing them in whatever direction they happened to go. Jim's slow, studied approach unnerved yet excited her. His chest, warm against her back, sent wonderful little tingles all the way to the tips of her fingers. She had an urge to reach down beside her ass, where his cock nestled against her side, but didn't. As curious as she was about what his cock looked like, the white strip of cloth that hung in his hands before her caught her curiosity. No one had ever tried this game with her. Probably because their foreplay hadn't lasted any longer than it took to take off their clothes. Tania's hesitation was fleeting. She nodded once, not trusting her voice. The white cloth, so innocent and pure, could not, by itself, hurt her. The butterflies in her stomach settled as she accepted the temporary loss of her sight. Her hands were not bound and if Jim did something she didn't like, she could rip off the handkerchief at any point. Thus desire beat down sanity with logic.

With her eyesight no longer giving her information, Tania relied on touch and sound to give her clues as to what Jim intended. She felt him slide his hand into hers and allowed him to lead her toward the loveseat. He prevented her from sitting on it, however.

"No, sit on the floor with your back against the seat."

His voice came from just above her head, to her right, and she smiled to show him she was intrigued by this game. Dropping gracefully, she stretched out her slender legs, demurely crossing them at the ankles and making herself comfortable. She heard Jim move away and was tempted to lift the handkerchief and see where he went. But the apartment wasn't large and if stealing from her was his intent, he'd find little of value.

She heard him rustling around in the kitchen. A plate rattled and she called out to him, "There isn't much, but go ahead and help yourself." The sarcasm dripped and she frowned, puzzling over his intentions. The fires that had ignited just moments before sank to a simmer as she folded her hands, cocked her head and tried to figure out just what this was all about.

Several moments later, she felt him return and kneel beside her. It sounded as if he put something down on the floor, then all was quiet for a moment. Her frown deepened.

"Open your mouth," he instructed her.

Hesitantly, Tania opened her lips, the frown still knitting her brow under the white cloth. What was he up to?

"Wider..."

Defiantly now, she opened her mouth wide. Something cold hit her tongue and gingerly she closed her mouth around the spoon.

"Taste."

Tania smiled as she recognized the round shape and taste of one of the white grapes she'd bought yesterday at the supermarket. Nice and sweet with just a hint of tart in them. Swallowing, she eagerly opened her mouth for another.

Jim laughed. "Oh, you think you're about to be fed, do you? Try this..."

Tania made a face as something pepperminty and squishy hit her tongue. She swallowed it down and wrinkled her nose. "Toothpaste!"

"Yep. This is all about sensations, Tania. About learning to slow down and appreciate every sensual aspect of life around you. It's also about learning to trust me."

Tania felt a spoon at her mouth. Trust him? Did he think he would have gotten this far if she didn't? What might he be planning? Hesitantly, she parted her lips and opened her mouth. Another spoonful of something. She closed her lips around the spoon as Jim fed her. This was something smooth with little bumps and the flavor burst in her mouth. "Tapioca pudding..." Grinning she bent her head down as she enjoyed the flavors mingling in her mouth. "I begin to understand."

She felt a brush against her breast and did not flinch from the soft and fuzzy something that stroked her skin. She could not identify it but decided it wasn't important. Only the sensuous caress mattered as Jim traced it over her breast, her belly, her arm, her neck.

Abruptly it was gone. She sat up, eager for the next sensation. What would he show her? Unconsciously, Tania changed positions as she became comfortable with their game. Instead of sitting with her legs straight out, stiff and closed up, she adjusted her position, now sitting cross-legged, leaning forward for what he would give her next. Although her fingers itched to lift the white handkerchief and peek at the food Jim had on the plate, she kept her hands at her sides and tried not to bounce in anticipation.

Tania jumped as she felt his fingers brush lightly against her breast and hover there. They were cool, as if he had dipped them in cold water on this hot afternoon and then rested them against her skin. But there was no pressure, indeed, he barely touched her.

Suddenly cold ripped through her skin and she gasped as an ice cube touched her flesh. He trailed it over the mounds of her ample breasts in diminishing figure-eights, not changing the pattern until he had circled around each nipple, the cold ice stiffening them and turning them into hard little nubs that ached for his touch. The remaining sliver of ice then slid down to her belly in trails of cold flame that made her squirm and cry out. Tania's hands came up in automatic defense, to push away the cold, but she touched only the warm skin of his bare arms. The ice cube paused with an implicit warning. Moaning, she forced her hands back to her sides and let him play with her body. Heat flared inside her to answer the call of the cold ice. Flames heated her skin and melted the cube into nothing.

Then warmth on her skin again, the tips of his fingers spreading the water from the melted ice over her belly and breasts, stopping to gently pull her nipple, twisting it and giving it a small pinch before dropping her heavy breast.

As each new sensation tore at her control, her whimpers turned to growls. Her ragged breath caught in her throat and her need broke loose. She could not keep up this torment. She wanted him and she wanted him now.

Her hands grabbed for the blindfold, but Jim was quicker. He ensnared her hands in his, holding them tightly, preventing her from taking it away.

"Trust me, Tania. Trust me."

The command in his quiet voice was hard to resist. For a moment she wanted what she always had—quick passion that burned hot and flamed out quickly. But her pussy throbbed in a way it never had before, and deep down inside, she didn't want him to end it too soon. This agonizingly slow pace held the allure of something worth waiting for. Sniffling back her frustration, she relaxed her hands and let him bring them down to her sides again.

Tania flinched as the ice again touched her heated flesh just above her navel. Three times he circled it around, dipping it once to rest in the little hollow until he'd forced another moan from the back of her throat.

Behind the blindfold, Tania's eyes closed as Jim slid the ice lower, tracing the outline of her mound and letting the water drip between the downy hairs to trickle and tease. Her nails dug into the carpet as she pushed her hips forward, her knees opening as far as her crossed legs would allow.

"That's it. Open for me."

Even as his encouragement made her feel like the slut he had thought her to be, her legs slid apart and spread wide for him, inviting his touch. She no longer cared what he thought of her as long as he didn't stop. Leaning back on her hands, she opened herself to new ideas and sensations.

The ice cube, mostly melted, slid easily between the pink lips of her pussy and with a quick push, Jim slid it into her opening. The cold ice along her hot slit sent conflicting messages to her brain, which, in response, promptly shut down all rational thought. The heat of her pussy melted the small piece of ice and cold water trickled from her.

With an oath, Tania ripped off the blindfold, her driving need finally outweighing her intention to obey. Jim sat beside her, not a stitch of clothing covering the hard, sculpted planes of his chest or the ropey threads of muscle in his arms. Whatever this guy did for a living, his body was incredible. What god had come down from on high to live on Earth and walk into her life? Not from Olympus, this one. The Greek gods were too civilized for the slow heat of James Delaney. A Celtic deity, Tania decided. The primal lust of dominant males echoed in the depths of desire that glimmered in his look.

She paused only seconds as her glance fell to his magnificent cock, which stood hard and dark with desire. The condom already in place didn't hide the ridges and sheer size of him. With a second oath, she straddled him before he could stop her, holding herself above his cock.

"Enough!" she commanded. "I want you inside me now."

Something flashed in his eyes—was it anger? Irritation? She was past caring. All that mattered right now stood just a finger span away from entering her and driving her over the edge. Her pussy twitched as her need ran hot. But Jim's hands tightly gripped her waist, preventing her from impaling herself on his upright cock.

"I'm not tamable, Jimbo." She had no patience for slow sensuality and she unleashed the feral animal that always drove her sexual encounters. "Hot and quick" was her style and she demanded it from him now.

But Tania had not counted on his strength...or his ability to say no to the desire that flared in him as obviously as it burned in her. Jim's lips pursed as he lifted her petite frame and dragged her to the floor beside him. He rolled over, effectively pinning her beneath him, his face inches from hers.

"We do this my way or not at all."

Tania's temper flared. Even as she spit the words out, her heart trembled inside. "How dare you? First you call me a hooker and insult me, and now when I give you what you want, you tease me? Do you want sex or not?"

Jim just grinned and repositioned his grip on her squirming body. Holding her wrists above her head with one hand, he slowly slid the fingers of his free hand down the side of her cheek, pressing against the flushed skin of her neck, not stopping until he reached her chest, where he grabbed a fistful of breast and squeezed. Flesh bulged where her breast escaped the cage of his fingers.

"I want sex with you, Tania. But my way." He tightened his grip and saw the need flare in her eyes even as she squirmed harder.

"Slow..." He leaned closer to her ear, whispering the words he knew would drive her crazy.

"Sensuous..." His tongue flicked out to leave a trail of fire along her earlobe.

"Erotic..." His hand released her breast, leaving white fingerprints behind. His fingers slid along the sinuous contour of her hip as he shifted and put his knee between her legs, forcing them apart.

"Oh, my God..." Tania turned her face to him, her eyes barely focused. Mesmerized, she fell under the spell of this Celtic god whose tongue danced around her ear and whose fingers slid over the hair on her mound and straight to her clit.

"I like seeing you turn to a puddle of jelly." Jim grinned down at her.

"I bet you do," Tania managed to say around her gasp as his knee pressed against the tender flesh of her thigh, spreading her legs farther apart. And when he slid his finger into her pussy, she couldn't stifle the moan that emerged from the depths of her soul. "Oh, yes. Fuck me, Jim. Fuck me with your fingers."

"No." Grinning, he pulled his fingers away, while using his other hand to keep his grip on her wrists. Tania squirmed and tried to pull free, but the man's hands were like iron manacles around her wrists. Anger flared in her. Just who did he think he was?

"You can't lead me along and then drop me over and over. Are we going to have sex or not?"

His eyes went sad. "We *are* having sex, Tania, if you would just slow down and enjoy it. There is so much more to sex than just rutting together like two wild animals. So much more than having a man stick his cock in you, coming, dropping into bed exhausted and being done with it. But that's all you know, isn't it?"

She didn't answer. She had no answer.

Jim saw the confusion and need mingling in her eyes. What was there about her that made him want to teach her the finer points of love? A woman was something to be savored and cherished, not fucked and left. Which, he was beginning to suspect, was all she had experienced.

He brought his fingers, still covered in the white, creamy juices of her pussy, up to her face. "Have you ever tasted yourself, Tania? Do you know what a sexy woman you really are?"

With his wet finger, he traced her lips, pleased when her tongue snaked out to lick them clean. Deciding to push her limits of patience, he held his fingers still. "Lick them clean for me, Tania."

With barely a moment's hesitation, she lifted her head and pulled first one, then the others, one by one, into her mouth to clean them off.

"This is all new to me, Jim." Her voice, husky with emotion and need, was barely above a whisper. "I can't just turn it off and on like you can."

For answer, he released one of her hands and guided it down to his still rock-hard cock. "I can't turn it off and on either. But I won't rush through sex with you. At least not this first time."

"First time?" Was he saying there would be more times? Suddenly it seemed two paths lay before her. One way lay the life she'd led this morning, right up until the moment she had seen Jim sauntering down the street. That path was neat and orderly, with few surprises. Every day she would go to her job, every evening she would come home to her empty apartment. Her life stretched before her in straight, disturbing sameness. Nothing would ever change. Even her sex life. Hot and quick with passions flaming, yes, but always the same. And ultimately, she'd be alone. No one stood in sight on the path, no one beckoned her further along.

The other path led...somewhere else. It wound out of sight quickly, the way dark and unfamiliar. It was untidy and a bit unkempt. Without being able to see far down the road, who knew what risks lay ahead? But Jim stood beside this path, his confident smile a bit cocky, yet reassuring that she would not be alone.

"I don't know, Jim."

And then his fingers slipped back to dance over her clit again, fingering her and sliding between her wet nether lips and driving sane thought from her mind as the banked embers flared into an all-consuming fire. "I can't do this." The whimper rapidly became a shout as the feral animal inside drove her wild. With sudden strength, she pushed him away, sitting up and snarling as the untamable force broke loose again. Passion's grip held her and Tania flung away all the carefully gathered shreds of her self-control.

She pushed him onto his back and straddled him, his cock pressing against her mound. "I want you now," she commanded. There was nothing left of the sane, rational woman. Just violent, incredibly primal need drove her now as she fought for completion. The hell with slow and sensual. She just didn't have the patience.

Jim gripped her hips, again preventing her from impaling herself. "My way," he commanded, his voice raspy with power.

"You can't always have your way!" Tania's voice rose to a screech. She sounded like a complaining washerwoman even to her own ears and lowered her tone. "I want passion...hot sex on a hot afternoon... and I want you to give it to me."

She was losing control of the situation and knew it. Even as she tried to command him, her voice took on a pleading quality that infuriated her. Why was she coming so unhooked by this guy? Confusion and frustration knit her forehead into furrows as the heat inside her banked again…the hot embers hiding beneath a thin layer of pride. Was it only this morning that she had wondered if there were any "take charge" types of guys left in the world? Jim Delaney offered her a sexual experience she'd never had, on his terms, his way. Why didn't she have the courage to accept it?

Fire spit from Tania's eyes as their wills clashed, but still Jim did not back down even as his own desire to thrust himself into that willing heat built inside his belly. This was a deal-breaker for him. If she could not slow down and accept his guidance, then all the earlier hopes he'd had for turning this into something more than an afternoon of sex were done. Granted, when he'd thought she was a hooker, all he'd expected was a "fuck 'em and leave the money on the table" afternoon. But there was so much more to this woman and instinctively, he knew she was worth fighting for.

"Fuck me now, damn it!"

Jim saw the change in her eyes as her last word came out as a plea and suddenly realized that he could win this battle of wills, but only if he played his cards right. One tip of his hand and not only would she show him the door, but she'd probably kick him down the stairs as well.

Still keeping his tight grip on her hips, he lifted her up and to the side a second time. Her entire body trembled and as he sat up, he pulled her into his arms in a tight embrace. He gave one hand free rein to brush over her skin, keeping the heat flowing from one sensuous part of her body to another, while the other arm held her close and prevented her from escaping. "This is twice I've had to stop you, Tania. If you cannot behave, I will have to leave."

"Behave?" She struggled to push him away. She wasn't a child to be scolded. And just who did he think he was? If only his fingers didn't feel so damn good. They danced over her skin, making it hard to concentrate on her pride.

"I intend to awaken a new passion in you, Tania. One that will run as hot and fiery as the one that likes quick sex. But 'quick' flames out too fast for my taste." His voice, soft in her ear, commanded her in ways she barely understood. When his fingers came up to her chin and lifted her face to his, she didn't resist. "This is all about sensation, Tania. You learned how sensual taste could be, let me teach you how erotic touch can be."

"I feel how erotic touch is. Your fingers..." She couldn't even complete the thought as his hand slid down to encircle her neck. For the first time, she glimpsed the power he had over her—and the power she still held. All she had to do was tell him to leave. All she had to do was say "stop" and he would get dressed and walk out of her life as quickly as he had walked into it. And yet, the vulnerable feeling of his warm fingers lightly pressing against her neck opened a channel inside. Her heartbeat drummed against his fingertips, her breath quickened as she faced the two paths, one safe, secure and lonely...the other dark and forbidding, but with him beside her.

Her head tumbled back as she gave him her neck and her will.

Tania trembled in his arms and Jim knew she was afraid. But she didn't run, didn't scream...and didn't tell him to stop. Bending down, he claimed a kiss from her parted lips, sliding his tongue around hers when she pressed against him and her lips opened in submission. Keeping the pressure on her neck only a moment more, he relished the sudden openness of her giving and plundered her mouth, claiming it for his own.

They parted and Tania's eyes opened, barely focusing. "More. Teach me more about touch."

He grinned at her demand. All right, he'd cave in to her command this time and let her win this one, since it gave him an opening to win the war. Still keeping his grip around her body so that she could not move away from him, he brought his hand away from the beautiful stretch of her neck and flicked her nipple.

Tania's head came up as the sting made her gasp. Again he flicked the nipple and she struggled to move away. But he was strong and held her tightly against his side. A third flick and she cried out.

"Ouch. Jim, that hurts."

He flicked it a fourth time. "And it excites you, doesn't it?"

Her cheeks colored. It was true. It hurt, yet her pussy was gushing. The banked embers glowed.

He switched to the other nipple, alternately squeezing it tightly between his fingers and flicking it hard. She tried to remain still and just let the sensations flow through her, but found it impossible.

"You see?" He lifted her chin again and held her eyes. "So much more fun than just rutting on the Oriental carpet."

She couldn't answer, tingles were flowing from her nipples to her fingertips and down through her belly to her pussy. For the first time, she didn't want to just jump on him and ride the sensation through to the end. These tingles were far too intriguing to let them go too quickly.

"More?" She looked at him, knowing her question was a plea and not a demand.

He smiled as his fingers now caressed her sore nipples. "Much more."

Satisfied that she would not try to rush things again, at least not for a while, he released her and stood. He held his hand down to her and when she placed her smaller, more delicate one in his, he pulled her up to stand at his side. "Keep that fire banked, keep control of your passion and breathe deeply. Whenever you feel yourself wanting to come, I want you to tell me."

"Why? So you can stop again and make me frustrated?"

He grinned. One lesson he was learning about this woman was that she was no doormat. "No, so I can guide you to the longest, hardest, most incredible orgasm you've ever had."

She cocked an eyebrow at him, her nipples pink and tingly and her pussy soaking wet. "You're on, Mr. Delaney. I'll let you know when I want to come."

"Bend over and put your hands on the chair seat."

That Sixties-style chair she had found at a garage sale last spring. The clothes she'd stripped off for him still lay, neatly folded, on the seat. Ignoring them, she leaned over. Bright orange vinyl stuck to her palms as she experimented a moment, finding a comfortable position.

"Spread your legs for me."

The words made her knees weak, even as she wanted to throw something at him for commanding her like she was some sort of slave girl. Shifting her weight, she parted her thighs, feeling the slight breeze from the open window caress the hot lips of her extremely wet pussy. Feeling open and vulnerable, her breath caught in her throat as a slow smile spread across her face. It had been a long time since anyone had taken her from behind, but her memories of it were pleasant indeed.

Jim's hands caressed her ass, the smooth skin of his palms warm against those rounded hills. Around her cheeks and up along her back, then out and down to her hips, his hands explored every inch of her skin. Completing the circuit, he began again, this time his fingers massaging her muscles until she was purring in contentment. His cock, still hard, brushed against her leg and she smiled. She was not the only one who would benefit from the waiting.

He set one hand in the center of her back. "Be still."

Almost a whisper, his voice held power and she held herself quietly, no longer arching or voicing her appreciation of his touch.

"Take a deep breath and hold it in. Don't let it out until I tell you to."

Closing her eyes, Tania dropped her head, pulling air into her lungs in a long, slow intake. Just as she reached her limit, she heard him instruct her again.

"Slowly let it out, and as you do, let the tension in your back flow out as well."

The calm before the storm settled over her and she closed her eyes. A languorous smile played on her lips as she released the tension in her shoulders, allowing him to guide her thoughts and movements.

"Take in another breath, and this time, think of your pussy as you do. Focus on your clit, and on the breeze that cools it..."

Serenity filled her soul as she listened to his voice. Inhaling again, she bent her knees a little, allowing the warm air to caress her pussy the same way his hands had run along her back.

"This is all about giving me control and letting me teach you about sensation. Feel how your pussy tingles. Feel how open you are...how ready you are for my cock. Hold your breath and feel yourself on the edge..."

She did. The abyss yawned but a step away. For the first time, she did not run headlong and jump. Instead, she stood where she was, content to hover close to the edge and savor the moment, content to wait for him to take her there at his pace.

The slap of his hand on her exposed ass shocked a cry from her lips as the abyss suddenly rushed closer. Shying away from it in confused betrayal, she shot up and turned to face him. "What was that for? What do you think you're doing?"

Jim stood silently behind her, one eyebrow cocked as if he expected her to know the answer. Frowning, she considered a moment and then realized that she did.

"Sensations. This is all about sensations."

His smile dimpled one cheek and Tania studied him a moment as she weighed this new tingle. Jim simply stood with his hands at his sides, waiting for her reaction. Smiling a naughty smile of her own, Tania made a show of turning her back to him again, bending over and carefully placing her hands on the vinyl seat. For good measure, she adjusted her stance, widening the space between her legs so he could see how turned on the spanking made her.

Jim waited until she settled, hiding his grin. She had turned the tables on him again, making it seem as if the game were her idea. No, this one was no doormat at all. She let him lead her, but once she decided she liked the path, she settled confidently into it as if it were her right to be there. Could this be the woman he'd always longed for? One who could not only allow him his need to dominate but who wouldn't lose her own delicious personality in the process? Too bad he didn't have any of his "toys" here. The heart-shaped cheeks before him made one hell of a spankable ass, but his hand was going to get tired much sooner than a paddle. He could do her so much more justice with the right tools.

For now, his palm would do, however, and he spanked her again, this time leaving very little time for her to gather her wits between slaps. Under his hand, the skin turned pink. When she moaned, he switched cheeks, watching the creamy white liquid pool between the lips of her pussy. And when it dripped, a thin line hanging...suspended...her moans turned to whimpers and she gasped out, "I need to come."

Jim let his hands hang at his sides again, the palms of his hands burning and as pink as her ass. His cock throbbed almost painfully and he knew neither of them could take much more. Grabbing her hips, he positioned himself at the entrance to her pussy, holding her hips still so she could not move.

"Oh, God...Jim! I need to come. I don't think I can hold off much longer..."

Still he held her hips in his deceptively strong hands, his cock quivering at the entrance to her pussy. He retained control, knowing he needed to force her to accept his dominance. Only then could he teach her all the wonderful sensations of sex, including one called "humiliation." She had tasted it earlier, when she had begged for his kiss. Except her begging then had only been a means to an end, not words spoken from her heart. A woman of her pride would fight, but her ultimate submission to him would send her emotions into a whirlwind that would make her flight unforgettable. His fingers pressed against her skin as he held her, her pussy hovering just centimeters from the tip of his cock. Growling his command, he pushed her limits.

"Then beg me."

A feral growl came in answer and she shook her head even as she squirmed in his hands, trying to take his cock inside her.

"Beg me, Tania. You want to be fucked? Then beg for it." He slapped her ass again.

Embarrassment and mortification mingled with frantic need and Tania cried out, tears of frustration pooling in her eyes. She shook her head no, and he gave her ass another spank. It almost sent her over the edge. How could he demand that she debase herself like that? How could he treat her that way? The image of a slave girl came to her again. Didn't he realize she was an intelligent woman? That she was independent. That she was...

His cock brushed against the entrance to her pussy and the tears of need slid down her cheeks as her pussy longed to embrace him. A wall crumbled inside her heart as her last coherent thought flew out the window.

"Please, Jim. Please fuck me. Let me feel you inside me."

His cock brushed against her again and his fingers tightened on her hips, his thumbs digging into her reddened skin as she writhed in agony, trying not to come.

But when his fingers reached underneath to find her clit, all her pretenses shattered. Tears coursed down her face and her heart admitted his dominance. Whimpering, pleading, she begged again—this time from the depths of her being. "Please, Jim. Take me. Let me hold you. Please?"

Her sweet submission drove him over the edge. Without another word, he gripped her hips and thrust his swollen cock into her opening, forcing himself deep inside. Her muscles strained to accept his width, stretching to take him. He pushed her body away and pulled her to him a second time and a third, plunging again and again to allow her muscles to pull from him the seed his body wanted to give her.

His cock filled her, struck the sensitive spot inside, and she cried out in wordless passion even as his groans ran counterpoint. She rode him viciously in her need, moving now in tandem with his thrusts, her fingers gripping the edge of the chair as his fingers dug into her hips, slamming harder and harder.

"Come for me now. Come for me, Tania."

The world stopped. Two breaths held...one glorious second stretched to two, stretched forever before they plummeted to the earth in mindless ecstasy. Muscles contracted and released and together their voices shouted to the world that they were one. All the pent-up passion she held on to spilled out in waves of glory that lifted her time and time again until, spent, she leaned her head on the vinyl chair seat and gasped for breath as Jim leaned his hips against hers, relishing the last echoes of his climax.

For the first time in her life, Tania felt sated and whole. And when her body settled, and Jim pulled her to him to lie in his arms on the carpet, exhaustion overtook them both. Sliding her arms under his, Tania laid her head on the packed muscle of Jim's shoulder, just listening to him breathe as she sorted out the confusion in her mind.

Jim returned to reality slowly. The afternoon of paid sex he had thought to get when he'd first sat down at Tania's table had turned out to be far more than he had bargained for. He felt the light weight of her on his chest and pulled her close, burying his nose in her hair, drinking in her scent. A woman with passion that ran so hot and deep was the type of woman who came into a man's life only once. For some, maybe never. He was not about to let this one go.

"Jim?" Tania's muffled voice sounded far away.

"Yes, Tania?" He was a bit surprised to find his own voice fairly dreamlike.

"We need to do this a lot."

Jim grinned down at the tawny hair spread over his chest and pushed it away from her face. "Does that mean you liked learning about the different sensations sex can have?"

"Yes, you cad. I liked learning about the 'different sensations sex can have.' All of them." She blushed. "Even the spanking." Lifting her head, she gave him a mischievous grin, reaching down to gently squeeze his cock. Briefly she wondered what he tasted like but decided that would have to wait until later. Right now she was far too comfortable to move.

He looked down at her and brushed a stray hair from her cheek, still flushed with the heat that had fueled their passion. He tilted her chin up and gently kissed the soft lips he was falling in love with. "Even the spanking? I was afraid you were going to send me packing at first."

"The thought did cross my mind."

"But you didn't."

She propped herself up on one elbow so she could see his face. "No, I didn't send you packing. And before you ask why, I really don't know. If you'd have asked me at lunch if I wanted to be spanked to an orgasm, I'd have told you to take a hike. But when you slapped my ass...I found it so...wonderfully erotic...that I didn't want you to stop."

Jim went out on the limb. "There are other sensations I can teach you."

"Oh? Like what?"

The afterglow still lit her face, and there was an endearing, open curiosity there that made him smile up at her from his comfortable position on the floor. A flash of desire sped through him as he imagined what he would like to do to her. But past experience had taught him that the limb he was moving out on was a precarious place to venture, so his words were gently said.

"Sensations that involve…ropes."

"Really?" Her brow furrowed. "What do you mean?"

The limb he stood on could break at his next words. Jim hesitated, his fingers idly playing with a lock of her hair as he considered the best approach. Deciding Tania was the type of woman who wanted information in the most direct way, he rolled over onto one arm so he could gauge her reaction when he told her his somewhat kinky preferences.

"Tania, I want to teach you how being open and vulnerable to someone else's will can be erotic and sexy. I want to make you vulnerable to me by tying you up. I want to teach you how the rope I weave around your body can hold you, how it can caress your skin. How it can bind you to me in more ways than just the physical."

Tania's lips had parted and her breasts moved in tandem with her quickened breath. "You want to tie me up and fuck me?"

Jim laughed. "In short, yes."

"With rope?" She eyed him carefully.

"Yes." He sobered. Would she accept what he proposed? Or would she show him the door?

A slow smile spread over her face as she considered the idea. "And chains?"

"And chains." Did he dare hope?

Her smile turned naughty. "And whips?"

He grinned. "And whips."

"I'd like to know more about whips. A lot more."

Jim's fingers traced the outline of her face, wonderment in his voice. "My God, woman, you are incredible."

She smiled up through lowered eyelashes. "Thank you. Does that mean you'll come back?"

Jim grew serious once more. "Tania, I would very much like to come back. I don't want today to be all there is for us."

"What are you saying?"

His hand reached out to cup her breast and he felt her heart beat harder even as her eyes narrowed. Was he misinterpreting her again? He'd already made one huge mistake today and he didn't intend to make another. Did he really dare hope that this woman could handle his politically incorrect attitude toward sex? He looked into her wary eyes and didn't want to pass up the chance to find the answer. Taking a chance, he put his feelings out on the line. "I'm saying I'm not seeing anyone at the moment. But I'd like to be."

"Me?"

She looked so surprised and so vulnerable that Jim wanted to find whoever had hurt her in the past and punch his lights out. "Yes, love. You." He resisted the urge to flick that cute little nose of hers.

"Good." Tania's heart soared. "I'm not seeing anyone either. At the moment."

"And you will let me teach you more about slow and sensuous sex?"

"And whips and chains? I'm counting on it, buster."

Much too exhausted by their afternoon to do more than kiss her gently, Jim smiled down at the beautiful woman in his arms. "Then what do you say we continue this and see where it goes?"

"I'd say I am very glad you walked by my table today, Mr. Delaney." Tania looked up at him through her long lashes, flirting with him. "And I'd say you need to kiss me again." *And maybe give me another spanking*, she added silently.

"Yes, ma'am." Jim's grin lasted only until their lips met and Tania seductively pulled on his lower lip, arousing his cock again. Jim suddenly wasn't sure who was leading whom in this partnership, and as the kiss deepened, he decided he didn't care. Whether she had hooked him or he had hooked her, this partnership would be unlike anything either of them had ever experienced. Pulling her into his arms and taking possession of her mouth once more, Jim knew he wasn't going to let this one go.

In the End

S. L. Carpenter

Prologue

The queen grasped at the sheets of her large bed. Clinging onto the edge of her sanity. "Oh, it's happening again, oh, yes."

The large, dark-haired man growled as he nuzzled his face between her olive-toned thighs. With each roll of his tongue over her fleshy pussy, he knew he had hit the spot to bring his queen to the point of ecstasy.

His large hand reached up, molding to her breast. One hand high and the other between her legs, spreading her lips open to ease his assault on her slippery flesh.

With a smooth glide, he inserted his finger inside her and began to swirl it around in a circular motion. Spreading her open more and more each time around. Constantly applying pressure to her clit with his tongue.

The queen began to squirm and shake, her mind a blur, climbing over the wall of her boundary, until finally, she jumped over.

Rising off the bed she cried out, stretching her muscles and then falling loose and relaxed. She had finally freed her desires and let go. The calm after a storm of pleasure.

"What am I going to do without you for two years, Jared?"

The handsome man sucked the tips of his fingers one by one, savoring the taste of his queen. "You'll manage. You always do."

"You and Tommy need to bring back the right woman, Jared. Be careful on Earth. The only reason I am sending you two is because all the other missions have failed and I trust you."

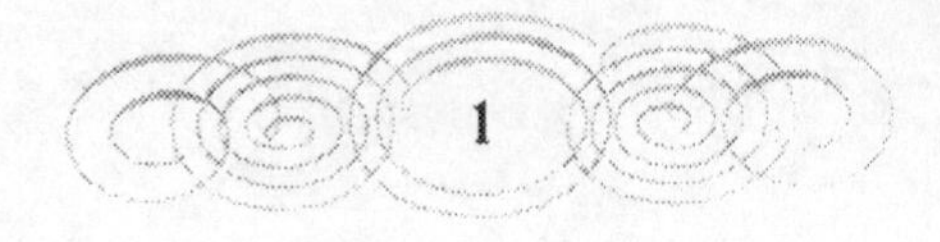

1

The double doors burst open and a stern-faced brunette woman boiled over in a fury.

"Damnit, Kirsten. You know I busted my ass to get those clients in here. You have the nerve to take credit for everything I do for this company." She clenched her fist, about ready to lash out. "I have had it with your backstabbing, money-grubbing bullshit!"

The supervisor stepped out of her office and gave a thumbs-up signal to the two women. "Great job, Kirsten. Those were some innovative ideas. You two should work together. Rene, you can learn a few things from Kirsten."

"Like how to kiss the boss's ass so much my lipstick is brown! Fuck this place. I'm going to open my own studio and bury this place. You'll see how much I add to this stale, dead-end company when I'm gone. Especially you, Kirsten. Live it up now, you're going down." Rene turned in a huff, holding back her rage.

Kirsten flung her long, fake blonde hair aside. "Oh, you should try going down more, Rene, maybe you wouldn't be such a bitch!"

The next sound was a grunt, followed by a slight crunching. It was Rene's fist embedding into Kirsten's face.

"There went that six thousand-dollar nose job, bitch. Fuck you." Rene shook her hand to ease the sting out. She wiped the spatters of blood off her knuckles on Kirsten's expensive business suit then stood up and walked past the other workers standing in their dull gray cubicles, mouths hanging open.

Rene's supervisor Bob rushed down the cubicle aisle and stopped when he saw Kirsten, bloodied and crying, and Rene standing in front of the large, tinted glass partition between the office area and management, applying lip gloss. "What the hell is going on here?"

Rene turned, puckered her lips then smiled widely, showing her pearly white teeth. "Kirsten fell into my fist. Oh, before I forget, fuck you, too, Bob. I quit!

"Ahhhh, I feel much better now." Rene smiled and whistled, walking past the few clients still standing inside the Ralston Interior Design Studio lobby.

She walked out of the building with a box of awards, memories and a few trinkets from her five years at the studio. Five years wasted on making a name for herself and having a blonde blowjob artist take credit for her. The soreness in her knuckles actually had a good feel to them. They reminded her of how great it had felt to hit Kirsten.

She got to her car, tossed the box in the back and stood with her arms resting on the roof of her car. Looking out through the smog-filled air toward the city skyline, she thought to herself, *I need time to relax and figure out what the hell is going on in my life. What's next? Maybe I should travel. God, I need to get laid again. I'm thinking I'll be a virgin because my hymen will grow back.*

Locking her car door, she sighed and headed toward the local row of coffee shops and bars looking for *whatever*.

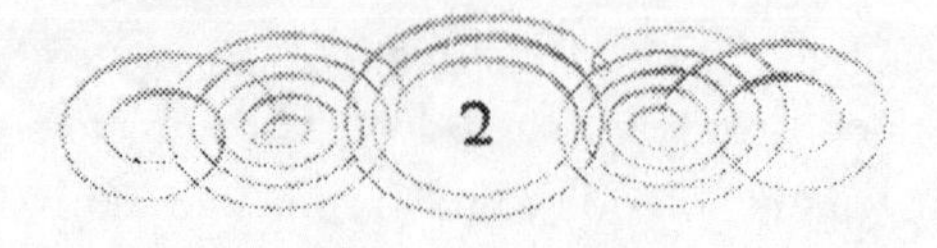

2

"There she is." A darkly handsome man motioned in Rene's direction. The blonde man turned and gave her a once-over.

The two men were aliens from another world. Humanoid—but aliens nonetheless. They had been studying Earthlings for two years. To blend in they dressed and acted like characters they had seen on standard television shows.

Back to reality...their mission was assigned, they were on Earth and had chosen their female. She had to come of her own free will. She couldn't be forced. The two men had some telepathic powers, but they were limited.

Most people would wonder how a race from another planet would look and be so similar to Earthlings. The answer was easy. On a secret mission to another planet long ago, three-headed, tentacle-armed freaky aliens abducted a small colony of humans on a deserted island. They were stranded after a storm left them on the island instead of being back after a three-hour tour...a three-hour tour.

The freaky aliens conducted tests and removed DNA. Things were beginning to look up. But one of the Earth subjects named Mulligan or something was a certified moron. He spilled the female DNA when trying to give a last sperm sample. Terrified by what would happen, the aliens didn't say anything and now Uranus was overrun with humanoid males.

That is, except for the few females who had been there from the beginning. These lucky ladies had been tasked with the job title of "baby machines" and only they could produce females. However, since they can each only have one child a year, things were getting tense in Uranus. Even the scientists with their advanced cloning techniques, all they produced were test-tube males. Talk about up shit creek.

Thus, the ruler Queen Senna sent these two selected males to study and bring back a woman. Many missions were begun, but like most things started by men, they fucked up. Each time they would go to Earth, they would pick up some Midwestern people who would freak out whenever the anal probe was opened. That and the aliens kept getting lost and refused to ask for directions. Really, is it *that* hard to find the third planet from the sun?

This was going to be a final mission, a last hope. The queen was getting pretty sore at the men's futility in all areas of their world.

The two men had seen her before, walking out from work, intrigued by the way she carried herself. Jared noticed the way she walked and how her clothes clung to her shapely form.

Tommy noticed how she needed to iron the seams. They were crooked and her jacket was wrinkled from all-day meetings, or at least that's what he assumed was the cause.

She wasn't perfect, yet there was a fire in her, an intangible. She was attractive and seemed at least from a distance, very confident. They had found the one they wanted—now they just needed to get her to go with them.

"Oh, please tell me she isn't wearing pumps with that hideous pant-suit...tell me."

Jared hesitated. "Tommy, she is. They are brown, too."

"I feel faint." Tommy laid the back of his hand against his brow. "Good Lord, I hope she doesn't need to pack before the trip. I don't think my stylist ego could handle another fashion fiasco like what she is wearing." Tommy fanned himself with his hand.

Jared shook his head, piping in, "Oh, come on, Tommy, she's not that bad. She's actually kind of cute."

"She needs a 'Tommy' special makeover. Highlights in her hair, a little makeup, a massage treatment and…Oh look, she went into the coffee shop. Yummy, I hope they have French vanilla cappuccino."

"Let's wait a few minutes. I don't want to look too suspicious. Why are you squirming in your seat?"

Tommy held both hands between his knees and swayed side to side. "I am excited, I can't wait."

Rene sat in the coffee shop. She was alone, scared and in a desperate funk of nothingness. She'd quit her job with no obvious prospects, her love life was nonexistent and to make matters worse, she burned the tip of her tongue on her coffee.

Whatever had happened to the "old" Rene?

The adventurous one who was afraid of nothing. The woman who had lost her virginity to a college man while was still in high school. The woman who won a few wet T-shirt and margarita-drinking contests in college. Who had fun no matter the situation, thrived for spontaneity and threw caution to the wind.

The same woman who had scraped and crawled her way up the interior design ladder and let her reputation and diehard enthusiasm speak for her. She had stood up for herself and gotten thrown down enough. Now she was lost in the middle of the rat race and didn't have cheese. She had crackers.

Her pride led her to this particular time in her life where she had become lost. She was free from everything and wanted to spread her wings…and her legs. She was in desperate need of two things.

One was a change in her meticulous, seemingly boring life. The other was a proper fucking and she wasn't sure just who it would come from.

"Let me pull the truck up front, a space just opened." Jared drove the truck over to the coffee shop.

Tommy hopped out as soon as Jared pulled into a parking space. Standing straight up, he brushed off his shoulders and adjusted the collar of his colorful silk shirt.

The two men walked in to see their target sipping her tall coffee in a meditative state. She appeared focused and calm. Her hair was hanging loosely over her shoulders and her eyes were closed. She was truly at peace. Funny how a caffeine drink could relax some and make others act as though they were on a cocaine binge.

Tommy swished up to the counter. Jared was more methodical and observant of the various groups of people jabbering away with their java fix in hand.

"Helloooo, I can see you, can we get a little service here?" Tommy reached out and rang the small bell on the counter a few times. The young employees behind the counter were all spastic buckets of nerves frantically trying to keep up with the coffee orders and discuss their weekend plans at the same time.

Rene glanced up and saw Tommy waving his hand limp-wristed to get some service. Her initial reaction was to giggle at how he acted. He was a good-looking man. He had shoulder-length blond hair, a medium build and was an exquisite dresser. Except for the red handkerchief in his breast pocket. Black would look better with the silken blue Hawaiian shirt.

When she turned to look at his companion, her eyes met his stare and the coffee's warmth became cold compared to the heat she began to feel between her thighs. *Hello*. It wasn't just the way he looked, which was pleasing, but it was something in that stare. A look that was deep, mysterious and definitely hot. He was tall, dark-haired, clean-cut and built like Fireman of the Year beefcake. She wondered if his hose could cool her fire. At least he could try.

The blond man received his coffee and held it tight in both hands, blowing the steam away to cool it. "Yummy, yummy, hot, hot, yummy, yummy."

The shop was crowded. The two men stood looking around for a table in front of Rene's and it was the perfect height.

Looking up she saw two men's crotches. Her reflex action was to grab the dark-haired man's because his had the biggest bulge. The horns of her wicked thoughts pushed her halo aside. *All of a sudden I have a craving for salami*, she thought.

She was in a perfect mood to do anything. Including taking this hunk of beef and fucking him into oblivion.

"You guys can sit here, I'm easy. I mean I don't mind." Rene's subconscious talked first with her mouth not editing the words.

"Hello, my name is Tommy, this is my friend Jared," the blond man brushed crumbs off the chair beside Rene's and sat down.

"Umm, Rene, my name is Rene." She was having a blonde moment and wasn't even blonde.

Jared spun his chair around with the tall wooden back against the table and sat directly across from her.

"Isn't this place just decadence at its most primal? A cup of coffee for five bucks and you don't even get a muffin." Tommy looked around at all the patrons. "Next time we need to open one of these, Jared. Jared?"

Jared's eyes stared directly at Rene. Their gaze was intense, intriguing and had the distinct emotion of lust. "Yeah, I could go for eating a muff right now." His voice was deep and penetrating.

Holy fucking shit, she thought, noticing the wetness of her panties. *This guy could melt ice with that look.*

Jared reached his large hand out, beckoning Rene to take it. Something was connecting between them. He wanted the connection to be complete. Like ten inches buried inside her complete.

Rene began to sense something in her head. A voice subliminally telling her to take Jared's hand.

His spell was cast and she followed his mental commands.

When their skin touched, heat radiated through her veins. Her mind began to cloud and her breath quickened, she was being possessed. *Who cared?* The flow of the heat seemed to follow one direct route, to the engorging center of her being, her pussy.

"Jared, no mind manipulation." Tommy broke his focus. "She has to come of her own free will."

"Give me two more minutes and I'll come everywhere." Rene hadn't realized she spoke out loud. Their hands parted and her pussy began to cry, longing for more.

Sighing, Jared knew Tommy was right.

"We *will* continue this conversation." Rene straightened her stature, sitting upright and proper.

"Look at her nipples, Jared. See what you do?"

"I am looking, Tommy. Damn, I'm horny, too." Jared was like a kid, wanting to play with a new toy.

Rene cleared her throat and tried unsuccessfully to hide her arousal. The chitchat was pleasant and she kept peeking over at Jared to see him staring at her.

Rene sat, smiling and shaking her head as the two guys, mainly Tommy, began explaining their real intent. Why they wanted her to come with them.

"Well, we are actually aliens. We have studied your planet for a few years and our queen has asked us to bring a female Earthling back with us. So Jared and I have been looking for someone that is strong-willed and single—with no ties. Someone free. Someone like you. Except for your choice of fashion, you are perfect for us."

"So you're aliens? Like from Mexico? Canada?"

"No, Uranus," Tommy answered.

"Aliens from my anus?" Rene replied, raising her eyebrow in confusion.

"Nooooo. Ur-anus. You know, one of the planets?" Tommy was miffed at having to explain himself again. "Are you sure you aren't a blonde?"

"You want me to find out, Tommy? I'll check." Jared looked down Rene's body and focused again toward her pussy.

"How about...*no*. We don't have time, Jared."

Who says we don't have time? Just give me thirty minutes! Rene liked the attention this Jared character paid to her. She also liked the effect he had on her libido.

Tommy continued his explanations to Rene. She sat mystified by Jared and confused by Tommy.

"If you're aliens, why do you look human?" She could only imagine that *everything* was like a human. She damn well hoped so.

"We're humanoid. You don't think Earth is the only planet inhabited, do you? Hey you...behind the counter. I need a refill." Tommy sighed and continued. "He's a cute guy but probably has his mother dress him. No style whatsoever."

"How'd you get your names? Jared and Tommy are rather normal names. Shouldn't you be called Pla-booger-345 or something weird?"

Shaking his head, Tommy put a hand on his hip and explained. "We picked more common names to blend in."

"Okay, I'll bite. What're your real names?" Rene was following along with what she thought was a charade.

Waving his hands on either side of his head, Tommy answered, "You really don't want to know. They just gave us numbers because we were cloned. Sort of like your Social Security system over here on Earth. We're just numbers. Nothing special."

"I know the feeling. Working in big business and trying to make it in this rat race makes you feel like nothing more then a drone." Rene sipped her coffee. "So where'd you get your names then?"

"I picked them." Tommy smiled ear to ear, giddy with himself.

"Ever hear of soap operas? He picked names from one of those," Jared answered.

"I was addicted to them. Those shows suck you in and right when you get to a climactic scene...they cut to a commercial."

"That's the story of my sex life. Just when it gets good, the guy needs a commercial break." Rene slumped into her chair.

"We'll have to remedy that," Jared said the right thing, again.

Is it getting hot in here or am I horny? Looking at Jared she knew, she wanted a nasty fuck, like right now.

After talking and flirting for a while, the three of them seemed to get along and the sexual tension between Rene and Jared was obvious. She was into him and he definitely wanted to get into her. In any hole possible. Hips or lips, he wasn't worried about where.

Rene figured she would throw caution to the wind and follow along with this game being played on her. These were a couple of really cute guys. She didn't have anything else to do. She had left her job, needed a change and this little adventure seemed like fun. Stupid...but fun.

As the three of them chatted and talked about a variety of things from the weather to bad television shows, the obvious connection between them grew.

"What the fuck. Let's go." Rene threw her hands up and began to get up from the table.

Also getting up, Jared knocked a napkin holder off the table. He bent over to pick it up and Rene's eyes stared at his muscular ass. Ache crept through her pussy. She imagined her fingernails digging into Jared's ass as they fucked.

"Anybody home? Hellooooooooo? I can't believe it. Jared bends over and you are a vegetable." Tommy obstructed her view. "Look... don't I have a nice ass, too?" Tommy posed in a standard jeans ad pose, sticking his ass out with his shirt pulled up.

"Well, yes, I am sorry." Blushing six different shades of red, Rene was caught wishing for Jared's pants to fall down.

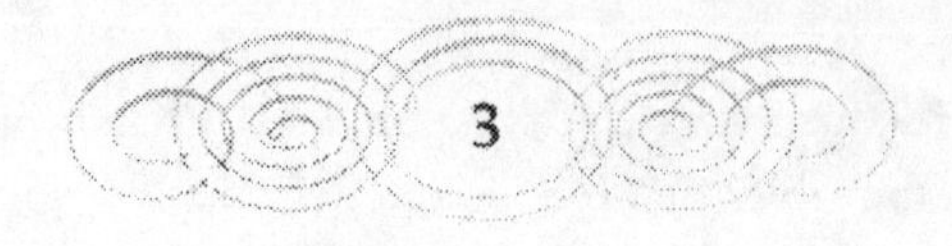

3

After following Rene to her apartment in the truck, the two guys stood in her small home.

"I just need to get a few things." Rene ran into her bedroom while Tommy and Jared stood in the middle of her tiny apartment.

"Ewwwww, and she does interior design?" Tommy looked around the room, analyzing the décor, his own ego and realm of expertise showing its face. The room was bland, with only a couch, loveseat and a small end table. On the wall hung a flat-panel television and a few unimpressive pictures.

"It looks as though she's never home. She must be one of those workaholic types." Jared walked into the kitchenette area. He glanced into the fridge and saw old pizza, some outdated milk and various flavors of yogurt and some pre-made salads. *No beer, hmmm.*

Tommy walked over to the large window, which led to a small patio. He opened the sliding glass door and went outside. "I love the night air," he said, leaning on the patio railing overlooking the city.

Jared moved toward the bedroom and saw the door ajar. With his finger, he opened it a bit more. Leaning against the wall, he saw Rene's reflection in the full-length mirror she had on her closet door.

Hmmm, interesting, he thought as Rene was pulling her blouse off and standing in her panties. She reached her arm back and unfastened her bra, letting it fall. Jared stood, admiring her nicely shaped breasts. He bit his lip, hungry for more.

Rene was oblivious to Jared's watchful eyes. She doubted whether she should go with these two strangers who seemed to have some rather strange kind of bond with her. Instead of behaving in her normal, "little miss careful" manner, she was throwing caution to the wind. Acting careless, like some bad actress in an even poorer B-rated movie. But she could really use a little make-believe adventure right about now. That, and a starring role in a hot, erotic, sex movie with two guys.

Her hands fell to her hips and began to roll the waistband of her underwear down. The silky fabric tumbled along her swaying thighs and legs.

Jared breathed in. Her fragrance was intoxicating. He couldn't pinpoint what it was but something about her stirred him.

Jared's thoughts raced through his head. *Nice ass. Damn, I am horny again. Look at that small patch of hair. What's that tattoo say on her hip? Why don't I just jump her? Why am I thinking all these thoughts? Echoooooo. Where am I? Who's talking to me? Oh wait, it's my conscience telling me to pay attention and quit fucking around.*

Rene turned and faced her bed. Kneeling down, she reached under and grabbed a travel bag. Standing naked, she knew she obviously needed clothes but what else? Just the necessities and some naughty stuff—just in case.

Let's see, condoms, strawberry-flavored lube, breath mints, my new vibe, a rainbow of thongs, the pocket instamatic nail file and knife with one thousand uses, some pepper spray in case these two looney tunes try something, my address book and Midol—can't go anywhere without THAT. I am forgetting something. Oh, Lord, my Swiss chocolate stash.

The hair on the back of her neck began to stand on end. A growing warmth began to swell inside her pussy, making her suddenly gasp. She tightened her thighs and couldn't figure out why she was having this sudden ache. An uneasy chill crept down her spine. She was being watched and could feel lustful eyes staring at her.

Turning around she saw nothing in her doorway, just a shadow disappearing off the wall. She had better hurry. There were only a few comfy clothes she wanted, so she grabbed them and stuffed them into the travel bag. She slipped into a pair of skin-tight jeans, a pair of nice boots and a red silk blouse that clung to her body. She had always enjoyed the feel of silk against her skin. The blouse tied at the bottom revealing a hint of midriff.

After she finished packing quicker than ever, she left her bedroom and walked into the living room.

Nobody was there. They must have left. Rene should have known it was a joke. She was getting into the idea of an adventure and spending time with these two characters. Especially Jared.

"You see over there, Tommy? That's Venus." Jared's voice echoed from the balcony.

With a sigh, Rene went out to the balcony with them. They all looked to the stars.

"You ready?" Tommy asked as he grabbed Rene's hand. "That's all you are bringing?"

"Yeah, it's not like I'll be gone that long. I'll take care of the bills and stuff when I get back."

"Okay, whatever you say." Tommy then slipped her hand under his arm and walked toward the door. "So you are going to wear *that*? We need to talk, Rene, we need to seriously talk."

Jared grabbed her bag and they left.

The three of them piled into the truck and headed toward the downtown area as night began to fall.

"Well, sweetheart—"

"Rene, my name is Rene."

"Okay, *Rene*." Tommy made quotation marks with his fingers. "We need to take you to our spaceship, actually the portal to our ship. Then we can zip off to our planet and never come back."

"This is a joke, isn't it? Some of the guys from the fabric department set this up, right?"

Jared piped in. "Nope, this is for real. We have been searching for you for quite a while. We need a certain type of woman. Somebody that is ready for change."

"Jared...pull over here...stop, stop, hurry!" Before the car stopped completely, Tommy leaped out.

"Oh, shit. Tommy, we can't. Later, we don't have time for this now!" Jared chased after Tommy.

Rene looked out the side window. Opening the door, she got out and started to walk toward the two guys. Jared tried in vain to move Tommy from his stance. Rene stepped up. "What the hell are you looking at?"

"I have been looking for this for months and months, you gotta let me get it, Jared. I'll do anything. I'll even fuck that ugly bitch you set me up with."

Jared sighed, knowing he had to give in. "Okay. But you don't have to sleep with that dog."

Tommy danced in the street. "Whoaaaaaa, yeah. Gimme, gimme the money."

He grabbed it from Jared's hand and ran into the small hole-in-the-wall store. It had a brick entrance and an old-fashioned décor with a Seventies feel of neon and bright colors in the window.

"That's really not a nice way to talk about women."

"Huh? Oh, well, we weren't talking about a woman. We were talking about an old woman's poodle. We got drunk and I dared him to fuck the dog. He said we all have limitations. I haven't heard the end of it since. He can be such a bitch sometimes." Jared shook his head, smiling.

"Hello, dahhhhhlings, don't you just looooooooove my new jacket?" Tommy stood seductively against the wooden doorframe in a purple crushed-velvet sports jacket. "Damn, I feel sexy now. Let's get to the pick-up zone."

They walked back to the truck. Except Tommy—who sashayed like a princess.

"Why do you guys act like this?"

"Well, all we get on our satellite is the infomercials and the cheap TV stations. And he watches reruns of that show where the gay guys do a makeover of a straight male. Tommy just loooooves the different characters. We thought we would blend in easier if we acted like people from television."

"Blend in? What planet are you from again?"

"Uranus."

"Pardon me?"

"We live inside Uranus."

"My anus?"

"Not my-anus...Ur-anus. You know, the planet. Didn't we go over this in the coffee shop? In the solar system. Don't they teach you humans anything in school?"

"That sounds about right for you two. I thought Uranus was bitterly cold. Life can't exist there. I'm getting a headache." Rene rubbed her temple and sighed.

"Well, on the surface it is just smooth and cold. But inside Uranus, it is warm. Many species live in the long tunnel of caves buried beneath the surface. It is a cramped, small area."

"Yep, you'll like it there. Uranus may be a little dusty but it's not much different from some of your cities."

"Holy smokes, what's that smell? Oh, jeez, it's horrible." Rene blinked her eyes tightly.

Tommy sniffed the air and looked over to Jared with an eyebrow raised. "It was probably Jared. Every time he eats pork, he gets gas. One time he ate a whole bag of pork rinds. Oh. My. GOD. I was scared to light a match."

"Let me guess. Jared is the male of this couple."

"Couple? Ohhhhh, you have us all wrong. We're Uranuses. We are here on a mission for the queen. She rules over all the male population. She wants us to bring a female Earthling to the planet. She has a job for the woman who comes to Uranus with us. So it will be you, the queen, a dozen breeders and about two million men."

"I like those odds. I need to get laid anyway. Maybe I can find one that isn't an asshole." Rene began to laugh.

"Oh, quit it. We only mate male to female for creation of more life or when the queen gets an itch for some beefcake. She is such a slut. I mean, you could probably fit a whole arm up there and have to open your fingers to feel the sides."

"That's just great. A black hole of sex."

Rene began to rub her forehead. "I'm getting a migraine. What does the queen do?"

With a sigh, Tommy began his little condensed speech for Rene.

"The queen basically rules Uranus. Think about it, when hasn't a woman ruled everything. So anyways, she only mates with certain men. Men like...never mind. It's rather complicated. She is like a merry-go-round, everyone gets to take a ride and it seems to last forever and you feel sick in the end."

"Hey, we just follow orders. I hear it is pretty bad now. She has like four guys at a time. I was one of her bodyguards before coming here to study Earth. Things were different before. Now I'd be afraid I would fall in," Jared piped in.

"That's disgusting!!!" Rene shook her head.

Angrily Tommy turned back. "Oh, I see, Earthlings are so much more sophisticated. I have seen some of your so-called entertainment. Girls with horses, midgets, guys with farm animals. Although, that one time with the cow was interesting. Besides, that was a long time ago."

Pausing, Tommy continued. "I wanted to be a woman for a while and thought I would *DIE* when I had a period. I would eat four gallons of chocolate ice cream and a dozen pepperoni sticks."

Jared interrupted. "You can't judge people without knowing them. Or aliens, for that matter."

"Can we hear some music or something?" Rene rubbed her temples, feeling a migraine coming on. *This is what happens from too much coffee,* she thought.

"Oh, sure, what would you like?" Tommy bounced in his seat.

Now lost in thought, Rene said, "Not the Village People. I don't care. Just something."

"Ewwww, they suck. I have a perfect disc that you'll love."

Jared reached out to cover the CD player opening. "*Not* Cher. I am so tired of that CD."

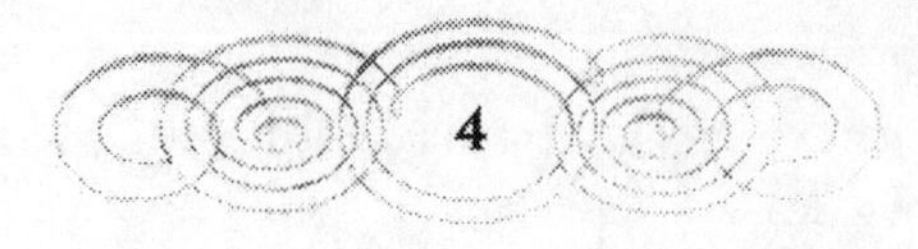

4

The truck pulled up to the downtown area. Jared parked it in a darkened alley beside a bar. Jared hit the ignition, ending Tommy's CD in the truck, and silence took over.

"Awww...shit." Tommy was peeved at not being able to dance anymore.

"A bar. You are taking me to a bar. Are you kidding me?" Rene quickly realized some free drinks might help. They sure couldn't hurt.

The doors of the bar opened as a couple left. Tommy was again in heaven, the silence was broken by the blasting sound of eighties music. Tommy shook his head and hopped out shaking his ass like a schoolgirl. "Wooohooo, I love this music."

"The transport is over there." Tommy pointed to an ATM booth under a corner streetlight. "We just need to wait until midnight then we can leave. Might as well have some fun."

A cloud of smoke billowed out the door as Jared opened it.

"Ah, my kinda place. Loose women and alcohol. What a great mix, and I need to get laid before the trip."

Tommy whispered into Rene's ear, "He always gets horny before space travel. Actually he is always pretty horny."

Rene almost said "likewise" but thought better of it.

"Let's dance. I wanna shake my ass to some tunes. Come on, don't get shy on me now. I'm a great dancer." Tommy tugged Rene to the floor as a techno beat filled the room.

Just as Tommy began to circle Rene, the music changed, as did the mood. The lighting turned blue and the music was a slow jam that had everyone filling the floor quickly and fully.

Rene turned to leave and was grabbed by the waist. Tommy pulled her close to him. "I said I wanted to dance." His voice was deeper than before.

Standing with her back to his front, Rene began to sway with Tommy's lead. He was warm, and for a guy who acted gay, he was beginning to push something against her backside from his groin area.

"Mmmm, you are a good dancer." Rene turned around to face Tommy. Looking up she noticed his smile, and his hands fell to her waist, pulling her close. His thigh rested between her legs and with each sway, she felt the tightening of his leg against her aroused cunt. They were close, the temperature was rising and Rene was enjoying the way Tommy felt. The inner slut was raising her head.

"Where's Jared?" Rene asked trying to gain control back.

"I don't know and don't care. He's probably looking for a redhead. He says redheads tend to keep him dormant longer for the trip. Personally, I think it's because he likes to have different flavors. He's such a man-whore." Tommy pulled Rene to him and she couldn't resist snuggling into him.

The song ended and with a sigh, Tommy and Rene parted. He led her to a small table in the corner. It was the only one empty, except for the leftover drinks and napkins scattered across it.

"Oh. My. God. This is gross. I need to clean this. I'll get us a few drinks, too."

Rene paused then ordered. "Get me a Screaming Orgasm."

Laughing Tommy walked away. "You're terrible, I'll see what I can do."

Rene scanned the bar. Darkness covered most of it with couples flirting and kissing. There was a group of women at the large table by the dance floor, looked like a party.

Something made the hair on the back of Rene's neck tingle. Someone was looking at her. She turned toward a pitch-black hallway in the back wall behind her. There she squinted to see a pair of eyes—Jared's eyes. Like before, they cut through her. But he wasn't alone.

"I see you found Jared." Tommy arrived with the drinks and brushed his jacket sleeve. "The dust and smoke in here are going to ruin my velvet jacket. Good thing we won't be here too long."

Rene peered back to see long strands of red hair swaying as the woman with Jared threw her head back. Jared was nuzzling into her chest. Whatever he was doing, the woman was enthralled to a fierce point of passion.

Rene swallowed, jealous and curious. What did this woman have that she didn't?

The lights from the dance floor turned red and made Rene's vision of the couple clearer.

Jared stood in the darkened hallway with the redhead. The swoop of her dress pulled taut down her spine as Jared groped her body. Rene could see the silhouette of Jared's hands unfastening his belt. The music was deafening but Rene sat with Tommy and watched.

Rene's back was to the crowded dance floor. Her instincts told her to turn away. It wasn't right to watch a couple in this way. Her eyes fell to the table and the drink Tommy had gotten her. Unable to help herself, she had to watch.

Her eyes fixated on the two of them. Heat began to stir within her body. The steady pulse of arousal began to fill her moist pussy.

"You know, Jared is an incredible lover. The queen favors him. He had a Venusian tutor in his middle years. She taught him things that most men never learn. She was exquisite and Jared's first love."

Tommy's voice filled her head. Jared's mouth kissing the woman's lips filled her eyes. The thought of him filling something else warmed her already hot cunt.

"Oh, my God," Rene uttered with eyes widened. A tingle of lust ignited her at the sight of Jared's immense cock in the redhead's hands.

The redhead was propped against the wall. She had her leg pushing the adjacent wall that Jared leaned into. The black hip boots hid some of their movements but from Rene's viewpoint, she could clearly see the woman stroking on Jared's cock. She had to use both hands to hold it. *Must be part elephant in Uranus' genetics.*

Gulping, Rene licked her lips. The fire burning inside her made the simple act of sitting almost impossible. Her ass squirmed on the chair while she watched.

A cool burst of air filled Rene's ear as Tommy's now soothing voice spoke to her. "You know, Jared and I are connected telepathically. I can show you something rarely shown to an Earth female. It is incredibly intense. You have to trust me and close your eyes."

Rene was torn. Scared at what might happen, she had her doubts, but her curiosity was stimulated almost as much as her sensitive clit.

Jared was licking the redhead's neck while she continued her steady stroking of his cock. He looked over to Rene and smiled. His eyes caused her to shudder and melt in her chair. He winked at her and then turned back to the woman he was with.

"Trust me. You wanted a screaming orgasm, let me help," Tommy whispered again.

Rene felt Tommy's fingers caress the tightened muscles of her neck. Her mind began to swim in a sea of calmness. The relaxing feel of a man's caress was soothing. His fingers traced the back of her neck and she felt Tommy taking deep breaths. His fingers reached her temples and the one word she remembered was, "*Now!*"

Rene's body felt lifted and a sudden fullness spread her pussy walls. The vision of Jared filled her mind. She was in place of the redhead. It was no longer a voyeuristic act—she became part of her own fantasy.

Her body began to tremble. Rene's jaw vibrated as she breathed in with the long, deep penetration of her soul. This was a true mind-fuck. If this was a fantasy, sign her up for daily sessions. Rene tried to stay focused, but was soaring to an unknown peak of ecstasy she had never felt before. Her pussy was filled to its limit and every movement of Jared's dream lover caused her more pleasure.

She found herself commanding the dream with wishes. Longing for Jared's large hands to cup her breasts as they fucked, suddenly it began to happen. The clouds around her took shape and the molding of his hands gently squeezed her breasts. Her nipples ached for his kiss and she felt the wet tongue of this fantasy suckle at them.

Jared was deliberate and forceful as he fucked. Long, hard, penetrating thrusts, touching the entrance to her womb. He was deliciously teasing her. She could feel the head of his cock swelling as he pressed into her. Over and over, he drove in and out.

Rene became lost in the dream state. If the redhead was feeling this for real then Rene was jealous. If this was only a fraction of the reality, then the woman must be dead from multiple orgasms.

This mental fuck was too much for her to handle. Rene's body began to shake and the first wave of her orgasm swept her deeper into the dream. She threw her head back, letting her legs widen and tighten. Like an epileptic fit, her body began to convulse and spasm.

"Rene, come back to me. Come to me." The voice echoed in her head as Tommy repeated it. "Come back to me."

Slowly regaining her consciousness, Rene felt weak. Her vision was blurred and a misty fog lifted from her mind. *Talk about giving mind to someone.* The smile spreading across her face spoke volumes. "I did come for you—I mean back to you."

Sitting up, she noticed coldness between her legs and on her ass. She was soaked through her underwear. "Oh, shit, I need to go to the ladies' room."

"What?" Tommy yelled back, unable to hear over the music.

"I need to use the ladies' room!"

Again he held his hand to his ear, showing he couldn't hear her.

With the fade of the music Rene yelled, *"I have to take a fucking pee."* At least everyone knew where she was headed now. She let her hand brush across Tommy's face, grinning at him.

"Okay, hurry back," he tapped his pink watch, "we don't want to miss our teleporter." Tommy sat watching the crowd shuffling around the dance floor, waiting for the music. He seemed very much in his element. People, dancing, music—Tommy appeared happy and ready to show off.

Rene turned, started toward the bathroom and saw the redheaded woman struggling to stand up. Jared was nowhere to be seen and she was obviously disoriented.

"Here, you need a hand?" Rene reached her hand out to help her up.

"Fucking A. Can you help me to the restroom? I feel drunk. My legs are gone." The redhead grabbed her small pocketbook from the floor where it had apparently dropped and staggered with Rene. She held her arm to maintain balance whenever her knees weakened.

Rene went pee, then to the mirror, cleaning herself up. She could hear the redhead sitting down and a slight sigh as she began to go to the bathroom. Now baseball players hold it for restroom breaks, concert performers do, as well as some speakers and stand-up comedians. This woman must have held it for days, like a camel.

The woman did the bathroom ritual. With a cleansing breath, she regained her composure and stepped up to the mirror beside Rene.

"Holy shit!" The redhead stepped back. "I saw you in my head."

"What are you talking about?" Rene asked, confused.

"That guy I was with. The, ummm, the fucking sex god. Before he stuck that monster in me, he told me to close my eyes. In my dream I saw you."

"He came here with me," Rene answered.

"Well, sweetheart, he came inside of me and I have never had sex like that before. I could swear I was in a dream. Over and over he just...shit, my Lord, I mmmmmm, can't describe the feeling. It was like he became a part of me. That cock entered me—hurt like hell—but he entered me like he was touching my soul. I was scared he'd explode through my diaphragm. You are one lucky girl." The woman had a blissful smile on her face.

"We're not lovers. We just met."

"Well, fuck the friends shit. You need to jump that horse and ride him like a rodeo. If I wasn't engaged and this my bachelorette girls' night out, I would. Hell, I thought he was my present."

After a few moments of girl talk and freshening makeup, Rene and the woman left the bathroom, laughing at their own private joke.

A large man stood at the end of the short hallway leaving the restrooms. He had a big smile that was directed at Rene. "Heya, sweetheart. I couldn't help but notice you walking in with those two faggots. You looking for a real man?" Arrogance filled the air. As did the smell of a few too many pitchers of cheap beer.

The other woman piped in. "Bubba, how would you know they are fags??? Are you a fag expert? Been doing your research?"

"Shut up, bitch. I'm talking to this little lady here. Not the bar whore."

"Fuck you, asshole." Apparently unsure whether to kick him in the balls or slap his face, the redhead reached her arm back and had it grabbed by one of her girlfriends who saw the argument beginning.

"Come on, Rose, he's not worth it." Her friend tugged at her arm.

"You come with us!" She reached out for Rene's hand and the man slapped it away.

"She's staying right here for now." His snarling smile was enough to make Rene ill.

"Who's that over there? He's waving at you?" Rene pointed her arm out, and the dumb lug turned to see Tommy waving to Rene. She saw her chance, ducking by the man and scooted to where Tommy was.

Turning away, Tommy didn't see the big goon grabbing for his shoulder.

Riiiiip...

Rene turned back to see the man with a handful of Tommy's new jacket in his massive paw. The man burst into laughter.

"Awwwww, pretty boy got a tear in his widdle coat?" He laughed aloud, causing everyone to turn to look.

Tommy looked down. His body tensing to the shame the worthless slab of meat was testing him with. "Apologize," he said quietly.

"*What*? You're kidding, right? For what? I tore your jacket, queer boy. Big fucking deal."

"I have been looking for a jacket like this for almost a year. They don't make this style anymore. It means a lot to me. If you would just apologize, I'll leave." His eyes began to lightly glow a magenta shade. His demeanor had become almost demonic. His glare was burning and anger radiated through him.

"Come on, Tommy, let's just go." Rene tried to move Tommy. She didn't want him hurt.

"Yeah, listen to the little cunt. She needs someone to tint her hair."

"Fuck you, asshole!" Rene was seriously pissed now.

Jared had finally pushed through the crowd and stood between the big bonehead and Tommy. The man was a little more intimidated by Jared's size, but a bellyful of beer made him dumber than a rock.

"What's this? You here to protect your little bitch boyfriend?"

A bunch of the guys from around the bar were laughing with him as the crowd grew.

"Actually I'm trying to stop you from getting...well, killed." Jared didn't want to sound too silly by warning a six-foot-five-inch, three hundred-pound musclehead about a five-foot-ten-inch blond man.

"Jared...he ripped my coat, my new coat. Now he won't apologize." Tommy's voice had lowered three octaves to almost a growl.

The man reached over and grabbed a full mug of beer. After taking a swig, he tossed the remaining beer at Tommy then threw the glass against the wall. "Why don't you just get the fuck out of here so I can kick this little bitch-boy's ass and get back to drinking?"

"Okay...I warned you." Jared patted Tommy on the shoulder. "See you outside in a few minutes. Don't make too much of a mess this time."

Jared grabbed Rene's arm and pulled her away from Tommy's side.

"You aren't going to leave him there alone, are you?" Rene was slightly panicked.

"Who? Tommy? You must be kidding. That guy doesn't stand a chance. I just hope he doesn't try to fight dirty, he'll just piss Tommy off."

Standing by the doorway, Rene yanked free from Jared's arm. "Stop. Just stand here. I don't want Tommy to get hurt."

A crowd surrounded the two men, leaving them a large circle of room to fight in. The man's friends all whapped his back and cheered him on. The bartender was frantically trying to contact the police on the phone at the bar.

"Go easy. Don't fuck him up too bad."

"After you kick his ass, can we fuck him like a goat?"

The banter was pathetic.

Tommy stood motionless in the middle of the floor. Beer dripped off his blond locks of hair. His anger causing his blood to heat and steam rose from his wet hair.

Rene stared at him. She could sense his rage—in fact, she began to become enwrapped in it. The mental mind-fuck had somehow linked her to Tommy and his burning anger began to boil within her also.

"Okay, bitch. Let's get it on."

Tommy looked up, eyes radiating a red ember like the coals of a fire.

The man stepped back and then lunged his fist in a roundhouse swing.

His large, pillar-sized arm swung hard and hit flush against Tommy's hand. It was as if he hit a brick wall, the man's fist cracked and broke. He swung upward with the other hand and hit Tommy flush in the stomach. Again, the man whimpered as he crushed his hand into a true six-pack of abdomen muscles.

The man wrung his hand and stood back. He wouldn't be humiliated by a smaller, less physical man. Apparently blocking out the pain, he rushed Tommy and bear-wrapped him in his arms. He raised him up, and Tommy arched his head back and firmly head-butted the brute, breaking his nose and causing him to loosen his arms.

Tommy punched him square in the solar plexus with a crunching sound. The man gasped. The goon fell to his knees, trying to catch his breath. With a thud, he fell to the floor. With a straight jab, Tommy smashed the man's nose further. Tears filled the goon's eyes as the pain swelled in his face. Blood drained from his broken nose and he was humiliated.

Reaching his hand back, Tommy swung his open palm across the man's face. The slapping sound made the crowd cringe. A hand impression glowed red across the brute's face. Tommy turned, leaving the man sprawled out on the ground in a bloody, gasping heap.

Tommy tossed him a napkin from a table and said, "Wipe your face, it's a bitch to get blood out of a cotton shirt."

Tommy walked toward the crowd that split apart in a caricature of Moses at the Red Sea.

Three of the goon's friends stepped beside their fallen friend behind Tommy. They were apparently torn as to wanting to defend their friend and getting their asses kicked by this slender man.

The goon held his arm up, motioning them to stand back. He pulled his body upright and groaned quietly in pain.

Behind Tommy, the shattering sound of a beer bottle echoed through the room. Bubba was going to fight dirty. "*Go fuck yourself*! Fucking fag, I'm gonna cut you a new asshole."

Tommy turned back around to face the large, bleeding hulk.

The watching crowd had grown, and the room felt alive with cheers and screams for the fight.

The big man spit blood on Tommy's Italian boots and waved the broken glass around.

"Ahhhhh, my boots! Do you realize these are Italian? Like from Italy, you fucking brainless, testicle-sucker!"

Rene felt his rage building stronger but could only watch as he stepped up to the man. A futile swish of glass cut Tommy's jacket. Before any more damage was done, Tommy grabbed the man's neck and tore his throat open. Blood began to squirt out from between the man's fingers as he tried to hold his wound closed.

Tommy then reached over and grabbed the big, bleeding moron's hair, tearing it loose from his scalp, making him turn around. The drunken guy was totally vulnerable with blood streaming down his neck, covering the front of his shirt.

Tommy raised his hand up behind Bubba's ear, tightening it like a tiger claw. With lightning speed, he struck the man's lower back causing him to lose control of his bladder and urinate in his pants.

Seeing an imported beer on the small table next to him, Tommy grabbed it and breathed in the scent of the barley and hops. With a tug and a tear, he yanked the man's pants down leaving him exposed and leaking. The man fell to the floor in a fetal curl with his ass upward. Tommy took a swig of the fine imported beer then shoved the beer bottle into the guy's hairy ass.

The crowd of onlookers became silent. The pool of blood from Bubba spread across the floor and his followers stepped away from their fallen warrior.

Tommy took off his jacket and flung it over his shoulder saying, "No...*YOU* go fuck yourself."

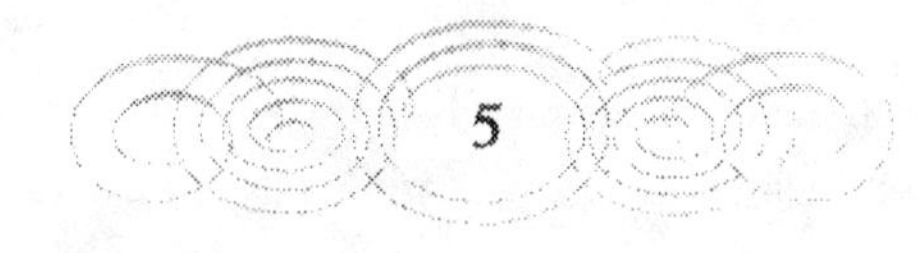

5

Rene shook her head as the three of them walked toward an ATM booth illuminated in a neon glow.

"Remind me to never piss you off," Rene joked. "How did you do that? Where did you learn to fight like that?"

"Can you fix this?" Tommy held up his sleeve showing the rip on the shoulder and the cut along the biceps. "I really love this coat." A tear seemed to fill his eye. Within three minutes Tommy changed from a menacing, violent monster into a caring, sympathetic...well, he was back to his old self.

"Of course. I owe you one. Thank you for everything." She leaned over and kissed Tommy's cheek.

"We need to get going. We'll miss the window for the transporter." Jared tugged at Rene and Tommy, guiding them down the sidewalk.

"Oh, shit! I need my bag. I need my supplies." Rene pointed to the truck as they walked past it.

"Okay, hurry up."

She grabbed her bag from the truck and they rushed to the ATM booth.

Tommy stepped into the booth first, followed by Rene and Jared. Rene felt like a hot dog with two sets of buns around her.

"Don't tell me we need money to go to your anus?" Rene snickered as she spoke.

Tommy punched a set of keys and nothing was happening except a droning beeping echoing through the cramped booth.

"I can't believe it. Dammit, Tommy, you forgot the ATM code again, didn't you?" Jared was angry and squished in against Rene's ass.

She didn't mind.

Tommy pressed in the code numbers for the third time and a faint screeching sound became louder and louder. Tommy turned and stuck his tongue out at Jared.

Rene second-guessed herself and for an instant thought, *Fuck this, I'm outta here,* but before she could speak, a blinding light filled the booth. She looked down at her hands, and they became transparent before her eyes and she suddenly felt euphoric. With a last blast of light, they were gone. Instantly she was in darkness and heard a clomping sound.

"Ouch, dammit, Tommy, you left the light off and I hit my toe on the table." Jared fumbled around for the light.

The room became bright with a neon-like glow. It wasn't much bigger than a walk-in closet. All that was there were a few hooks on the wall and a bench on either side.

"How did you guys do that? How did we get here? Where the fuck are we? You must have drugged me." Rene dug into her bag for her pepper spray.

"This is the ship we take to travel to Uranus. It's like a probe ship. Four weeks travel and we go up through the back hole to home." Jared shook a chill from his spine.

The more she looked around, the more things began to sink in. She dropped her bag and snapped.

"You mean, you guys really are aliens."

"Well, duhhhhhh, that's what we have been telling you all day." Tommy rolled his eyes.

"This is...Oh, good God, fucking A, shit for luck, sonovabitch, mutherfuckin' bullshit, eat my pussy 'til I scream, unbelievable, anus-licking, cock-smoking—"

Jared leaned toward Tommy, "I think she's going to explode."

"I hope not, I kinda like her," Tommy answered.

"Me, too."

"—cunt-munching, hairy-balled liars, you bastards lied to me!"

"Hello??" Tommy did the quotes again with his fingers. "We told you. You weren't listening. You were too busy looking at Jared's cock."

He was right about that part.

"I—I am in a spaceship. Suddenly I don't feel well." Rene sat on one of the long, smooth, white benches. "Please don't use one of those Martian anal probes on me."

"Now that's disgusting. The elders used to do that but the people got all scatterbrained and weird. Of course those probes were huge and opened their assholes to the size of a coffee can. Just thinking about that makes my butt hurt."

Tommy scrunched his eyebrows together and continued. "Rene, we just want you to come to our planet. We're not interested in your ass."

"Speak for yourself," Jared piped in, winking at Rene.

Sitting there, Rene was in shock. She was on a spaceship, leaving her own planet and had no idea what to do. The reality of the situation finally hit. Up 'til now she had foolishly thought it was just fun and games.

Jared sat beside her. "Don't be scared. It's not like we are from Mars or anything."

"Men are from Mars, women are from Venus is what I heard."

Tommy and Jared burst into laughter.

Jared began to speak. "What moron said this? They are some really uptight aliens. They are all freaky and into bondage and short. About two feet tall with tiny sex organs and it is red everywhere. Picture pissed-off pygmies with a bad attitude and small-cox virus. The guys from Mars are complete assholes."

"I'd think the assholes would live in Uranus." Rene didn't notice the stern glare from the guys.

"The Venus part is more accurate. Venusian women are…well. Mmmmmm…" Jared closed his eyes for a brief moment of peace.

"You and your Venus trip." Tommy snapped his fingers in front of Jared's face. "He spends a year on Venus with three hundred thousand Venusian women and he is hooked for life."

"Sorry, everyone fondly remembers their first real love. The difference between a Venusian woman and Earth women is anatomy design.

Venusian women have their pussy going across instead of front to back so when you spread their legs apart, it gets tighter." Jared motioned like he was breaking a wishbone with his hands.

Tommy interrupted. "They also have three breasts."

"Yeah, one for each hand and one for your mouth." Jared began to laugh and Rene was not amused.

She'd wanted an adventure and now it was on her doorstep. Just like a bag of dog poop lit on fire.

"You guys don't eat people, do you?"

"Sometimes. If she asks for it." Jared smiled and licked his lips.

BINGO, hot flash.

"Oh, quit it, Jared."

"Come here, Rene. I'll give you a tour." Tommy took her hand and led her out the sliding doors to a wide-open room.

"*Wow*, this is...wow." Rene stared as the main room was a vision of elegance and style.

The main living room area had a burgundy-colored wraparound sectional couch. There was a very expensive Persian rug under the couch and angular coffee table. From anywhere on the couch you could see the enormous flat-panel television hovering against the wall. The room was painted a very light peach color, accentuating the couch and cherry wood table.

"Sonovabitch! Did you decorate this?" Rene looked over to Tommy.

"Yep, it's all me." He puffed his chest out proudly. "There are no damn windows on the ship except in the control area so I couldn't do curtains. Oh, how I love curtains and wall coverings. But you can't hang anything on terilium metal so I got screwed."

They walked away from the living room and toward a hallway.

"Over here is the bathroom." Tommy pushed open the blue door to the right. "Dammit, Jared, you left the seat up again."

Peeking inside Rene saw marble everywhere. It had a tropical theme with blues and splashes of bright colors on the walls.

"This is the sleeping chamber past this wall. We have a kitchen-type area with dehydrated food—it's opposite the sleeping area. Most foods only take a few minutes to make. I'll show you sometime. I can make a killer soufflé."

"He is a good cook. But his chili is *hot*. It burns going in and burns worse coming out." Jared strolled in and walked toward the television area.

"Ahem, to continue, the black door down the hallway there leads to the engine room and cockpit. Cockpit...cockpit...I just love that word." Tommy paused and walked away.

"Cockpit," he sighed and walked over to the door on the right. "I'm going to get undressed, Jared. I am bushed."

He peeked back into the room and yelled, *"Cockpit,"* then was gone.

Rene walked around in a daze. While it contained items familiar to her, they were all placed in an obvious alien setting. "You know, I have always loved science fiction movies but never thought I'd be in one. This is something I'll have to write down.

"Okay, so now what?" she asked Jared who was rubbing his stubbed toe and looking around the room.

"Where's the damn remote? We always lose the remote for the Celestial vision. I missed the Uranus playoffs, and now I'm going to miss the Big Bang Game. This sucks!" Jared shrugged and faced Rene. "Take your clothes off."

"Excuse me?" Rene's eyes opened wide.

"Get naked." Jared made those obnoxious quotes with his fingers like Tommy had earlier.

"For space travel we need to be naked so we don't get all tangled in our clothing when we sleep," Jared continued.

"Ohhhhh, so, um, what do we wear instead?"

"Ummmm...nothing." Jared began to unbutton his shirt.

"So to travel in space we need to be naked?" Rene began to undress while talking.

"Are you sure you're not a blonde? I said we travel naked, nude, bare, unclothed, in our birthday suits."

"Oh, shut up, it's just weird. I never saw any of the shuttle missions in the nude. Of course most of those people look better clothed." Rene shuddered at the thought of middle-aged naked astronauts.

"Well, they travel around a little. They don't have to travel asleep for a prolonged time like we will be. The sleep chamber just makes the trip a helluva lot easier to take. Four weeks is four weeks, no matter how you look at it." Jared kicked off his shoes and socks then wiggled his toes. He looked down on the stubbed one and frowned.

"Where's Tommy?" Rene looked to the door just in time to see Tommy leap inside.

"What do you think?" Tommy stood, posing in a tiny pair of fuzzy, leopard-colored underwear.

It left little to Rene's imagination. Jared and Tommy had one large thing in common. She was amazed he could fit everything into the underwear that reminded her of her own fuck-me undies.

"What do we have to eat? I'm hungry," Jared said rubbing his eyes. He was undressing and Rene was watching her favorite program, *Beef TV*.

"Me, too," Rene said, looking down at Jared's large cock. "You have any wieners?"

"Yeah, I've got a foot-long one right here." Jared motioned in typical male fashion to his cock.

"Damn, I wish I could just get laid and relax." Rene sat there, eyes open realizing she was speaking instead of thinking.

"Me, too," Jared piped in.

"Oh, brother," Tommy mused. "You two have a one-track mind." He slid his underwear off and shot them across the room like a rubber band.

Rene was still, glancing side to side. Her eyes looked downward, drawn to their cocks as though they contained eye-attracting magnets. To her, if she had to wait four weeks and not get laid again for who knows how long, well, what the hell.

"So, um, guys?" Rene wanted to be tactful. "What about you two? Don't you ever, you know? You guys want to, um, well, the three of us, um..."

Acting stupid, the two guys stood naked, semi-erect and torturing Rene to say the words she longed to speak.

"Can we fuck?"

"Fuck? You mean like real humans do?" Jared smiled at first then wiggled his eyebrows.

"No, like koala bears do."

"That's a weird thought. Koalas screw in the trees. Did you know the koala bear—" Rene put her finger over Tommy's lips, silencing him.

"I just can't see spending all my time with nothing new and different to experience. I mean I did agree to take this trip with you. At least give me a good reason to be here. Something like that woman in the bar felt."

"Well, I am normal and think about sex a lot, too, you know." Tommy seemed a little perturbed by everything.

Jared shrugged and sat back, finally finding the remote control for the TV. "Aha, I found it!"

Tommy shook his head and took Rene's hand. They headed toward the sleeping chamber for the trip. When the door opened, a burst of cool air made Rene shiver. Her nipples paid particular attention to the cold. *Hello, girls.*

The light was dim but had a comforting glow of blue. The chamber was like a cloud-filled sky. Large silken waves rolled across the floor. It was a giant pillow of satin. Rene wasn't sure if she was stepping into heaven or what. The ceiling changed into a 3D view of a sunset. It was so real she could feel the sun's rays on her skin.

Tommy stopped and faced Rene. Taking her cheeks in his hands, he gently leaned into her and brushed his lips to hers. "Just because I act like a gay male doesn't mean I am one, nor am I immune to a female's needs. I appreciate beauty in both sexes. You are attractive, sensual and totally unique. That's why Jared and I picked you."

Rene's knees buckled and her eyes closed with another kiss from Tommy's soft lips. The stiffness of his cock began to rise against her pubic bone, which pressed into his warm body.

I can see he wasn't kidding.

Rene could taste sweetness. Something likened to strawberry syrup. She now began to understand the appeal of this man. He acted gay but was outfitted with all the equipment to be a lover for any woman to become addicted to. He also could decorate her house and dress her stylishly, too.

The taste of his tongue made her happy. In fact, she wanted more.

The more she accepted his advances, the harder his cock became. Tommy rocked into her body with subtle, unconscious thrusts. His hands began to explore her body. Firstly, they touched her hips then slowly lowered to her ass. His firm hands cupped her cheeks and pulled her against him. He then moved them up, cupping her firm breasts in his warm palms. He smiled and rolled the aroused tips of her nipples with his fingers.

Rene liked how warm Tommy became. Heat radiated from him and through her. Naked and standing in a dimly lit cloud, Rene was oblivious to everything else. Even the fact that, along with Tommy having a grip on her breasts, something else had grasped her hips and was pulling her back away from Tommy.

The enormous head of Jared's stiffened cock rested between her ass cheeks and Rene had become a hero sandwich. She was between two hunks of beefcake and loved being the cream filling. She was supplying the cream between her slippery thighs.

Her back began to mold to Jared's wide chest. His hot breath caressed the sultry slope of her neck. Silent whispers of air slid in her ears, searing the nerves to her brain. Her entire body became energized and aroused.

The two men touching her simultaneously caused every piece of her aroused soul to burn.

Reaching her arm up over her head, Rene began to run her fingers through Jared's hair while he kissed her shoulder.

Tommy began to lower his mouth down the front of her body, taking painfully long breaks between kissing the hot flesh of her breasts.

Rene's nipples were so tight she couldn't stand the rising tension.

Each kiss on her chest made a shiver of excitement jolt to her pussy.

Tommy's tongue swirled around the firm tip of her nipple, toying with it. When Tommy enveloped her right nipple in his warm mouth,

Rene almost came from the precious release of a moan. A moan so deeply rooted it was unearthly—yet utterly real.

The thick length of Jared's cock began to press into Rene's lower back. He was immense and a dab of wetness brushed her skin.

Rene reached her hand back, grasping the length in her palm. Her deepest fantasy was becoming reality. Two men paying absolute attention to her wants. This was going to be a long, slow, deep trip. With all the extras.

Tommy's mouth found her left breast and Rene could swear she had fallen off an ocean cliff. A rush of a sea breeze cooled her skin, and then the heat of the sun raged through her blood.

Rene became weak and leaned slightly forward.

Jared's hard cock rested between the lips of her dripping-wet cunt. She was so ready to just submit to their advances. She was enthralled by the extremity of her arousal from simple touches and kisses. Jared's cock wasn't anything to be scared of. It was something to be enjoyed and admired. As long as he hammered it deeply into her until she died from pleasure.

"I can't stand up anymore, my knees are useless. What are you guys doing to me?" Rene was enlightened to the point of ecstasy and had no way to control herself.

Jared lifted her legs and Tommy rested her head down on the pillows of air below them.

Rene blinked a few times and looked up at Tommy.

"My God, you are so beautiful." Tommy's words cut through to her bone.

A glow filled her eyes as Tommy lowered his face to hers. He was upside down to her face and he kissed her forehead first. Rene closed her eyes as Tommy kissed her eyelids. Then he kissed her lips ever so softly. He was romantic, slow and driving her crazy.

Rene's entire body began to shake as joyous pleasure shot through her spine. Jared's mouth was buried between her legs. His fingers reached up and tugged at her nipples. Rene would jerk and shake as Jared began to aggressively lick and suck her soaked cunt.

Rene arched her head back, burying it into the soft silk. Her neck thrust upward as Jared found her clit and began his assault on it. He sucked it between his lips and with every pull, Rene elevated her hips higher into his face.

With Jared consumed in her cunt, Tommy kissed her mouth. She felt the pressure of his tongue spreading her lips apart and she welcomed him.

The instant Jared's tongue licked across her clit and Tommy's tongue met hers, a wave of pleasure swept through Rene's body. The three of them merged together and she was stuck in the center of a tidal wave of sexual pleasure.

When she came, Rene saw the back of her skull as her eyes rolled back in her head. She was increasingly aware of every nerve ending on her entire physique and the intensity of their merging sent electric shocks through her soul. She collapsed, weakened, drained and permanently smiling. She was spent.

She thought.

Jared grasped her hips and pulled her limp body to his. The head of his cock rested between the wet folds of flesh. She seemed so fragile, so petite but was so beautiful that Jared couldn't help but crave her more and more.

"No, no, Jared. We need some type of protection. You're alien for heaven's sake." Although Rene was on the Pill and she didn't want to stop, that safe sex part of her upbringing held up a warning sign. Also, his sperm might be silver and have teeth.

Whispering, Jared eased Rene's mind. "There's no need to worry, us Uranus men are immune to all viruses and disease. We get shots before space travel that make us repel germs and bacteria." With a direct thrust, he entered her cunt.

Moaning, Rene was content and tossed away her concerns.

Jared was more like an animal than a man. He wasn't after the slow softness of love. He wanted the furious fulfillment of primal sex. As he penetrated her to the hilt of his thick cock, Rene could only thrash her small body to the majestic peaks of this fantasy. Rene screamed in a mix of painful release and a pleasurable excitement from the stretching violation of her body.

Jared was immense and it took a few strokes for her to adjust to the unleashed passion of the man. She began to feel spread wider than ever before and the slow, steady thrusts pulled her cunt back and forth. The rigid shaft pushed deeply in and as he withdrew, the hard length dragged against the hood of her clitoris.

Tommy wiped the tear from Rene's eye. She was blissfully excited and sweat began to seep from her skin.

"Kiss me, Tommy, kiss me again," Rene pleaded, needing a sense of compassion in contrast to Jared's more masculine force.

Jared's muscles tightened and flexed as he thrust hard into Rene's welcoming cunt. The tightness gripped every inch of his cock, holding it tightly inside, not wanting to let go. The slap of their skin echoed through the chamber.

When Tommy kissed Rene, she lowered her hand between his legs and caressed his tightened balls. Tommy pulled up his head. Then he began kissing her again as Rene stroked his length in the hot skin of her palm.

Tommy moved to kiss Rene's breasts and with her head arched back, she licked the tip of Tommy's erection. The jarring thrusts from Jared inched her closer to Tommy's swollen cock.

Rene pushed back on Jared and rolled onto her belly. She knew what she wanted to do and wasn't going to let this moment go.

Jared grabbed her hips and as she pushed her ass upward, he entered her cunt from behind. His groans of pleasure only accentuated the joy he was bringing Rene.

Her soul was peaking with excitement as she let her mind drift into the gratification of Jared fucking her. Long, powerful thrusts she swore would never stop. Pleasure like this seemed devious and a sin, but the unearthly delight it brought was exquisite.

Tommy sat in front of them and Rene lowered her mouth over the thick head of his cock. His body sank deeply into the fluffy pillows, his hardened cock standing proud like a flagpole.

The flick of her tongue, the amount of sucking in, it was all in tandem with the pleasure she was receiving from Jared.

With each hammering pound from Jared, Rene's mouth would dive down on Tommy's throbbing cock. She held herself up on her elbows and her head bobbed up and down in unison with Jared fucking her.

As Jared began to breathe between his teeth, trying to hold back, Rene flexed her ass and sucked hard on Tommy, seeing his balls tightening. She knew she was close and so were they. A salty taste trickled from the tip of Tommy's cock and the anticipation of his ultimate release excited Rene more.

Jared grunted and arched back. The plunge stretched Rene to her limits of pleasure. She was coming again and didn't want it to end.

Tommy began to squirm in an attempt to hold back bursting from the blowjob Rene was giving him. When Jared hit her cervical opening with a deep, driving thrust, she jerked forward and felt Tommy's cock hit the back of her throat. In unison the three of them erupted in a climactic blast of sexual expulsion.

Falling into myriad heated passions, Rene blacked out. She awoke to Tommy patting her cheek and Jared stroking the sweaty flesh of her ass. Rene lay in a limp state of exhaustion with only enough energy to say one thing.

"Okay, who's sleeping in the wet spot?"

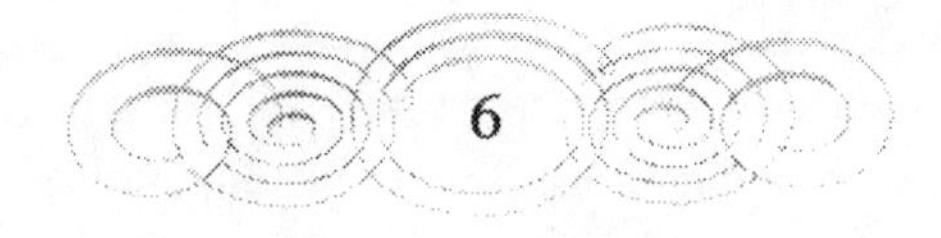

6

Tommy came back to the chamber with three glasses filled with a glowing pink fluid. "This will help us sleep during the trip. It may make you have some pretty weird dreams, but it will prolong the time you sleep and make it so you don't have to tinkle so much."

Rene sniffed the glass. "Mmmm, strawberry. My favorite." She let the scent fill her nose and watched as Jared and Tommy downed their drinks before drinking hers.

The smooth flow of the drink slid down her throat and as it coated her insides, her body became relaxed. She also became extremely horny. More than the usual itch she'd get for a hot guy. She was becoming *hot*.

Here she was on a spaceship with two good-looking men, she was hornier than a schoolgirl at prom and she was drifting into a deep, soothing sleep. Life just wasn't fair.

After the ship was docked in Uranus' port, Tommy and Rene awoke from their four-week nap. Jared lay facedown in a pool of drool, snoring. She had never been so content or relaxed in her life. They tried to unravel the pretzel-like entanglement of their limbs.

"Oh, no, oww, owww, owww, my leg's asleep." Tommy was half laughing and half crying at the numb feeling of his leg.

"Aw, which leg?" Rene asked.

"The right one—don't touch it, it tingles so bad."

A mischievous smile crossed her face and Rene lunged at Tommy's leg and began rubbing it. She poked at the limp limb as Tommy fought to get away.

"Ahhh, you bitch, stop, stop, it tickles!" Tommy was laughing and tossing around in agony. His leg finally awoke and so did his *other* leg.

"Pee time. Be right back." Tommy limped out of the chamber.

Mumble, mumble, "No more onions on my burrito," mumble, growl.

The beast was waking from his hibernation. Jared was the type of man who woke up grouchy, hungry and probably horny—or so she hoped. Rene began to massage Jared's wide back muscles. Her own body was awakening and the soreness between her thighs was a reminder of their sexual encounter before the trip.

"Not again, seven times is my limit," Jared grumbled under his breath. He slowly awoke and made a smacking sound with his mouth.

"Talk about bad morning breath. I feel like I just ate a cat." He grinned. "Or a pussy."

"Yep, you're awake," Rene snapped back.

"Hey, Jared, I had the weirdest, most intense dreams on this trip. Is that normal?"

He rolled over onto his back and looked at her. As usual, he had an erection and Rene noticed. She had to—it flopped against her arm like a tree branch. "Sometimes the sleep aid will make people feel funny. What kind of dreams?"

"Well, they were fantasies, I guess. Sexual stuff." She slowly let her palm brush against Jared's wondrous cock. Her mouth was dry, but her pussy was becoming wet. "You and Tommy were in them. All we did was have incredible sex for hours on end. Over and over and over. I swear I must have had a four-week orgasm."

"Um, those weren't all dreams, Rene." He paused. With Rene now stroking him in her hand, he reached over and toyed with the moist folds of skin between her legs. "Tommy and I merged with you. Soooo, well, we sort of *did* have sex with you for four weeks. In our minds and with our bodies."

Blinking a few times Rene looked back at Jared. "You mean we...?"

"Yep, quite a few times actually. Tommy isn't much for a lot of sex, but you had him going pretty good."

"That explains it then. That feeling like I had been riding a horse. My inner thighs are killing me." Rene crawled around and climbed on top of Jared. "Speaking of riding a horse..."

"Damn, Rene, I thought I was bad. You are so fucking hot." His voice was rough and deep and all Rene wanted to hear was him moaning with pleasure along with her.

She lowered herself down the thickened shaft of Jared's now iron-hard cock. "Ohhhh, yeah, I remember thisssss. Mmmmm, Jared, you feel sooooo goood."

"Aw, oh, Christ, not again!" Tommy stood covering his eyes, dressed in a silken shirt and tight black leather pants. "Dammit, you two are like a couple of fucking rabbits. I thought after the trip you'd have had enough! I mean, you did have both of us for four weeks, Rene."

"Awwww, Tommy, just one more ride, mmmm, maybe two." With a slow groove, she rolled her hips atop of Jared who lay moaning with pleasure, letting his hands rest on her swaying hips.

"I'll be back in an hour, I need to get our stuff ready anyway." Walking off, Tommy mumbled under his breath. *Why bother packing clothes, they never wear them anyway. Fucking humans. Hey, that's what Jared's doing now, fucking a human. Ha ha, I just made a funny. Why am I talking to myself? Why am I answering my own questions?*

7

They all readied themselves to leave the ship. Tommy had already packed their bags and had clothes laid out for them in matching colors like his. As the hatch opened, Rene noticed a distinctly odd odor in the air. It made her eyes burn and reminded her of her father's bathroom.

"Okay, who farted?"

The guys looked at each other and shrugged.

"Whoever smelt it dealt it," Tommy piped in, and started walking down the ramp where their ship had docked.

"No offense guys, but this place smells like shit."

Jared replied, "Well, it is Uranus."

When she saw a NO SMOKING sign flashing in red, she understood what the smell was—methane gas.

There were a dozen or so docks like theirs that all connected to a round opening to a tunnel. As they went through the tunnel, it opened onto a brightly lit city street. On the street, numerous eating establishments lined the sidewalks. It was like Disneyland. Burrito King, Beans-R-Us, Fiber Hut, Colon Burger and a single Oriental restaurant with the name Wong Hole on it.

"Well, I guess we better introduce you to the queen. She has to meet everyone that is new inside Uranus." Jared seemed a little depressed instead of being excited to be home. "Come on, Tommy. Back to the old grind."

"Jared?" Rene grabbed his hand. "What's wrong? You seem...well... you seem a little down. Aren't you happy to be home?"

Tommy interrupted. "He hates it here. He gets to live in the palace but he doesn't like his job."

"I am sort of the sexual concierge for the queen."

Rene backed up. "What the fuck is that?"

"It's kind of like a proctologist. I deal with assholes all day. I make sure all her men stay in line. I protect her and stay with her wherever she goes. It's really boring. She hardly ever goes out and when she does, I have to go everywhere with her. I despise shopping and she loves it."

"I would die to spend all day shopping," Tommy gushed, rolling his eyes.

"What do you do, Tommy?" Rene asked.

"Don't ask. I am in charge of decorating the palace. I feel like a maid, though. I have to pick up after her and she leaves shit everywhere. Being the queen of Uranus is a dirty job." Tommy sighed, and they all started walking along the narrowing street.

The street ended and in single file, the few people walked through the small tunnel. Rene noticed small debris hanging along the walls. "What's that?" she asked.

"Cling-ons. Don't mess with those, they stink and stick to everything."

Walking through the end of the tunnel, it opened up to a brightly lit space. All around were flowers, trees and greenery. It was extremely contrasting to the streets of Uranus. "Where are we?" She tapped Jared on the shoulder.

Pointing to a sign hanging from the shiny archway, it read "Welcome to Bowel".

"Bowel? You have a city named Bowel? This is a joke, right?" she laughed as she spoke.

"This is the entrance to Castle Bowel. The queen lives in the Bowel. What's so funny about that?" Tommy seemed a little confused at Rene's humor.

"If I have to explain it, it must not be funny."

The threesome continued down the road.

"Can we go shopping? I'm just famished." Tommy rubbed his belly and smacked his lips together.

"I need to go check in at work. You two go ahead." Jared held on to Rene's hand and slowly pulled away. Their hands touched until only their fingertips lingered in a final caress.

"Oh, enough of this lovey-dovey stuff, let's go shopping." Tommy was all giddy like a woman with a new credit card at the mall.

Rene stopped dead in her tracks. *No way!* she thought, wondering if her eyes had deceived her. Stepping back two steps she looked through a glass window and saw a line of men standing naked and at attention. They dangled in various stages and lengths.

"Oh, the queen is looking for tonight's victims. Must be a full moon again. Actually, it's always a full moon with twenty-seven of those things circling the planet." Tommy tugged at her arm but she wasn't moving. "Come on, Rene."

Rene wasn't budging, she was window-shopping. Thoughts of a charge account with no spending limit crossed her mind, as did the thought of which stud to use for each night. One, two or three at a time, the queen had a tough choice.

She stared through the window to see an incredibly statuesque woman walk from a hallway and into the open room of men. She was elegant and had her black hair pulled back, exposing her perfect facial features. As soon as she entered, all the men became erect. In their stance and their…well, erection.

Rene didn't notice her hands pressed up against the window. Nor did she realize her tongue was dangling and licking at the cold glass. Smorgasbord time.

The queen had run down the lineup, touching each man with her hand. Judging each man like a fish. She wanted a whale, not minnows. Her pussy was the bait.

Hearing a squeak, the queen turned to see Rene dragging her hands down the window. Her hands were sweaty and the flesh stuck to the glass.

Rene shook free from her hormonal rage of lust, then looked at the queen. A subtle smile crossed the queen's face. She was lovely.

Then she flipped Rene the bird and motioned for her to get away.

"Rene, we need to go. The queen gets rather possessive of her men. Good lord knows she won't share Jared. If she knew about him and... well... She wouldn't be too happy.

"Ohhh, look, a boutique. Let's get some scarves and some oils. I have something special to show you." Tommy shooed the clerk away like a fly. "They are no help. Hmmm, this blue one is nice but the burgundy fits your outfit better. Here let me get you one." Tommy knew his color schemes.

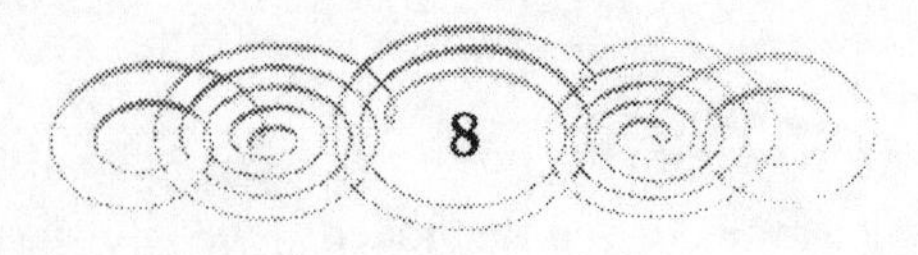

8

Rene and Tommy spent the day shopping. She was running with a marathon shopper and was a short-distance runner. She was exhausted.

Tommy's apartment was a blend of what appeared to be antique furniture and modern art hanging on the brightly colored walls. It was warm and all *him*. The place was cramped but just enough for a single man to live in. Everything was too pretty to touch and had its certain place.

"You can come in the kitchen, dear." Tommy stood mixing some type of drink that looked like a strawberry milkshake. "Want some?"

"No, I'm fine. That taco about did me in. I just want to lie down and relax."

"Oh, no, you don't. I'm not finished yet. Let's go to my bedroom."

Rene didn't know what to expect and really didn't care. "Okay, Tommy. Whatever you say."

"Oh, I have been waiting to give you a Tommy special massage since we met." Tommy led Rene by the hand to his bedroom and pointed to the large white bed. "Let me get my oils and we'll start with a massage."

Rene slowly began to undress. Each button on her blouse popped open as if begging to free her body. She had a weakness for massages. The slick feeling on her skin, warm hands caressing her flesh, it all made her wet. In every way.

Rene was naked, sitting on the edge of the big white bed and waiting for Tommy. She began to understand what men sometimes felt as they waited for their woman. After an eternity, Tommy opened the door.

"Now, I need you to lie down." Tommy had a tray with various colored bottles in different sizes and shapes. There was a radiant glow from each bottle. Like bottling fireflies, the flickering light in the liquid moved.

Rene looked at Tommy in a short silk robe, which barely hung low enough to hide something Tommy had dangling between his legs. "Facedown or face up?"

"Doesn't matter to me. Let's start on the front."

The bed molded to Rene's body. She was naked, on her back and Tommy opened his robe to reveal his toned body above her. Maybe she was in heaven.

Tommy smiled as he looked down on Rene. Pouring the pink glistening liquid into his palm, he set the glass down and rubbed his hands together. She was spread before him in a perfect position to fuck. After four weeks of neglect, her pubic area looked like a forest and Tommy would need a machete to trim the bush down.

Leaning down, he rested his chin in her pubic hair and asked, "You think I look good with a beard?"

Rene giggled and Tommy spread some of the oil over the soft hair. It smoothed out against her skin. His caress was soft and soothing in some ways, but the attention was causing Rene's body to stir.

The lips of her pussy were shiny from arousal but Tommy wasn't looking for a fuck. He wanted to give her pleasure.

He then began to massage Rene's belly. He spread the slick lotion on her skin making it warm. The circles were small and he made them bigger and bigger.

"This feels nice, Tommy. What is in the lotion?"

Tommy picked up the pink bottle and read it while continuing to massage Rene's flesh. "It is a base for the blue lotion. Not sure what's in it. This relaxes the muscles, the blue oil causes the stimulus reaction when it is mixed."

With another handful of oil, Tommy moved up to her chest. The oil smoothed over her breasts and erect nipples, causing her to moan. Tommy let her nipples rise between his fingers then closed the space, almost pinching the sensitive tips.

Tommy could see the soft caresses from his hands were giving Rene pleasure. His hand slid down to between her thighs.

Instinctively Rene spread her legs apart, anticipating Tommy's next move.

With one hand, he began to massage the pink oil into the silky flesh between her legs. He grabbed a green cylinder from his oils and shook it, making it glow.

Rene looked down her oily skin to see Tommy wipe some of the pink oil onto the glowing green cylinder. It was about eight inches long and had a mystical glow radiating from within it.

When Tommy began to insert it within her pussy Rene couldn't keep her eyes open. It was as if her entire insides were being opened and stimulated at once.

"Oh, my God. What are you doing to me, Tommy?" Rene moaned out the words. Even if she was being aroused to the ends of her limits, there was a relaxing feel to the pleasure.

Tommy grabbed her leg, letting it rest against his chest. His hands slid up and down, covering it with the oil. When he switched to the other leg Rene felt a different leg brushing against her bare skin. He continued his massage until her front was completely covered with the oil.

Tommy reached over to the tray and grabbed the blue oil. The green cylinder began to throb and swell inside her pussy with rhythmic tones.

Rene wanted the real thing but did want to remember to ask Tommy for one of these things to keep at home, just in case.

She looked again into Tommy's eyes. They stared appreciatively at her nude body.

Tommy poured a large handful of the blue oil into his palm. Rene saw that his cock was hard as iron and she wanted him, badly. She now saw him in his purest, natural way. Naked and a feast for her eyes. Tommy was a slender man. He was in great shape without an ounce of fat on him. *The bastard*. His muscles were well defined and everything was perfect. Everything.

He slowly began to rub the blue oil onto his skin. He was tanned and Rene found herself longing for his hands to touch her like he was rubbing the oil onto himself. Each ripple of his muscles made her twitch and the throbbing increased inside her cunt.

Licking her lips, she tried to speak, "What's that?"

"Oh, sorry, this is the catalyst. It makes the pink oil react. You'll see." Tommy giggled as he rubbed his legs. "Sorry, I'm ticklish on my legs."

Kneeling down he climbed above Rene, holding his body above hers with his strong arms.

"You know, I have never felt like this with a woman before. You are more like a flower, most beautiful when it is about to bloom." He then lowered his body to hers.

The reaction of the blue oil to the pink was lightning shooting through the skin wherever they touched. Rene buckled in half and wrapped her arms and legs around Tommy. He looked down at her wrinkled smile and kissed her. Her body jerked and shook with the electric jolts through her flesh. Her nipples were so tight she was afraid she would poke through Tommy's chest.

All he could do was moan with pleasure. The mixed oils tingled all over his skin. Tommy knew Rene was aroused by how she squirmed and her body flexed. The scent of her pussy was like perfume. She was exquisite and Tommy admired beauty.

With each touch, her simplest reactions made him excited and hard. She got to him more then any other woman had.

"Just hold me, just hold me," Rene was trying to regain her control.

"Okay, time for the back." Tommy pushed up off Rene.

"No more, I can't. You are driving me crazy, Tommy. You act like you are gay but make me want to fuck you so bad I can't explain it." She was feeling tense and horny. This massage was having a different reaction than relaxing her. It was arousing her. Rene gasped as the green cylinder began to expand and throb harder.

Tommy rolled her over and poured some more of the pink oil in his hand. Laughing he poured between her shoulder blades into a pool to spread it thicker on her back. Each time he reached over to rub her back the head of his cock would press onto Rene's ass.

Tommy grabbed the pink bottle and let a small amount of the liquid fall to the crack of Rene's ass. It slid between the cheeks and into the opening of her anus. With his finger, he encircled the tight opening. He glided his index finger into her anus, causing Rene to moan. He felt the gentle throb of the green toy inside her pussy.

Rene turned her head back and looked up at Tommy.

"Let me see the blue oil?" she asked.

She rolled to her hip and poured a small amount into her palm. Looking back up to Tommy, she reached out and grabbed the end of his cock. The dab of moisture on the tip showed her his excitement. She began rubbing the oil onto the head and shaft making Tommy smile.

Rolling back onto her belly, Rene turned her head away and arched her ass up into the air.

There was no need for prompting—Tommy knew what to do.

His fingers traced the line of her inner thighs making Rene moan softly. The throbbing cylinder within her cunt began to hum loudly as Tommy slowly withdrew it. It was dripping with the wetness of her arousal.

He let it sit halfway out. The throbbing toy vibrated against the lips of her opened pussy and her now exposed clit.

Grasping her hips, Tommy angled his cock to her ass. For a moment he laughed, seeing the blue glow from the oil on his cock. But his smile turned into a gasp as he pushed the head inside the outer rim of Rene's ass.

Moaning, Rene remembered the usual pain she felt during anal sex, but this was different. It was more a pressure followed by an adjustment. The oils relaxed her muscles and sent a tingling excitement through her.

Tommy slowly pressed on, feeling the inner muscles of her ass tight and holding on to every inch of his descent into her.

Pausing, he rubbed in the oil on her lower back and he pulled back a bit.

"Don't stop," Rene whispered under a gentle moan.

Tommy's hands again grasped her hips and he sunk deeper inside. The green cylinder followed suit, being pressed back inside her cunt by Tommy's legs.

"Oh, Jesus, I can feel the throb inside of you. Oh, it is vibrating against my cock." Tommy was receiving as much as getting.

Rene kept her eyes closed. The fullness from double penetration stretched her limits physically and mentally. Each time Tommy would thrust into her, the excitement built to a new crescendo.

Sinking to his balls inside her ass, Tommy stopped and reached under her. Grasping her full breasts, he let his toned muscles lay against Rene's back. "You feel incredible."

Rene smiled hearing Tommy's soft words.

His gentleness was thinning because the lust building within him began to take over. With more force and a deeply rooted grunt, Tommy began to consume.

Her legs weakening, Rene could barely hold her body up. She reached between her legs to grab the end of the vibrating toy within her pussy.

Each time Tommy thrust within her, his balls would smack against her pussy, pushing the toy back into her now swollen cunt. Tommy became increasingly more excited by the feel of their flesh hitting together. His balls were tightening as he climbed further and further to his ultimate climax.

Breathing through his teeth, Tommy sucked in all his control and held his breath.

Tommy clamped onto her flesh with such force it hurt her hips. He was about to climax.

With a hard thrust, he slid the toy to a point where it was throbbing directly on her clit. Rene peaked.

"Oh, shit, I'm...Oh, Tommy..." The orgasmic convulsion of her body began at her toes and reverberated through her legs and with a final plunge from Tommy, her body locked and he blasted his seed into her.

Tommy could only arch back, letting her anal muscles milk his spewing cock.

Rene felt her cunt squeezing tight and the toy pushed out. With a groan, she fell to the bed, her shaking body covered by Tommy's sweaty frame. He slid out of her ass and they lay in a clump, entangled and warm.

"I see why Jared has such a hard time letting you go."

Rene paused, thinking for a moment. "What do you mean letting me go, Tommy?"

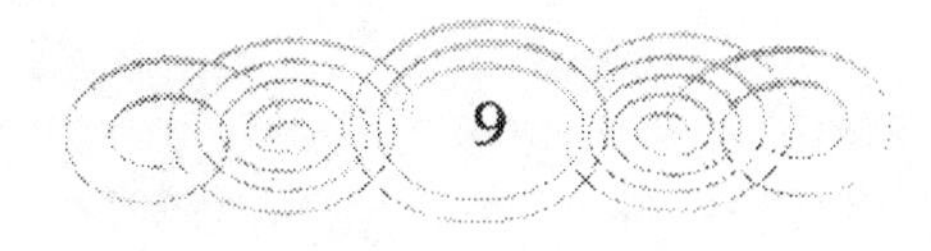

9

Jared stood watch as the queen entered the room. His wide chest filled the white shirt covered with the brown jacket. The matching brown tie strained around his thick neck but added the look of professionalism to him. His white slacks clung to every part of his lower body. Jared was a man with no need to accentuate his physique. He was big and strong.

"Well, it's been a long time, Jared. Almost two years?" She waltzed around him, stripping him naked with her eyes like a woman sizing up a side of beef.

"Yes, my queen. Tommy and I arrived this morning." He was at attention and kept his eyes forward.

The queen smiled and stood right in front of him. "After all those nights together all you can do is act like a servant? We've been more than that Jared, much more. Remember, I am the one who paid for that Venusian nanny. The least you could do is show me again what you learned." She reached around his large frame and hugged him. Much to her dismay, he didn't hug back.

Hanging his head, Jared couldn't do what she wanted. For the first time, he didn't want the queen. Of course knowing how many men she had while he was gone, made him afraid he might fall into her black hole of sex and be lost forever. With Rene, he felt every part of her body encompassing him. Quite a few times.

Thoughts of the trip home began to stir in his head—both heads.

"Leave us!" she commanded the other semi-nude men in the elegant chamber. "What the fuck is wrong with you? You know you belong to me. It has been such a long time, Jared. Nobody has been able to make me feel like you did. I trust you with my life—trust you with everything."

She paused. There was something different. Something strange. A barrier between them now that wasn't there before. She could feel it, didn't want to acknowledge it but suspected what it might be and it hurt her. "I sent you to learn and observe Earth and find me a new female servant and assistant, did you do that?" Becoming upset by Jared's obvious lack of interest in her, she was more sharp with her query.

"Yes, my queen, but—"

"No buts. Where is she?"

Tommy answered the voice modulator on the wall. Jared's voice echoed in the apartment. "Bring Rene to the queen's chambers."

"But, Jared, I have a peach loaf in the oven. It's almost done."

"Well, hurry up, you know how impatient she is. Did you pinch it to see if it was done?" Jared asked, knowing what a great cook Tommy was.

"Okay, it's done. I just pinched a loaf and it's ready to come out."

Rene blinked as she stepped into the kitchen, wondering what she just walked into. *Never mind, don't say it,* she thought.

"Jared says the queen wants to meet you. We better go—she can get pretty bitchy at times." Tommy made sure his food was finished.

"Let me grab my bag, Tommy. I may want to freshen up before meeting the queen. I want to make a good impression."

Jared met Tommy and Rene at the door of the Bowel Palace. "Tommy, take Rene back to Earth. She can't stay here."

"Jared, what's wrong?" Rene saw the look of panic in his eyes.

Tommy knew this side of Jared. "Oh no, what now? Jared, you didn't tell her, did you?"

"Jared, bring them in. I want to meet this Earth woman." The queen had followed him into the hall.

Turning to let Tommy and Rene in, Jared was torn in what he should do next. "Rene, this is our queen. Queen Senna, this is Rene."

Jared introduced the two women and stood like an idiot looking back and forth at them.

"I have seen you before. Where was that?" The queen started the conversation as she looked Rene up and down.

"I was the woman you flipped the bird to when you were sizing up all the men. Looked like a wiener roast and most of the guys had foot-longs cooking."

"So when can you start?"

Rene had a confused look and had no idea what the queen was asking about. "Huh?"

"I see Jared procured a dumb woman. That's good, makes her easier to control and have do what I command." Pausing the queen continued. "She does have a somewhat large ass. We'll have to get that worked on."

"Bitch, say what? I know you aren't talking to me that way." Rene had worked hard and long enough to be proud of who she was. Even if she did have a little cushion on her ass, it was *her* ass. No anus queen was going to smack her down a notch.

"You obviously don't know who you are talking to. I am Queen Senna of Uranus. You were brought here to work for me. I need a sexual slave to satisfy the men in my stable. Each of them needs to be kept happy and I can't be the only one anymore." The queen rubbed her butt.

The queen began to explain. "I need to breed more people here. We need to find out if the women of Earth can have our offspring. If so, we will bring more here to breed. All of our other alien encounters have gone bad. So you will have sex with as many of the men in my stable as necessary to breed more females. Our DNA is predispositioned towards making males, allowing only the rare female to be born."

"Say what?" Rene's jaw dropped, realizing what was being said.

"Also the men here seem to all be accustomed to gay sex so they need to be broken of only anal sex."

"Just because this is Uranus doesn't mean you only have anal sex." Blinking a few times, Rene scrunched her nose a little thinking about what the queen had said.

Rene continued. "Also, I am not going to be a hooker for these guys. I choose who I have sex with." Her eyes seemed to be drawn toward Jared. She knew she liked what he did to and for her. Her affection was obvious in her gaze.

And the queen saw it.

"I don't believe it. You and Jared—and Tommy? There's no way… I won't have this— I feel faint."

"Uh-oh. The last time she got like this there was hell to pay and the shit hit the fan. Literally, she beat the shit out of the guy and threw it at the fan. What a mess." Tommy pinched his nose and waved his hand, fanning his face.

"Is there someplace we can talk?" Rene asked the queen gently. "We need a little girl time." She grabbed her purse from the floor beside her and moved toward the queen.

"Girl talk? Can I come along?" Tommy asked, clapping his hands.

"No, Tommy, not this time."

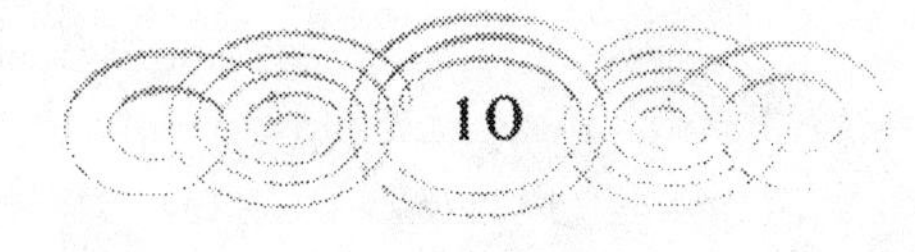

10

Walking down a gorgeous, stained-glass hall, the queen motioned to Rene to walk beside her. They went through a large wooden door. It was the entrance to the queen's chamber and was beautifully decorated.

"*Whoa*...this is magnificent." Rene stood in awe of the decadent furnishings.

"Tommy did this. It was much more than I ever expected. Come over here, let's sit down."

Rene paused then set her bag down, thinking she should start. "I am no threat to you. I'm just a regular girl, no frills and was looking for an adventure when these two great guys popped into my life. They have shown me more than I ever would have seen myself, and I have really grown to care for both of them. And, good Lord, they are great in bed. Hell, I am sitting in Uranus, for Christ's sake. Do you know how stupid it sounds to say that?"

"I am unaccustomed to sharing my men. I sent Jared and Tommy to Earth to find me someone to take over with all the daily shit I deal with including the breeding program. Here it's the same thing. Sex, Crapball—our planetary sport—and more sex. And this fucking infatuation with anal sex. What is it with men and screwing someone up the ass."

"I think it has something to do with prison and being confined." Rene shrugged "It's not my cup of tea either."

"This all happened after we brought the first DNA here. That idiot Mulligan or Gillian or whoever fucked everything up. He lost all the female DNA so we have all these men and no women. I only took over after my husband passed away during a freak masturbation experiment with duct tape and a hamster." The queen paused then continued.

"Think about it. This many men and that much testosterone in a small place. You are going to end up knee-deep with some serious butt love and blowjobs going on. I just thought I'd try to bring the men back one by one to what sex was supposed to be like. For reproduction, but they are all so used to gay sex, they only get aroused by anal. It's a royal pain in the ass. All the previous missions were disasters. I wanted to make sure this last one would work. That's why I devised the plan with Tommy and Jared." The queen stopped and sighed.

Rene could tell this whole episode was hard for her.

"I sent Tommy and Jared on this mission because they were the only two I trusted to not fuck up."

"Why them?" Rene asked.

"Because they were the smartest and to be honest, Jared has a gift."

"He sure does," Rene answered, speaking what her thoughts were.

The two women sighed in unison at the thought of Jared.

"Things aren't much different on Earth. Except the Crapball. I don't think I want to know what that is. Sounds messy."

After a moment of thought, the queen began. "I want to just rule Uranus. I want my people happy. I want these fucking post-menstrual cramps to stop. Damn, I hate this part of the month. And I really want to have one of those mind-blowing orgasms I see on all those Earth porno channels."

The queen became frustrated as she talked. "I have tried. I mean, I have had sex with almost every man on the planet. It feels nice. They don't seem to have any problems getting off. I just don't. I have with... well, one person, but that was a while ago. Of course, there was this other guy. He was from Pluto. Dumb as a rock but...dear me, it was this fucking long." The queen held her hands apart like sizing up a fish.

The two girls laughed and Rene wiggled her eyebrows. "You have his number?"

Touching Rene's hand, the queen asked, "Jared is really special. Do you love him? He is important to me for more than the obvious reason and while I'm not at all happy with the thought of him with another woman, I also want him happy. I just want...I don't know. There is something between you two. I want that."

The queen looked down, knowing Rene could give Jared more than she ever could. "He and Tommy are like peanut butter and jelly. When you have one you have to have the other. They both spread really well. Tommy is a great cook, too. He has great taste in clothes and decorating. Look what he did to my palace."

Rene sighed, "He gives great backrubs, too."

"Backrubs?" the queen asked.

Quickly Rene changed subjects. "Dear Lord, your ass must feel like a sponge. Don't worry though. Most women on Earth don't always have orgasms." Rene paused. "The men all think they do, but that's not reality.

"If I didn't have my toys I'd have gone nuts. You ever try a vibrator?" Rene fumbled through her bag.

"Vibrator? Well, yes. But mine is old and after the batteries died I just couldn't see being intimate with something made from a foreign planet."

"Some women just have their clits buried a little deeper and need the treasure unearthed." Rene found what she wanted in her bag. She pulled out a large, pink vibrator still in its wrapper. It was smooth, glowing and had a clit stimulator on it.

Rene opened the wrapper and turned the base to start it. The slow hum vibrated through her hand. She handed it to the queen.

The queen closed her eyes and gently moaned. "Wow, this is...well, this is nice." The queen rubbed along the shaft. It was slick but soft to the touch. "It's a lot different from the one I have. Mine looks like a tree stump. What all can this thing do? Can it fix a garbage disposal?"

Rene leaned over and whispered into the queen's ear. Raising an eyebrow the queen had a wicked grin. "Multiple orgasms? Rechargeable batteries? This thing reminds me of this guy from Pluto I went out with. Except it didn't hum like this. It squeaked."

The queen leaned over and opened a drawer beside her bed. "See, this is mine."

Rene jerked back and stared at the old-fashioned vibrator. It was a good twelve inches long, was thick and dark brown.

"So, is it true?" the queen asked Rene.

Still staring she replied, "Is what true?"

"You know, about the darker men of your planet. Are they bigger?"

"Uhhhh, well, it's a myth actually. But I did accidentally walk into the men's room at work when I started and saw this guy Russell in there. Damn, he was hung like, well, like this toy. He moved up quickly in the company. The women's division.

"You know something. I think we can help each other out here. You ever have chocolate?"

"What's chocolate?" the queen was sincerely confused.

Rene sat upright and looked back at the queen. "Are you sure you aren't a blonde?"

"Why do you ask?" she answered.

"What kind of fucked-up, ass-backwards world do you live in? You don't have proper vibrators or chocolate?" Rene rustled some more in her purse. Scanning the room like a spy, she pulled something out and dropped into to the queen's hand.

It was small, wrapped in gold foil and the one thing Rene knew would break any planetary boundaries between them. Like money, only better. It was Swiss chocolate.

The queen popped the small morsel into her mouth and made a funny face.

"You need to take the wrapper off first." Rene shook her head. *Maybe Uranus is full of the real assholes and idiots.*

Taking the wrapper off, the queen put the small, dark brown candy in her mouth. With a low, guttural moan, she closed her eyes and smiled. It was a true oral-gasm.

BINGO! Rene knew she had her.

"More." The queen almost purred.

"We both have something the other one wants and needs. How about we make a deal?" Rene looked at the queen as she smiled wickedly back at her.

"More." She beckoned again.

Rene had a small stash she always kept handy for those premenstrual times when the angry bitch inside her raised its head. She handed the queen another one.

Quicker than a fly on cocaine, the foil was torn away and the queen moaned again. She was hooked. Just because it seemed this place was a fudge-packing planet, chocolate was the universal bond between all that was female.

"Mmmmm, where can I get more of this? Damn, I can see why the elders hid this source of pleasure from us women. I could really get used to having this around." The queen seemed totally at ease. This was Rene's chance to bargain.

Epilogue

Riiiiing.

"Good afternoon, T. R. & J. Designs. Yes, she's here. One moment please." Putting the phone on hold, the petite blonde receptionist leaned toward the hallway. "Rene? The Samuels are calling again, line three."

"This is Rene. Yes. Okay, I understand. I'll have a talk with him again. I am sorr— Of course, he'll be over to do your bedroom tomorrow. We should be finished by next week. What's that? Yes, Jared does all our installs of showers. I see, your mother is leaving this weekend. All right, I'll have Cynthia make your appointments for next week."

Jared walked into the office, shirtless as usual. With a sigh, Cynthia stared and looked him up and down. The moistness returned between her legs. Like a schoolgirl she became flushed and warm.

"Hello, Cynthia, is Rene here?" Jared looked at Cynthia. A blank stare was in her eyes. "Cynthia? Hello?"

"Oh, sorry, was thinking of lunch. Cockdogs…I mean hotdogs today." Wiggling in her chair, she cleared her thoughts and continued. "Rene's in her office."

As Jared walked down the hallway Cynthia remembered she needed buns for her hotdogs.

Knock, knock.

Jared opened the door to Rene's office. She was on the phone as usual and he walked in, pulling his hand through his thick hair. Rene smiled and held her finger up, having him pause.

Jared walked behind her and looked out the window at the open park that was outside their new design office.

"Yes, I ordered that last week and we are waiting for the fabrics." Rene was becoming upset and Jared could not only feel her tension but it showed in her neck.

Raising an eyebrow, he smiled and stepped directly up behind her. He rested his hands on her shoulders and pulled her head back. It rested snugly against his lower abdomen. With expert motions, he began to massage her temples.

Rene let out a cleansing breath and allowed her body to relax as the man on the other end of the phone tried his best to bullshit his way out of his fuck-up.

The smoothness of Jared's movements calmed Rene as usual. It also beckoned something in Jared as her head rested against his now hardening cock.

"We can't. We have too much to do. We can't fuck right now. Later tonight we will." Rene was torn.

"We can't *what?*" the man on the other end was suddenly paying attention.

"I'll call you back. Just take care of this." Rene hung up the phone and turned her chair around. She was eye level to Jared's one-eyed snake.

"We received another complaint from the Samuels. You made their grandma pass out again. I tell you every morning to wear underwear when you wear those workout shorts to do bathroom installs. She rolled her wheelchair into the bathroom and you were hanging out again."

"Hey, those are comfortable. It gets hot putting those stalls in."

"Well, you are making a lot of things hot. The women especially." Rene smiled and gave Jared a hug.

"You make me hot." She kissed him and turned to her desk.

"Queen Senna needs her next chocolate shipment. She's going to balloon up like a blimp if she doesn't slow down. That's three cases this month. Oh, yeah, batteries, she needs two cases of batteries. The rechargeable kind, winter is coming soon and with the frozen months she'll be cold and in need of something to warm her up."

"Good thing we bought this building close to the portal." Jared sighed. "But if she asks for another of those male movie stars again, I mean the one guy left the movie set for three months."

"Well, he is pretty sexy, yummy." Rene licked her lips seeing Jared scowl at her.

The door burst open and Tommy leaped into the room wearing a sailor outfit. "Hello, dahhhhhlings. I went shopping with T.J. and am here to introduce the newest member to the firm." Putting his hand on his hip, Tommy opened his eyes wide and glared at the two of them.

"Oh, my God, he's walking." Rene stood up smiling ear to ear like new mothers do and staring at their miracle baby.

In a matching sailor outfit to Tommy's, the little boy waddled into the office. "Awwww, he looks so cute. Thank you, Tommy." Rene picked up the baby and leaned over, kissing Tommy on the cheek.

Jared grinned and rubbed his hand over the little boy's head. He then kissed Rene on the neck and patted her on the ass.

"The Maples absolutely went nuts on the decorating job you did, Tommy."

Blowing on his fingers like a pro, Tommy replied, "Well, some people have it, some don't. And I got it *ALLLLLLLLLL*. Now come on, let's go to lunch. My treat."

"Okay, I have a few things to tidy up here. Give me ten minutes."

Rene gave T.J. a big hug and rubbed noses with him, bringing a smile to his tiny face. She set the baby back down and blew a few kisses his way.

He looked at Rene and Jared, then to Tommy.

"All right, but don't dawdle. We'll wait out here." Tommy held the little boy's tiny hand with his finger and slowly walked toward the door.

"Wave 'bye-bye' to Mommy and Daddy. Uncle Tommy is going to show you how to make quiche later tonight."

Smiling, Rene watched as T.J. waved "bye-bye" as they walked out the door.

The doors closed behind them and Rene sat back down to finish up.

"I think we have everything." Rene pushed back from her desk and grabbed her sweater from the coat rack.

Jared looked over to Rene and sighed. "Okay, where did you find some more women willing to have sex with two million men, all day and night?"

"Oh, it was easy. I got some professionals. These girls had been working the streets of New York and wanted out of the hooking business. So with the money the queen was willing to pay to have surrogate babies, I got them to give a group rate. Hell, some of them stayed there. Not that I blame them. Ten thousand to one odds of men to women. There has to be one good one out of all the assholes."

"Hmmm, I would like to see their résumés." Jared winked at Rene.

"I bet you would." Rene wrinkled her nose and pointed her finger at Jared.

"I did find one special girl to break in the Elders. The three-headed, freaky aliens. Those fuckers are really demented. I thought those women that take double insertions had it tough. These guys have three penises, one for each brain, and fill all holes at once." She shuddered. "Makes me queasy just thinking about it."

"Well, who gets the dubious honor of feeling like an overstuffed turkey?" Jared had a puzzled look on his face.

"I knew the perfect girl who would do anything to think she was moving up in the world. I used to work with her. The fucking, backstabbing bitch...her name is Kirsten."

Mistress Charlotte

Chris Tanglen

Author's Warning

Though the tale you are about to experience is called *Mistress Charlotte*, nobody named Mistress Charlotte appears until...oh, I'd say about halfway into it.

It's no big deal. Plenty of stuff happens before that, much of it involving people having sex. My only concern is that you might be reading one of the sex scenes that have been thoughtfully provided for your reading convenience, and you're getting more and more aroused, and maybe you're even whispering, "Oooh, yeah, right there, do it just like that," when you think, "Hey, y'know, I'm 11,278 words into this thing and there's been no reference to Mistress Charlotte! What's up with that?" and suddenly the whole erotic spell is broken as surely as if you'd stepped in dog shit.

(For those of you who would rather not have references to dog shit in their erotica, please note that the previous reference is the only one contained in this book.)

So, are we all clear? Let me recap, just to be sure:

1. This book is called *Mistress Charlotte*.

2. You won't be introduced to anybody named Mistress Charlotte for a while.

3. There will be scenes of a sexual nature to tide you over until then.

Also note that because I'm not being paid by the word, this warning cannot be considered a shameless attempt to boost my word count. It is being presented solely with the intent to maximize your potential enjoyment of *Mistress Charlotte*.

I'm just that kind of person.

Anyway, thank you for reading *Mistress Charlotte* (or, if you've changed your mind, thank you for at least reading this introduction). It's the culmination of years of work, all of it compressed into a last-minute "Deadline? What deadline?" panic. I hope you enjoy it as much as I enjoyed the one hundred and sixty-three cups of coffee that went into its creation.

—*Chris Tanglen*

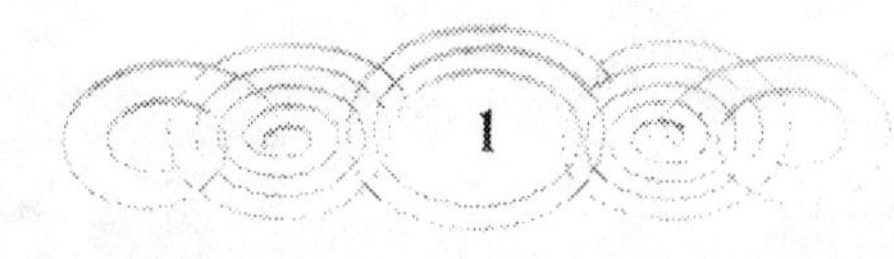

1

Jenny and Brian were both virgins when they got married at age twenty-five. Brian was a virgin by choice. Jenny was also a virgin by choice, if you wanted to get technical about it, but she had much less enthusiasm for the decision.

Brian was sixteen when he vowed that he was going to abstain from sexual relations until he was married. It was a popular decision with his parents, who were happy together and loved their son, but whose wedding took place primarily due to their failure to abstain from sexual relations. His friends, however, expressed concern and outrage over this decision, despite the fact that none of them were even close to getting laid anytime soon.

Everybody expected Brian to renege on his vow as soon as the opportunity for sex arrived, but it didn't happen. He grew into an extremely handsome young man, and during his college years no fewer than eight female students expressed a desire (ranging from subtle hints to graphic dialogue) to fuck him. He refused. Granted, it was not without a lot of anguish and a lot of hand lotion, but he stayed true to his vow.

It wasn't a religious thing, which is what everybody thought. In fact, he used religion as an excuse on several occasions just because it made it easier to explain. The truth was that he wanted a true *bond* with his future wife. He wanted them to have shared their bodies with each other and nobody else. And he wanted that special moment when they made love for the first time to take place on the night that they were finally joined as husband and wife.

He got teary-eyed describing this scenario. The few women he did share it with felt that it was the most romantic thing they'd ever heard. It made three of them want to fuck him even more, but he refused.

Also, Brian had a six-inch penis when fully erect, but porno films and misinformation from friends had convinced him that this was ridiculously small and laugh-worthy, something that would cause women to yawn and polish their nails during intercourse. He was much more comfortable talking about *not* having sex than talking about sex itself, and so on top of his vow of celibacy he was frightened that he had a tiny little dick.

The big problem with this particular vow was that throughout college he never met anybody he was even remotely interested in marrying. Nor did he meet anybody during the two years after graduation, while he worked as a graphic designer for a local magazine. He began to worry that maybe he'd be a thirty or forty-year-old virgin seeking a maiden bride, which was really going to narrow the pool of applicants.

A week after his twenty-fourth birthday, he met Jenny.

Jenny's virginity was not due to a vow of celibacy. In fact, she felt like she was *really* ready for sex. Lots of it. She was ready to find Mr. Right and ride him until the mattress ripped in half. But she hadn't yet found Mr. Right, or even Mr. Mildly Acceptable. She'd found Mr. Would Probably Be Willing To Bang Her on a few occasions, but horny as she was, she didn't want to have sex with just anybody.

She was five-foot-one and thirty pounds overweight. She was on a perpetual diet and got plenty of exercise, but it was as if the numbers on her digital scale were just painted on. On her good weeks, she was twenty-nine pounds overweight. On her bad weeks, she was thirty-one. Genetics had made its decision and was sticking to it.

Jenny was also painfully introverted. During her college years, she always sat in the back and never participated in class unless a cruel teacher called on her. She didn't attend a single party in four years, usually ate by herself in the cafeteria and even paid extra to keep from having a roommate.

After graduating college, she got a job as a waitress at a crappy diner. Six weeks later, she got a much better job writing documentation for a computer game company. She made some casual friends at work, went out on a few dates and had a couple of not-very-appealing offers for bedroom antics that she felt it necessary to decline.

On the Friday night that she met Brian, her refrigerator died. Or, to be more specific, on the evening that she met Brian she *discovered* that her refrigerator had died. Its actual death occurred at an unknown date and time, during the week she spent out of town visiting her mother. Among the contents of the refrigerator were milk, eggs and raw chicken.

When she walked into the apartment just before midnight, the smell hit her like a runaway sports utility vehicle to the face. She gagged, dropped her suitcase, gagged again, staggered a bit, gagged, staggered, gagged, staggered and then rushed into the bathroom. She expended an entire can of Lysol before clearing out the contents of her refrigerator and carrying them out to the dumpster. Then she made an emergency trip to the nearest convenience store.

She stood at the counter, waiting patiently as the clerk argued with a college student who was trying to buy extremely cheap beer without an ID.

"Okay, I don't mean to be nosy," said the guy behind her in line, "but I've *got* to know what you're doing with that stuff."

She turned to look at him and was momentarily stunned. He was tall, dark-haired, clean-shaven and devastatingly handsome in a boyish way.

"Huh?" she asked.

He touched the items in her arms, counting them. "You've got one, two, three, four, five cans of Lysol. One, two, three plug-in air fresheners. One, two, three, four, five, six, seven candles."

Jenny nodded, still too entranced to speak coherently.

"Those just don't seem like typical midnight purchases."

"My apartment stinks."

"Must be one big apartment."

She shook her head. "It's small. It just stinks really bad."

"Did somebody die in it?"

"My refrigerator."

"Ah, I see. And so all of your Lysol spoiled?"

Jenny stared at him. "What?"

"I was making a joke. You know, implying that you kept your Lysol in the refrigerator and it went bad, so you were buying more to replace it."

"Oh."

"But I know that you don't *really* keep your Lysol in the refrigerator."

"Okay." Jenny shifted uncomfortably.

"You don't, right?"

"No."

They were silent for a long moment. Finally Brian spoke. "That joke sucked, didn't it?"

"No, it was cute," Jenny insisted.

Brian shook his head. "You don't have to spare my feelings. I know when I've told a crappy joke. In fact, I wouldn't blame you if you bought your stuff, left this convenience store and never spoke to me again."

The college student stormed out of the store, beerless. Jenny moved forward and placed her items on the counter.

"Okay, I'm not going to spare your feelings," Jenny said. "It was the worst joke I've heard all day."

"Understood."

"Probably all week."

"Equally understood."

"Maybe all year."

"Now you're just being mean."

"In fact, I take that all back." Jenny tried to keep her expression serious but wasn't having much success restraining the smile that was trying to break free. "I wouldn't even call it an actual joke. It was like something that tried to *sound* like a joke but forgot to include the humorous content, sort of like if somebody slipped on an apple peel."

"I don't get it."

"The joke would be slipping on a banana peel. Slipping on an apple peel only sounds like a joke, but isn't really."

Brian shook his head. "See, you tried to ridicule my joke, but now your argument doesn't hold up to close scrutiny. Slipping on an apple peel could be humorous in an ironic way, because it defies traditional humor expectations. And I'm going to disagree with your assessment of my joke. I've already admitted that it wasn't funny, but that was because of *weak* humorous content, not non-existent humorous content." He turned to the cashier. "What do you think?"

"I think you two should just get a room."

Instead, they went to the twenty-four-hour restaurant that was two blocks away, where they ordered banana splits and chatted until it was time for breakfast. Then they ordered waffles.

Jenny had never in her life felt this comfortable around somebody. She was talkative, witty, sarcastic...practically an extrovert. He was clearly too attractive to be in her league, but he *did* seem to genuinely like her, and not just out of pity.

They left the restaurant around seven-thirty, when Jenny realized that it was either go home and get some sleep or pass out onto her syrup-covered plate. Brian asked if she wanted to go to the movies that evening. She did, very much.

Jenny returned to her apartment, practically floating on air, at least until she opened the door and very suddenly remembered exactly why she'd gone out in the first place. But a can and a half of Lysol and seven burning candles later, the apartment was habitable and she went to sleep.

She slept *extremely* well, at least until she suddenly woke up out of a sensational dream involving Brian and his penis, realizing that she'd left seven candles burning. She got up, blew them out and returned to her restful slumber.

She didn't wake up until early evening. She showered and tried to decide which pair of panties to wear.

Officially, it didn't matter. As attracted as she was to him, she wasn't going to put out on the first date. Bad idea. He might even be freaked out by her virginity.

Still...she wore the sexy black ones.

The movie sucked, which was fine. After the first predictable plot twist they found themselves holding hands, and by the end credits they were snuggling.

"I had a wonderful time," she said, beaming, as they stood at the door to her apartment.

"Me too," said Brian, putting his arms around her. "Would it be all right if I kissed you?"

"It certainly would."

The kiss was electric. Sizzling. Jenny's toes curled. Her heart raced. And, much to her chagrin, her nipples stiffened.

Oh God, he had to be able to feel that.

And, worse, she was getting wet.

Maybe she *would* put out on the first date.

He'd be a gentle lover, she just knew it. And a skilled one. Tonight was going to be the most memorable night of her life. Thank heavens she'd worn the sexy panties.

Their kiss lingered. He caressed her shoulders.

Finally, their lips parted. "Do you want to come inside?" she asked.

Brian nodded but then quickly shook his head. "I can't."

Jenny's heart sank. "You can't?"

"I mean, I *can*, but I can't...you know. Look, I made this vow..."

He told her all about it.

Jenny thought it was beautiful.

And it made her want to fuck him even more.

Then, blushing, she confessed her own virginity.

They stayed outside of her apartment for another twenty minutes, laughing and kissing.

Then Brian left, and Jenny realized that she was already in love.

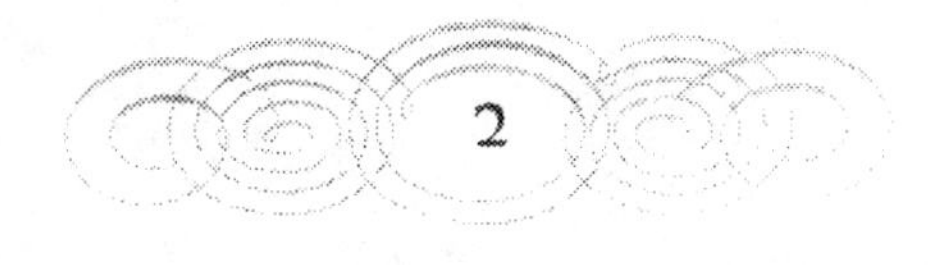

2

Jenny actually said the words "I love you" two weeks later, after they kissed next to Shaker Pond. It was said that if you kissed your lover at midnight and then gazed into the pond, you would see an image of your future together materialize in the water. But it was two in the afternoon, so all they saw was a fish jumping.

"Do you really?" Brian asked, looking surprised but extremely pleased.

Jenny nodded. She'd planned those three words all day, even rehearsed the intonation, and she was happy that they'd come out as "I love you" instead of the babbling gibberish she anticipated.

"I love you too," he said.

They kissed again.

Seventy-three days after they first met, they slept together. Brian in his underwear, Jenny in a nightgown. She could feel his erection pressed against her leg as they held each other under the covers, but he'd made it clear that he wasn't changing his mind.

They only slept together on weekends, with Jenny missing him horribly when his side of the bed was empty. She tried to suggest loopholes to the whole maintaining-their-virginity thing, such as oral sex. He could lick her into several dozen mind-blowing orgasms and she'd remain, technically, a virgin, and thus no vow was broken.

He didn't go for it. Through-the-clothes fondling was okay, but that was as far as he was willing to go.

One hundred and twenty-eight days after they met, he changed his mind, licking, sucking and nibbling her large breasts with great enthusiasm. She'd never had anybody pleasure her in this way, and the sensations were beyond anything she'd ever imagined.

He sucked one nipple while gently pinching the other between his thumb and index finger. His cock looked about ready to burst right through his briefs. If she hadn't encouraged him to buy new underwear just last week, she was confident that it *would* have ripped through the fabric.

She lay on the bed, arms stretched out over her head, legs spread, soaking wet beneath her panties. Brian moaned as he sucked. Jenny moaned even louder.

It felt *so* good.

He switched his mouth to the other breast and she thought she was going to scream in ecstasy.

Jenny squirmed, writhed, whimpered and knew that if she didn't get some kind of release, she was going to explode. And since they were in Brian's bed, he'd be stuck cleaning up the mess.

She reached down and slipped a finger into her panties.

She stared at Brian as she did this, wondering if he'd be shocked or offended. But he was too busy tending to her breasts to notice.

She ran the tip of her finger over her wet pussy, shivering at her own touch. She liked to masturbate and was good at it, but she had never, ever been this sensitive in her life.

She slipped a second finger into her panties and began to move her arm with exaggerated movements. She wanted Brian to know what she was doing. Wanted him to watch.

He noticed and pulled away from her breast. For a horrifying moment, she thought that he was appalled, but instead he broke into a wide grin. Without a word, he adjusted his position on the bed, giving himself a better view of her hand, and then returned to sucking her breast.

She stroked her clitoris, slowly, wanting to draw out the pleasure as long as possible...

But then it became abundantly clear that she was too horny,

too turned on, and she was going to come whether she was ready or not.

So she stroked vigorously. The orgasm hit almost immediately. She squeezed her eyes shut, arched her back and howled in pleasure while Brian continued working her breasts. She came so hard that she thought she was going to catapult herself right off the bed.

They slept together that night. Jenny changed into a fresh pair of panties.

Six months later, she walked into his apartment with an armload of groceries. Brian took them from her as he greeted her with a kiss, and then set them down on the kitchen table. As they began to put the groceries away, she noticed a DVD resting on the counter. The handwritten label read *The Price of Time*.

"What's this?" she asked.

"Ah, an old friend of mine sent it. I think I told you about him. The aspiring filmmaker?"

Jenny shook her head. "I don't remember hearing about him."

"Well, he finished his first short film and sent it to me. He's coming to visit next week, so you'll get the great joy of meeting him. I'll probably invite him to stay here with me, if that's okay."

"Of course. Is the movie any good?"

Brian shrugged. "I haven't watched it. I'm guessing that it's pretentious crap. I mean, what kind of stupid title is *The Price of Time?* Knowing him, it's probably *The Prince of Time* and he just wrote it wrong on the disc."

"Well, let's watch it. I've never known anybody who knew somebody who made a movie before. It might be an all-time classic."

"I'm guessing that it's not. I don't want to damage our relationship by making you watch it. I'm supposed to be protecting you from such things."

"Oh knock it off," Jenny said with a smile, picking up the DVD and heading into the living room. "How bad can it be?"

It was very, very bad. The movie, shot on video, consisted of two very poor actors sitting on chairs in a barren white room, speaking very slowly to each other about fate. Every thirty seconds or so, the movie would cut to a shot of a clock, unmoving.

After five minutes, Brian began to fast-forward.

"Is that a good idea?" Jenny asked, teasingly nudging him with her elbow. "What if he quizzes you on the plot twists?"

Brian fast-forwarded for a few more seconds and then let it play again. The actors were still talking about fate, and their performances hadn't improved.

"I bet you can't wait to meet this guy, huh?" asked Brian.

"I'm sure he's more interesting than his movie."

"No, actually, this movie is a pretty good representation of his personality."

"I fear fate, and yet I don't fear it," said the actor. "But should fate be feared or not feared?"

"I also fear fate," said the actress. "But it is not a question of whether or not it should be feared but—"

Suddenly a third actor came on screen. It was Brian. "Okay, both of you, quit babbling about fate! Nobody wants to hear this shit! Get off those chairs, both of you!"

The actors sheepishly stood up. Jenny's jaw dropped and she gaped at the real-life Brian, who looked far too pleased with himself.

"Get out of here," Brian said on the television screen. The actors left. "And somebody fix that clock!" He addressed the camera. "Jenny, we haven't known each other that long, but I feel like I've known you my entire life. And I can't imagine not living the rest of my life without you." He began to fish in his pockets. "Where did I put that thing?"

"I've got it," said the real-life Brian, taking a small box out of his pocket.

"Oh good," said the television Brian. "Actually, why don't you take it from here?"

The television screen went blank.

Brian knelt down in front of Jenny, who was still in a state of shock, and opened the box. Inside was an absolutely gorgeous ring. The diamond was small, but to her it seemed to be the size of a mountain.

"Jenny, will you marry me?" Brian asked, voice trembling.

Jenny burst into tears and cried so hard that it took her nearly a minute to be able to answer "Yes!"

It was a small, intimate wedding, and it went perfectly. Brian gazed at the woman he loved more than anything else in the world and knew that he could be happy for the rest of his life.

And tonight, finally, they were going to make love.

It had been a difficult vow to keep at times. On one hand, his intense love for Jenny made it easier, because it was a vow meant to bond them even closer as husband and wife. On the other hand, she was sexy as hell, and pleasuring her breasts or kissing her through her panties just about made him lose his freakin' mind. There had been many, many, many times when he wanted to just yank down her panties, bend her over and take her from behind, but he'd resisted the urges.

And now it was going to all be worth it.

When was this reception going to *end*?

Their honeymoon was local. Instead of paying for airfare to some exotic location that they'd be too busy fucking to appreciate, they booked a week in a hotel suite with a hot tub.

They walked down the hallway, hand-in-hand, Jenny still in her wedding dress, Brian still in his tuxedo, both of them feeling nervous but excited.

Jenny retreated to the bathroom to change. Brian quickly got out of that miserable outfit, wishing that Jenny had taken him up on his suggestion to make it a shorts-and-t-shirt kind of wedding. He stripped down to his blue silk boxers and then stretched out happily on the king-size bed. A bottle of non-alcoholic champagne and a fruit tray rested on the dresser.

It took Jenny over half an hour to emerge from the bathroom, but Brian was neither impatient nor surprised, mostly because he'd fallen asleep.

Jenny returned to the bathroom, shutting the door loudly.

When she emerged again, moments later, Brian was wide awake. She stood before him, practically glowing, and gloriously naked.

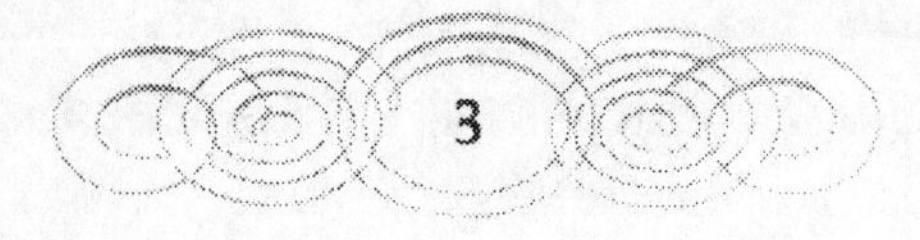

3

He'd seen her completely naked before, but only in quick glimpses. Just a brief peek as she got out of the shower, or a glance as she changed out of her clothes. He'd tried to avoid it as much as possible...and now, as he stared at his bride, it had been worth all of the frustration, agony, torture and frantic masturbation sessions.

She was absolutely gorgeous. He looked at her wavy brown hair, draped over her shoulders. Her blue eyes, shining. Her smile...she'd had her teeth whitened before the wedding, and the dentist had done one hell of a job.

He looked at her full, large breasts, the nipples already perky. And her tummy. She'd actually managed to battle genetics and lose some weight before the wedding, but she still carried some extra padding, which made her look even sexier to Brian...like a *real* woman. Her arms, with her hands on her hips.

And he looked at her pussy. The neatly trimmed curls, darker than her other hair. Those sexy folds that he would get to touch for the first time, to taste, to be within.

He wanted to take her all in, head to toe, but he found himself preoccupied with her pussy.

"Like what you see?" asked Jenny, biting her lip nervously.

"Oh yes," said Brian. "Come over here and join me."

"Don't you want me to turn around?"

"My mistake. By all means, turn around."

She did, lifting her arms in the air as she twirled. He gazed at her sexy ass, hardly able to believe that tonight he was going to knead it, nibble it...

She turned to face him again. "Your turn. I want to see that big, wonderful," she hesitated for just a split second, "cock."

Brian grinned. She'd never used that word before. In fact, she rarely said anything stronger than "dammit!" unless there was physical pain involved. "I think I can fulfill that request."

He got out of the comfy bed and pulled down his briefs, letting his erection pop free. He tossed the underwear aside.

They stood before each other, ten feet apart, completely naked.

And then, simultaneously, they stepped forward and locked themselves in an embrace.

In the approximately 47,310,881 times she'd imagined this scenario, Jenny had envisioned gentle, tender kisses. But these kisses were passionate, almost rough, and it was every bit as good.

They both moaned as they kissed. She slipped her tongue into his mouth and he accepted it hungrily. As he clenched her tight, he quickly ran his hands all over her back, sweeping down toward but never quite reaching her ass.

She pressed her breasts against him, adoring the sensation, wanting his hands on them, his mouth, his teeth.

Jenny couldn't believe that she was finally here, finally married, finally officially committed to the man she loved.

Finally going to get laid.

His kisses were so intoxicating that she almost felt like she was in a dream-state, like she was falling...

No, wait, she *was* falling.

Shit!

Her legs slipped out from underneath her, and only Brian's tight grip around her waist kept her from landing on her newly married ass.

"Are you okay?" Brian asked, genuinely concerned but also highly amused.

She nodded. "How about we move to the bed?"

"Good idea."

He took her by the hand and led her to the bed. They climbed onto the mattress together, as they had done so many times before, but never as husband and wife.

They kissed some more.

And then, slowly, Brian began to move away from her lips. He kissed her cheek, her ears, her chin, her neck, her shoulders. As she lay on her back, he kissed a path down her left arm, caressing her skin with his hands as he did so, kissing each finger.

He did the same with her right arm, and Jenny felt her nervousness fade. It wasn't gone altogether, but it was nothing more than a gentle tug at the pit of her stomach, nothing that would ruin the most wonderful night of her life.

Brian cupped her breasts.

"You are so beautiful," he whispered.

She grinned. "Thank you."

Brian licked the underside of her breast, loving the way it felt against his tongue. He'd licked her breasts before, but this felt somehow different. Better.

He took her right nipple into his mouth, circling it with his tongue. She sucked in a deep breath. Moments later, he switched to the other breast, his tongue darting over the nipple, teasing her.

But only for a few seconds. They'd been teasing each other for months, and the time for teasing was over.

He kissed a path down her belly, finally crouching between her legs.

She opened them invitingly.

She glistened. Brian ran his index finger through the top of her pubic patch, loving the gentle tickle. He took in her scent, a wonderful combination of being fresh and clean from the shower, and something else, something aroused and womanly.

He lightly traced his finger around her pussy while she whimpered.

He kissed it.

And then did a tentative lick.

Jenny thought that she was going to shriek when his tongue touched her. She clenched her hands into tight fists and struggled to maintain her sanity.

Oh God, what if he didn't like it? What if he thought the taste was disgusting? What if he got completely grossed out and never licked her again?

Brian licked her again.

"Mmmmmmm..." he moaned.

Jenny relaxed.

Brian licked slowly, still entranced by the sight of her this close. He'd seen the female parts in great detail in porno flicks, but even watching it on his friend Ralph's wide-screen television couldn't come close to presenting the beauty in real life. Its effect on all of his senses was almost overwhelming.

Jeez, what if he came just from licking her?

He forced that thought out of his mind and focused entirely on his wife's beautiful pussy. He wasn't completely sure that he liked the taste, but he *did* like the heat, the wetness, the way it felt under his tongue...and most importantly, her reaction.

He continued licking, top to bottom. He tried to listen, to see what was getting the strongest response, but *everything* seemed to be eliciting a strong response from her, so he just licked everywhere.

It was better than Jenny could ever have believed. Every movement of his tongue sent waves of pleasure through her. One of her friends had said, "Y'know, if he doesn't know what he's doing, he can lick down there for hours and it ain't gonna do a damn thing for you." Jenny didn't know if she was just excessively responsive, if Brian knew what he was doing or if her friend was just a bitter old hag, but this was absolutely *incredible*.

It felt so good that she thought she might be headed toward an orgasm.

No. She didn't want that. She wanted to come with him inside her.

She let him continue to lick her for several more moments, until she knew that if she didn't make him stop, she wouldn't be able to control herself. She scooted back on the bed.

"I want you inside me," she said.

Brian began to caress her legs, looking a bit uncomfortable. The tip of his cock was covered with pre-come. "Look, I can tell right now that I'm not going to last more than a stroke or two."

"Why? You horny?" she asked with a smile.

"A little."

This was one of the problems with both of them being virgins. She was likely to experience some pain, and he was likely to suffer from premature ejaculation.

She decided that she'd better give him a release.

"Lie on your back, hubby," she said.

Brian did. She took his hot, hard cock in her hands. Oh yeah. This was hers now, to do with as she pleased.

Right now, it pleased her to run her tongue along the underside. As she did so, she noted that it seemed to be pleasing Brian as well. Very much so.

She kissed the tip and then took him into her mouth.

She'd never tasted his penis before, and she had to admit that she liked it. A lot. Her darling husband would be receiving many more blowjobs in their years together.

She felt his cock twitch in her mouth. "You'd better move away," he said. "I'm almost there."

She pulled away just long enough to say, "No, it's okay," and then she sucked him in deeper.

"I'm gonna come..." he said. "I'm gonna..."

He cried out as he exploded inside her mouth. The taste was surprisingly mild, but the quantity was much more than she expected. As he continued coming in her mouth, she worried that she might not be able to swallow it all. She didn't want it running down her chin like some porn slut on their wedding night, although there'd be a place for that in their future, she guessed.

She kept her lips around the head of his cock, forming a tight seal as his orgasm subsided. She closed her eyes and swallowed half of what was in her mouth and then swallowed the other half.

Done. That wasn't so bad.

She slowly ran her mouth up and down his shaft, cleaning him off.

Then she gave his cock a quick kiss.

"Oh wow," said Brian, leaning up to look at her. "You have no idea how much I needed that."

"You deserved it." She gave his cock a playful stroke and then crawled on top of him. And now for the first major test of their marriage: Would he kiss her afterward?

He did. Passionately.

He was still very hard, and she was still very wet. She straddled him and then sat up. She took his hands and placed them on her breasts as she raised herself and pressed the entrance of her vagina against his cock.

She was so wet that there didn't seem to be any resistance.

She slowly slid down, not very far, working him inside her. It felt like pure bliss, but now the nervousness was creeping back in. Would it hurt badly? Would it hurt at all?

God, she was horny.

Okay, she was going to take the same approach as swimming in a lake. Just dive in, get the ice-cold sensation over with and enjoy the swim.

She braced herself.

What if it *really* hurt?

Brian moved his hands from her breasts to her waist. "Do you want to wait?"

She shook her head. This was ridiculous. Everybody fucked. No big deal.

Maybe she should roll on her back and let him do all the work.

No, no, she wanted to be in control, just for this one moment. It felt so good right now that the pain couldn't possibly overpower that, right?

She slid down onto his cock just a bit more, a fraction of an inch.

And then she impaled herself.

The pain was like a soft conversation that took place during the Times Square celebration on New Year's Eve...it was there, but it was drowned out by everything else. There were a million things she wanted to shout, but all she said was: "Oh!"

He was inside of her.

Inside her body.

The intimacy, the love, the bonding...all of it expressed in this one act, accompanied by physical pleasure so intense that she thought her heart might give out.

She made love to her husband in slow, long strokes. She sensed that the wetness might not all be her lubrication, but that didn't matter, all that mattered was that she was truly joined with Brian, and that she had reached a state of absolute bliss.

Then her thoughts became a little less romantic: *Holy shit, I'm finally getting to fuck!*

Oh yeah, she could get used to fucking him.

She continued with the slow strokes. Brian looked into her eyes as she fucked him, and his expression was pure joy.

His erection didn't seem to be diminishing.

She rode him for several minutes, never picking up the pace. Now she was starting to feel a bit sore, but that was okay, the pleasure was still the strongest sensation.

She moved his right hand from her waist and guided it to her clitoris. "Touch me."

He stroked her wet clitoris with his thumb, and she gasped. "Faster," she whispered. "I want to come."

He stroked faster. She guided his thumb just a bit lower...moaning as he hit the perfect spot. "Right there!"

She kept fucking him as he worked her clit, and it wasn't long at all before she felt the oncoming rush that she'd previously only achieved through her own fingers.

Now she picked up the pace. "I'm gonna come!"

When it hit, it was the most intense orgasm she'd ever experienced. She moaned through clenched teeth and grinded her pussy into him, feeling like the orgasm was shooting through her entire body, from her curled toes to her fingers, which she now realized were digging a bit too hard into Brian's chest.

She pulled them away, leaving red marks.

"Sorry," she said.

"I didn't even notice," Brian admitted, rubbing his chest.

They went back to their cheerful fucking. Brian had stayed nice and hard, and not too long after her orgasm, he wiped some sweat from his brow and groaned. "I'm almost there again."

Jenny rode him harder.

He came with a loud gasp. She could feel him coming within her, filling her, and it was almost enough to send her over the brink again.

When he was done, she collapsed on top of him, and they just held each other, satisfied and happy, but not nearly ready to call it a night.

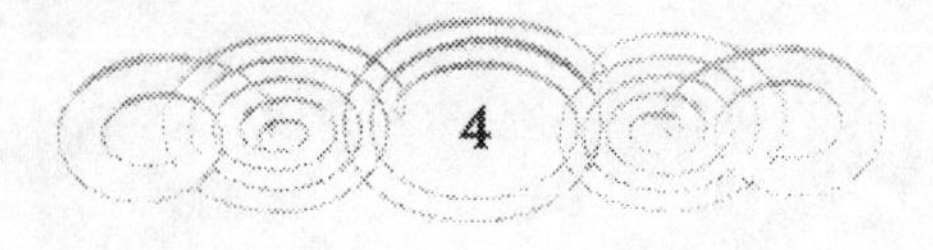

4

There was a bit of a mess to clean up, but Jenny didn't mind. It made for a perfectly good excuse to share a hot shower with Brian. Of course, she discovered fairly quickly that sharing a shower is one of the more overrated erotic acts, unless one had a shower with two nozzles, but Brian was a gentleman and let her enjoy the majority of the hot water spray.

Once they were nice and clean, they got rid of the top sheet and returned to bed. They lay together as she stroked his limp penis.

"That was fun," she said.

"I absolutely agree."

"We'll have to do it more often."

"I absolutely agree."

"You know, I don't think most women come during their first sexual experience. I must be special."

Brian kissed her shoulder. "It probably helped that you weren't doing it in the backseat of a car worrying that your parents were going to catch you."

"No, I'm going to stick with the 'I must be special' theory."

"I can go with that."

"So what did you think, Mr. Ex-Virgin? Disappointed?"

"Not a bit."

"Was it everything you hoped for and more?"

"Well, no, I kind of hoped that I'd be able to go for hours, that you'd come sixty-five times and that we'd break the bed. But this was pretty good too."

"There's still time. Our honeymoon has only just begun."

They kissed some more, tongues sliding over each other, hands roaming. Before too long, Brian had moved back down between her legs for a second session of delightful oral sex. He reached under her, cupping her buttocks in his hands, and kneaded them as he licked, and licked, and licked.

"Oh yeah, keep doing that," she said. "That's so good. Oh it's wonderful. I love you. Yes, right there, just like that!" Positive reinforcement was important in these situations.

She considered suggesting a nice round of sixty-nine...but no. He was doing a splendid job licking her pussy, but having it pressed on top of his face might be a bit much to handle this early into his non-virginity. Of course, she could offer to be on the bottom, but having his cock in her face like that would *definitely* be too much to handle. Gagging wasn't sexy.

She pinched her nipples as he licked.

And, yes, another orgasm signaled its approach. This was going to be a big one, she could tell.

His tongue moved rapidly, all over.

"Lick my clit!" she suggested—demanded, louder than she'd intended.

He lapped at her clitoris, and she knew that the approaching orgasm had not been a false alarm. In fact, it was feeling more like a the-skyscraper-is-burning emergency. As she prepared herself for her second orgasm of the night she wrapped her legs around Brian's back and closed her eyes.

This one was even better than the first. She cried out so loudly that she suddenly worried that they'd be evicted from the hotel room and forced to fuck elsewhere. For future orgasms she'd use a pillow to muffle the sound.

Brian kept licking, but she wanted him inside of her again. "Kiss me," she said, and she checked out his cock as he climbed back up to kiss her. Firm but not quite hard enough. She took it in her hand and stroked it as their lips met.

"Feels like you're almost ready," she said.

"Mmm-hmmm."

"But a bit of assistance is in order. Kneel, hubby."

Brian moved into a kneeling position, while Jenny got on her hands and knees in front of him. She began to suck his cock again, reaching around to clench his ass as she did so. She could feel him stiffening in her mouth. He brushed her hair aside to get a better view.

"That feels amazing," he said.

It was impolite to talk with her mouth full, so she didn't respond.

Very little oral effort was required on her part before his erection had returned to its former glory. So she pulled her mouth away, rolled onto her back and spread her legs as wide as she could. "Time to fuck some more," she announced, surprised by how comfortable she was saying something like "Time to fuck some more". But they were married now, and she could be as filthy as she wanted. Fuck it.

Brian got on top of her in the traditional missionary position and slid into her easily. There was a little pain this time as well, but again it was overpowered by the intense pleasure his cock brought her. He thrust into her, over and over, being gentle but not *too* gentle. She hooked her feet around his ankles, locking him in place.

They continued making love in that position for quite some time. Brian had to slow down a few times, and even stop altogether, but that was fine, he'd learn control during the huge amounts of sex they'd be having, and just being joined with him was enough for now.

Brian couldn't *believe* how good this felt. It was unquestionably helped by the intense love he felt for his wife and the emotions pouring through him, but still, the fucking itself just felt *amazing*. And he was performing pretty well for a virgin, he thought. At least he hadn't had trouble getting it in.

He fucked her and kissed her and knew that he wanted to be with Jenny for the rest of his life.

The bedsprings creaked.

He felt like he was going to come again, and this time he didn't think slowing down or stopping his thrusts was going to do any good. So he picked up the pace, pounding into her, fucking her hard.

"Oh *God*!" she cried out. "Don't stop! Don't stop!"

Of course, he'd started fucking her harder because he *had* to stop, but she'd understand. He slammed into her a few more times and then came, shuddering as he spurted within her, pressing his face against the mattress.

And then he was spent.

They kissed some more and then lay in bed, talking softly about nothing in particular. Jenny finally fell asleep, her head against his chest, her hand on his cock. He lay there, taking in her scent, and then fell asleep shortly thereafter.

They both woke up in the middle of the night, horny again.

This time, Brian crouched by the side of the bed while she sat on the edge of the mattress, legs spread. He lapped at her hungrily. This man seemed as if he were becoming addicted to performing oral sex, and that suited Jenny just fine. She would make no efforts to get him off the wagon. In fact, she'd be an enabler.

She let him lick her for as long as she could stand it and then scooted forward and got on her hands and knees, raising her ass in the air. Brian climbed onto the bed behind her, and she could almost see his hard cock jutting out in front of him, ready to penetrate her.

Jenny knew it would be tighter in this position. Would it feel even better?

He pressed his cock against her, and she braced herself. She moved her legs farther apart and he slid into her. Her wet, slick vagina offered no resistance. Oh yeah. Definitely tighter. She could see why so many people favored this position.

I was a virgin this afternoon, and now here I am getting fucked doggy-style. Woo-hoo!

Brian fucked her with long strokes, his hands on her ass cheeks. Sustaining her balance was a bit of a problem, and she had to subtly shift her position a couple of times to keep from toppling over, but before too long she was all set for a nice extended session of fucking.

And, much to her surprise, that's exactly what it turned out to be.

Brian had quickly developed amazing longevity for somebody this early in his sexual career, and they went at it for quite some time. Of the three sexual positions she'd added to her repertoire, this was most definitely her favorite.

She wanted to reach back there and play with herself while he thrust into her, but she wasn't quite comfortable enough to try to sustain her balance with one hand. She'd have to work on that.

Brian was in heaven. He was getting an absolutely perfect view of his wife's beautiful ass, and her pussy was so warm and wet that he never wanted to leave. He'd have to leave eventually, he suspected, if only to allow the hotel staff to clean the room, but for now his cock was delighted with its new home.

And he was very relieved to discover that he was *good* at fucking. Not an expert yet, but a certainly a promising beginner. With practice, he felt confident that he'd be winning awards any day now.

He considered saying that out loud, strictly with humorous intent, but decided against it.

Jenny seemed to be having one hell of a time. Was there any sound in the world more exciting than listening to her squeal with pleasure? He thought not.

"Fuck me harder," she said.

Okay, maybe hearing her say "Fuck me harder" was more exciting.

He fucked her harder, being an obedient husband.

Finally he could hold out no longer, but he didn't want to come this way. He wanted to come while he was kissing her. He pulled out and gave her a very light, playful slap on the ass. "Missionary," he said.

"Where? Send him away! We're busy fucking!"

Jenny rolled onto her back and Brian quickly mounted her. He entered her and resumed his rapid thrusts as he kissed her on the lips. He came seconds later, his cry of pleasure engulfed by her mouth.

She hadn't come, which Brian felt was unacceptable. He might kiss her after a blowjob, but he wasn't about to lick her pussy after his orgasm, so instead he used his hands. She gave him very specific directions regarding location, pace, pressure and number of fingers to utilize, and he happily complied.

But Jenny was in no hurry for another orgasm. She wanted to draw out the pleasure that his fingers were giving her, wanted them to bring her almost to the brink and then move away. Brian was very good at following directions. She asked him to slide one finger completely inside of her, then two, then three, while he gently stroked her clitoris with the index finger of his other hand.

They kept this up much longer than the intercourse, until she began to sense that his fingers were getting tired. So she had him focus all of his attention on her clitoris, which was so swollen and sensitive that it took only...

She came so hard that she forgot all about the pillow.

They fell asleep shortly after that, and this time they slept until late the next morning.

Jenny and Brian had a lot more sex over the remainder of their honeymoon. Though they did leave the hotel on various occasions to go out to eat, most of their time was spent on the bed, or in the hot tub, or on the sofa, or on the floor, or against the wall.

Oh my God I'm a nymphomaniac. Jenny's moment of realization occurred as she was bent over the edge of the bed, her husband ramming her from behind. No, no, not a nympho. Just somebody with a hell of a lot of lost time to make up for.

Tragically, the honeymoon drew to a close, and they sorrowfully packed their suitcases and checked out of the hotel. They returned to Brian's apartment, where they would be living for the next month until they moved into their new house.

The first thing they did was fuck.

The second thing they did was unpack their suitcases, but it was interrupted by the third thing they did, which was fuck.

They made love constantly during the first month of their marriage, even meeting for lunch during the workweek so that they could do it in the back of Brian's car. They had sex in every room in Brian's apartment. That didn't sound impressive because it wasn't all that big of an apartment, but the feat took on a greater significance when one considered that they managed to have sex in a very, very small closet, though not without an emergency trip to the chiropractor immediately thereafter.

The first night they *didn't* have sex was the first night of moving into their new home. It was unseasonably hot, Jenny had acquired a lot of heavy crap during her twenty-five years of life and they lay in bed too exhausted for even a quickie.

They made up for it after the moving was done. They fucked in every room of the house, which was more impressive because of the number of rooms involved, although doing it in the walk-in bedroom closet wasn't quite as astonishing.

The first year of their marriage was a constant sex-a-thon.

Things slowed down a bit in the second year, but that was to be expected. They still had a far above-average amount of sex, at least according to the women's magazines.

The third year, Jenny got a new management job working under Satan (or his human counterpart). The pressure at work was unbelievable, her stress level shot way up, and more often than not Jenny would come home late wanting nothing more than a foot rub and some sleep. Brian was always happy to provide the foot rub, and they still had sex on weekends, as long as they weren't too busy.

The fourth year, Brian got laid off. He'd loved his job and despaired that he'd never find another one nearly as good. He was right. After a lengthy search, he settled for a decent job that paid well but offered no real fulfillment and no control over his future. So he decided to go back to college while he worked full time. Their marriage remained strong, and they remained happy together but sex became a low priority.

The fifth year, they made up a sex schedule.

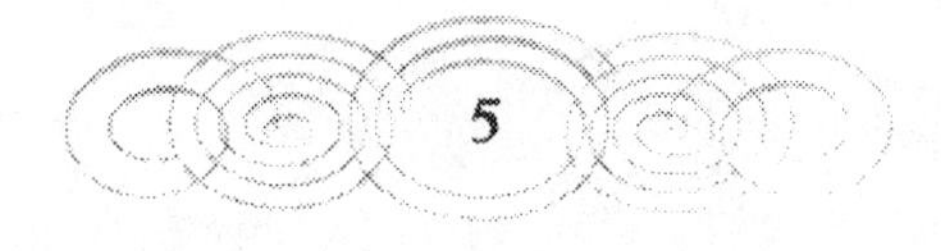

5

I can't *believe* we have to resort to a sex schedule," said Jenny as they sat at the dining room table. "Isn't that for people in their forties with eight kids? We're such losers."

Brian shook his head. "This doesn't make us losers. Lots of couples do this."

"Yeah, well, there are lots of loser couples."

Brian sighed. "It's no big deal. We just aren't in the mood most of the time. If we plan to have sex at a certain time each week, maybe we'll look forward to it and *get* in the mood."

"I guess so."

"It doesn't bother you that we haven't had sex in two months? And when we do, it's half-hearted missionary. We can't let this go on."

Jenny nodded. "No, no, you're right. You're absolutely right. I just never would have thought it would happen to us, y'know?"

"Me either, but we're here, and we'll deal with it. We'll do it once a week, every Saturday night, what do you think?"

"I was thinking Sunday night. That'll put us in a good mood for the upcoming week."

"Good point," Brian agreed. "Okay, Sunday night. Eight o'clock?"

"Do we really need to schedule a time?"

"I guess not."

"I mean, I'm not totally against the idea, but you never know, some weeks we might be interested in a quick romp on the kitchen floor, and some weeks we might be up for a six-hour marathon."

"All right. No time then. But Sunday nights. That's our special sex time."

"God, this is pathetic," said Jenny.

"It's not pathetic. If you keep thinking it is, this won't work. I love you, and I don't like that we do nothing but talk about work and my classes every evening and then collapse into bed. It's not healthy."

"Maybe we should take a vacation."

"Of course we should take a vacation. But since I can't get any vacation time until this project ends in May, I think that the sex schedule will have to tide us over." Brian sounded a bit irritated with her, which was very much unlike him.

"I know, I'm sorry, I'm not trying to be difficult, I just..." She trailed off, and then leaned over and gave Brian a hug. "I love you."

"I love you too."

They kissed.

"And I think that once a month we should do something kinky," said Brian.

Jenny giggled. "What do you mean, kinky?"

"Kinky. Sex in public. Bondage. A really freaky sex toy."

"A third party?"

"Not that kinky."

"Okay," said Jenny, "we'll do it. This Sunday is bondage night. You can tie me up and do with me as you please."

"Ooooooh yeah. Can I wear a black leather mask and bring a branding iron?"

"Depends on your plans for the branding iron."

"I thought I'd brand 'Property of Brian' on your ass."

"How about a temporary tattoo instead?"

"That's almost as much fun." He gave her a kiss. "Bondage Sunday it is!"

On Bondage Sunday, their errands took much longer than anticipated, the lawnmower broke and Jenny's older sister called and cried for two hours because her son was skipping school. Brian and Jenny agreed to postpone Bondage Sunday until next week, though they did have some pretty good sex before going to sleep.

Brian stood alone in their bedroom, staring at the bed, trying to figure this out. If they had a four-poster bed this would be nice and easy, but instead they had a flat headboard that didn't have any place to attach handcuffs or a silk scarf. As far as he could tell, they'd have to loop something underneath the mattress, maybe a rope, to give him something to cuff Jenny to.

So...if he had two ropes, he could wrap them all around the mattress, one at the top, one at the bottom. Then he could handcuff Jenny's hands and feet to the rope.

That would work, wouldn't it?

He was a graphic designer, but he was much better at making things look good than he was making them functional.

Yeah, this would work.

He went to the local hardware store and bought a coil of nylon rope. Then, a bit embarrassed and blushing furiously, he went to the sex shop and picked up four sets of fur-lined handcuffs, one for each appendage.

When he got home, Jenny was in the kitchen, pouring herself a glass of apple juice. "I thought you were going to be gone until six," he said.

"They let us go early." Jenny had been at a mandatory team-building weekend for work, which she'd complained stood little or no chance of building a team. She'd become rather cynical about matters pertaining to work.

"Oh. I was going to have everything all set up." He held up the plastic bags with the bondage accessories.

"Ooooh, is that our stuff?"

"Yep, it's our stuff."

"Well, we should get started! Let me go take a shower and we'll start some bondage a-plenty!"

She gave him a lingering kiss and then retreated into the bathroom, shutting the door behind her. Brian went into the bedroom and tossed his bags on the mattress and then returned to the kitchen to seek out the necessary supplies.

He opened the freezer door. Ice cubes. Check.

Then he looked in the refrigerator. Strawberries. Check.

The feather duster was in the closet, and he had a silk handkerchief in his top dresser drawer to use as a blindfold, so all of the supplies were in order. He hurried into the garage and grabbed his large pocketknife and then went back into the bedroom.

He uncoiled the rope, figured out how much would be necessary if he wanted it to loop around the mattress a couple of times, and then cut two separate pieces of that length. The rest he shoved under the bed. He lifted the mattress with one hand and tossed the rope across the box springs with the other, then lowered the mattress, walked around to the other side and pulled the rope most of the way through.

So far, so good. He'd be a Bondage Master in no time.

He tossed the rope over the top of the mattress, walked back around to the original side of the bed, lifted the mattress with one hand, and tossed the rope under the mattress again. He walked back over and pulled it tight.

Perfect.

He tugged on the rope to test it.

Not perfect.

Shit. It was too loose.

He pulled it tight again. He'd have to tie the ends to something, maybe the legs of the bed. Damn. He wasn't good with knots. He knelt down and tried to remember his Cub Scout training. But he'd been a crappy Cub Scout. He hadn't even made it past Wolf, which was the second rank, higher than Bobcat but less than a Bear, and certainly not a mighty Webelos...

Focus.

He tried to focus.

It didn't have to be a pretty knot, anyway, it just had to keep the ropes tight. He wrapped the end of the rope around the leg of the bed a couple of times, then tied it into a bow.

He stood up and gave the rope a tug.

Still loose.

"Dammit!" Bondage wasn't supposed to be this complicated. He untied the bow, pulled the rope as tight as he could, and then tied the bow once more.

The rope remained too loose to restrain his wife. It almost seemed to be laughing at him, mocking him, which was a pretty impressive feat for a rope.

Okay, desperate times called for desperate measures. He went out into the garage and got the duct tape.

Jenny wrapped a towel around herself after her very hot, very thorough shower. She was so excited! From what she understood, a little light bondage was typical with most couples, so she really wasn't sure why it had taken her and Brian so long to give it a try. In the early years of their marriage, they'd been passionate but not all that creative.

She still wasn't completely comfortable with the idea of a sex schedule, but she had to admit that it *did* give her something to look forward to all week. She dried herself off and looked at herself in the mirror. Yep, she could pass for a submissive slut. She pushed her breasts together, made a sexy face and then left the bathroom and headed into the bedroom.

"Uh, what are you doing?" she asked.

Brian was crouched down beside the bed, using duct tape to attach a rope to the mattress. "The rope was too loose."

"You couldn't just tie it tighter?"

"No. I could not."

Jenny frowned. "I'm not trying to criticize your setup or anything, but, uh...could you explain your setup?"

"We don't have posts to attach the handcuffs to," said Brian. "So I wrapped these ropes around the mattress, and we'll attach the cuffs to the rope, and you won't be able to move."

"I'll be able to move side to side the whole length of the rope."

Brian stared at the mattress for a long moment. He was pretty sure that somebody who wasn't a complete idiot would have noticed this substantial glitch much earlier. "Oh."

"It's okay for me to move side-to-side, though, isn't it?"

"No, that wrecks the point. How about I just duct tape you to the mattress?"

Jenny giggled. "You're cute when you're frustrated."

"I'm not frustrated. I'm just using sarcasm as a defense mechanism to cope with my own crippling failure as a bondage setter-upper. I mean, I really suck. Why the hell would I have thought that a rope would work? Of *course* you'd be able to slide from side to side with a rope setup like this. When did I become such a dullard? Why didn't you warn me sooner that my brain was eroding? Maybe I have some rare form of—"

"You can go on for hours like this, can't you?"

"Oh yeah. Easily. I may not be able to figure out a way to work these handcuffs, but I can ridicule my inadequacy all night long."

Jenny put her hands on her hips and surveyed the bed. "This shouldn't be too hard to figure out."

"We could move to the kitchen. I could cuff your hands to the cabinet and do wicked things to you from behind."

"Then I could move around by pulling the cabinet doors open."

"*Shit.*"

"We have the shower curtain rod," said Jenny. "We could take that down, put it under the mattress so that it sticks out on both sides, and then attach the other ends of the handcuffs to it."

Brian shook his head. "Yeah, but the handcuffs would just come right off the ends. Ha! It's not so easy, is it?"

"If you're not careful, you'll be the one tied to the bed and I'll be administering the spanking."

"That might be fun, actually."

"Not when the blisters form."

Brian grinned. "Is this the way people are supposed to talk when they're getting into the bondage lifestyle? Isn't it supposed to be a lot of 'Yes, Master' and 'Ow, Master'?"

"Well, I think we've already established that we're not very good at the bondage lifestyle."

"I'm gonna have to agree with you there. Wanna fuck the regular way?"

"No way," said Jenny. "You're not getting off the hook that easily, buster. I *will* be handcuffed tonight, whatever it takes."

"Now, see, we're still screwing up. The handcuffee is not supposed to be the one giving the orders."

"Tough noogies."

Brian gave her a kiss. Despite his jovial tone, he had to admit that he was genuinely flustered by his inability to set things up. Hopefully news of his inferiority complex didn't reach his penis.

Oh great. No better way to ensure a limp evening than to worry about an inferiority complex reaching his penis. Jeez. What else could he mess up?

Several dozen things quickly came to find, and so he didn't feel so bad.

He did his best to come up with the sternest expression he could possibly manage. Brian wasn't particularly good at stern expressions, mostly because he wasn't very good at being stern, but he knew that if he had a mirror, the face reflected in it would look most stern indeed. He hoped. "I said that the handcuffee will not be the one giving the orders," he said, sternly.

Jenny's smile vanished and she nodded, although the smile didn't vanish from her eyes. "I understand."

"Good. See that you continue to understand. Now tell me what a superb job I did setting up the bed, lest thee feel my wrath."

"I wish not to feel thy wrath. You did an excellent job setting up the bed. If you were to cuff me to those ropes, I would be incapable of mobility of any form. In fact, it is unlikely that I would even be able to breathe or complete a heartbeat, so restrained would I be."

"A fine answer," said Brian. "Now get your naked ass on that bed."

Jenny got her naked ass on the bed. Brian grabbed one of the ropes by the center and pulled it free of the mattress, which was embarrassingly easy. He tossed the rope aside and then got rid of the other one with similar ease. Jenny, respecting his astounding authority, bowed her head and said nothing.

"There," he said, satisfied. "The ropes that were perfectly set up and would have served their purpose with nary a problem have been removed, simply because it pleased me to do so."

"It pleased me as well," said Jenny.

"Hush, naked one." Brian glanced around the room. What had he done with the blindfold?

Oh great, now he couldn't even remember where the blindfold was. This evening was going to be a continued disaster, and they were going to throw away their sex schedule in favor of a life of celibacy, and he was going to start wearing his hair like a monk and then...

Wait, it was in the top drawer.

He went over to the dresser, opened the drawer and, yes, there was the silk handkerchief. He picked it up and returned to his wonderfully naked wife. He liked seeing her naked. She needed to be like that more often.

"Close your eyes," he said.

"I will do so, but only because it pleases you, my ever-powerful husband."

He'd kind of expected them to take the whole bondage thing a bit more seriously, but hey, there was nothing wrong with silly sex.

Brian placed the handkerchief over her eyes and tied it around the back of her head. Yes! It went on without any difficulties, not even in the knot-tying portion, and he was pretty sure that she couldn't see a thing.

The evening was looking up. Now it was time to have a hell of a lot of fun.

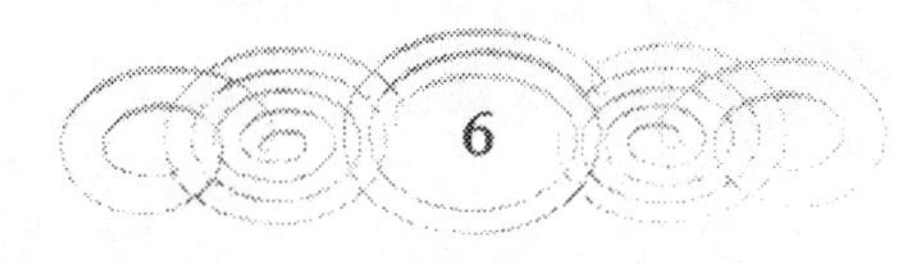

6

"Lie on your back," he said in an even sterner tone of voice than before.

Jenny did so without even mouthing off. Her right leg was bent at the knee, blocking his view of her pussy, though he doubted it was intentional.

He loved the way her breasts looked when she was flat on her back.

It was time for the furry handcuffs. He still didn't have anything to cuff them to, but damn it, he was going to get some use out of these things. They weren't cheap.

He picked up the first pair and rubbed the fur on the inside with his thumb. Mmmm. Soft.

"Stretch your arms over your head," he told Jenny.

She did, making her breasts rise and look even better. He cuffed her hands together at the wrist.

"You just keep them right there," he ordered. "Pretend I duct taped them to the bed."

"Yes, sir."

He walked to the foot of the bed, still looking at her great breasts. He gently took her right leg and straightened it out and then cuffed her feet together.

He admired his handiwork. Maybe it wasn't some freaky S&M setup, but, hey, she was sort of restrained.

And now she was all his.

"I'll be back," he said. "Don't move."

"I won't."

"Talking counts as moving."

"Sorry."

"'Sorry' counts as talking."

Jenny was silent.

"Silence counts as thinking about talking."

"I guess you'd better spank me then."

"I'll decide when and if you get spanked, thank you very much."

"Yes, sir."

"Roll over."

Jenny quickly rolled over, raising her ass slightly in optimal spank position.

"See, I've decided not to spank you." Brian left the bedroom and hurried into the kitchen.

Why was he hurrying? By golly, if he wanted to *saunter* into the kitchen, he would, and she'd wait for him.

He took a small bowl down from the cabinet and then opened the freezer door.

It was ice time.

Jenny raised her ass just a little bit more. She had to admit that it was pretty exciting being blindfolded. He could be anywhere. He might have faked leaving the bedroom and could be hovering over her at this very moment.

Of course, she'd heard the refrigerator or freezer door open, making that scenario unlikely, but maybe he'd installed a remote control.

She heard Brian walk back into the room.

"Did you behave while I was gone?" he asked.

Jenny wiggled her ass. "Not for a second."

"Put that cute ass where I can't see it," said Brian. "Roll over."

"I just got comfy," Jenny protested.

"I could make you much *less* comfy."

"You'll catch me if I roll off the bed, right?"

"Of course."

Jenny rolled onto her back, keeping her arms stretched out over her head. Though she'd been joking about him catching her, it *was* a bit disconcerting to be rolling around on the bed without being able to see, even though she knew she was in the center of the bed and it would take three or four rolls to topple off the side.

She could hear Brian approach the bed.

Then he was hovering over her.

What had he gotten from the kitchen?

Something cold. She knew that much.

A food item? Whipped cream?

A very cold drip of liquid landed on her stomach, and she let out a yelp.

Then an even colder piece of ice lightly brushed across her lower lip.

She opened her mouth slightly. The ice slid across her upper lip, and she flicked out her tongue to meet it. Brian held the piece of ice in place as she licked it. A trickle of water ran down her lip as it melted.

Brian placed the ice on her tongue and she took it into her mouth, sucking on it as it rapidly melted away. She heard the ice cubes jostle against each other as he picked up another one, and she extended her tongue expectantly.

But this piece didn't go on her tongue.

She shivered and sucked in a deep breath as it touched her nipple, causing it to stiffen instantly.

The intense cold was uncomfortable, but yet it felt good.

Real good.

Brian moved the piece of ice in a circle around her nipple, making her squirm. Oh wow. The ice might be freezing her breast, but it was sure warming up her pussy.

He moved to the other nipple.

Something like this should *not* be pleasurable, but somehow it was.

A small trickle of cold water ran down her left breast. The ice had already almost melted away (most likely her intense body heat at the moment was a major contributing factor) and Brian lifted it from her breast and touched it to her lips. She sucked on this one just like the first.

Then something else cold touched her nipple, but it wasn't ice.

She could smell it. A strawberry. Your classic sex-play fruit.

Brian circled each of her nipples with the strawberry. She wanted him to lower it down to her pussy, even though she was so wet that eating the strawberry afterward would be a weird experience.

Instead, he brought it to her mouth. She took a bite, relishing the intense, sweet flavor.

She chewed it slowly. "Mmmmmmm."

"Good strawberry?"

"Oh yeah."

"They're in season."

"I can tell."

"Want another one?"

She nodded.

He brought her another cold strawberry, this one between his teeth. She bit into it, kissing him deeply as she did so. His chest pressed against her still-cold breasts as they kissed, warming them up nicely.

Brian pulled away and she finished chewing and swallowing the delicious strawberry. *Let a chocolate course be next. Hot fudge, white chocolate, chocolate chips, a chocolate bunny...just let there be chocolate!*

The next course was not chocolate.

Nor was it food.

"Oh shit!" she cried out. "Shit! Shit! Shit!" She rolled onto her side, trying to get away from whatever was tickling her knee.

"Don't resist," Brian warned. "You'll only make it worse."

Jenny continued rolling and shouting profanity through her involuntary giggles. "Shit! Shit! Shit! Damn! Shit!"

Brian continued attacking with the tickle device, which was clearly their feather duster. He was merciless. She kept rolling.

"Stop rolling," he said, placing a hand on her side to brace her.

"Stop it!" she cried. "Stop it now or I'll kick your ass with my cuffed feet!"

Brian ceased his vicious tickling. "Okay, the safe word is 'Lysol'. If you really need me to stop something, say that word."

He resumed the tickling.

Jenny said "Shit!" some more, laughing so hard that she was almost in tears. She rolled back and forth, trusting that her dear sweet husband, as cruel as he might be in regards to tickling, would not let her roll off the bed and break herself.

The feather duster was withdrawn and replaced with something much friendlier: Brian's lips. He tenderly kissed her belly.

She hoped he wasn't trying to put her off-guard before another tickle onslaught.

Well, okay, she hoped that he *was*.

And he was indeed. His lips had just touched her navel when the feather duster brushed against her knee. She yelped. He quickly rolled her over on her stomach and began to tickle her butt.

"I don't think my butt's ticklish," she said.

"I'll be the judge of that," said Brian. He brushed the feather duster against it for a moment. "Okay, no, your ass isn't ticklish. Pity. I had such great plans for it." He placed his hand on one of her butt cheeks and squeezed gently. "Of course, they don't have to involve tickling."

"Is that so?"

"It's very much so."

"And what else might they involve?"

"That's for me to know, and you to find out when you're screaming in ecstasy."

"Uh-huh. Don't get *too* bold, mister."

They'd never done much in the way of anal play. Brian had always appreciated her ass, but he'd never expressed any huge desire to get into its nooks and crannies. He'd used his well-lubricated fingers a couple of times, but that was it.

"Why on earth not?" he asked.

"I may be cuffed and blindfolded," Jenny informed him, "but I still get to decide what we do with...oh my..."

He'd slipped his tongue between her ass cheeks. He began to lick as she trailed off.

Oh. Oh this was nice. If he was going to make fine decisions like this, she'd have to put him in charge more often.

He licked her gently. It felt sensational.

She wanted to say "Lick my ass, you stud!" but couldn't quite bring herself to do it, so she thought the words instead. They had a strong marital connection. He'd probably get them psychically.

Oh *wow*.

She actually sort of wished that her feet weren't cuffed, so she could spread her legs apart and give him even better access. Although he seemed to be doing perfectly well with the access he already had.

Oh *WOW*!

"You can do that whenever you want from now on," Jenny informed him. "At the grocery, in the movie theater, at my work...anyplace but my mom's house. Sound okay?"

She felt Brian nod without removing his tongue.

"Don't stop," she said. "Please don't."

Damn. The wrong thing to say. She didn't want him to stop just to exert his imaginary authority.

She thought quickly: "Losyl!"

He stopped licking and pulled away.

"No, no, that was Lysol backward! The anti-safe word!"

"Very clever," said Brian with a chuckle, and then he went back to work.

He put in a long shift.

Finally, Jenny couldn't take it anymore and she lifted her ass up higher, encouraging him to lick someplace else but someplace just as convenient. His tongue felt absolutely wonderful on her pussy.

She came before she even realized that an orgasm was on its way.

It was the kind of orgasm she hadn't felt in quite some time, one that soared through her entire body, one where she barely even noticed how loud she was crying out.

When the pleasure finally began to subside, she went limp.

"Excellent job," said Brian. "That's exactly what you were supposed to do."

"I did it only for you," Jenny told him.

"Uh-huh. Roll back over."

"You're starting to make me feel like a dog with all of these roll over requests."

"Roll over or I'll roll you over. No, wait, I'll roll you over anyway."

He placed his hands underneath her side and with one swift motion rolled her onto her back.

"Ooooooh...you're strong," said Jenny.

"Hell yeah."

"I like to fuck big strong men."

"And this big strong man likes to fuck you. Do you want the blindfold on or off?"

"On."

"Too bad, I'm going to take it...no, wait, I wanted it on. Fortunately, your desire matches my own, or you'd be shit out of luck on the blindfold issue."

"I'm very pleased to not be shit out of luck."

"Spread your legs."

"I can do that."

Brian mounted her, carefully manipulating his legs so that they were between hers, her cuffed feet wrapped around his calves. He slid into her slowly, going in all the way, and she moaned with enjoyment.

She looped her cuffed hands around him, hugging him.

They kissed as they made love.

"I changed my mind," she said. "I want to see you."

"Then I changed my mind too, since I suck as a dom." Brian stopped thrusting and carefully removed the blindfold. Jenny gazed at him adoringly as they went back to fucking, leaving her cuffed.

It wasn't all that different of an experience with the furry handcuffs on though. Had she not been restrained, she probably would've been doing exactly what she was doing: Lying there with her arms and legs wrapped around her husband, thrusting up to meet him and making plentiful noises of enjoyment.

She came the second time as they made love. It was a mild, almost relaxing orgasm, and she sighed loudly as it flowed through her.

Brian began to fuck her harder, raising himself up and adjusting his angle just perfectly. Each new thrust elicited a sharp cry from her, and she quickly realized that this was going to be another wonderful multiorgasmic intercourse session.

She racked up three orgasms total before Brian came himself, gasping as he filled her. They lay together, still joined, for several minutes without speaking, just enjoying the afterglow.

"That was nice," Jenny finally said.

"Indeed."

"Although we didn't do much with the whole bondage scenario."

"No, we didn't," Brian admitted, pulling out of her. "Still, it was a fun session, once you got past the bumbling incompetence element."

"Yes, it was."

Brian rolled off of her. "Maybe we'll try again on our Kinky Night next month. That'll give me four weeks to research this and figure out how to do it like, y'know, somebody who isn't an idiot."

Jenny kissed him. "But you're *my* idiot."

"There's nobody else's idiot I'd rather be."

The following week, they violated the sex schedule by fucking on Wednesday night. Complaints were minimal.

The next Sunday, Brian and Jenny took time to spend the afternoon relaxing on the couch, watching television and relaxing in each other's arms. The doorbell rang, they did a quick "Rock, Paper, Scissors" to see who had to get up off the comfy sofa, and Jenny lost.

She opened the door to reveal a very short, plump woman in her late forties or early fifties. The woman smiled and winked.

"Hello there, Jenny," she said. "I'm Mistress Charlotte."

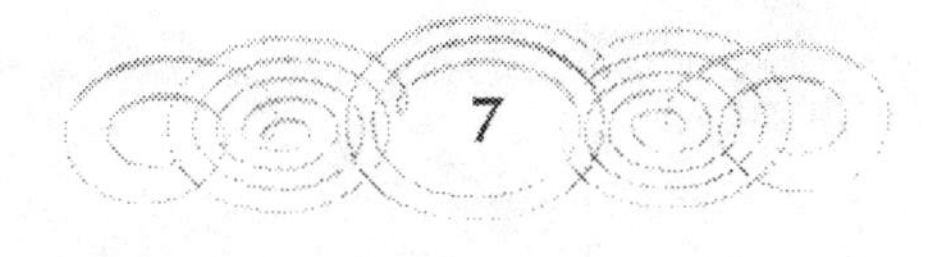

Uh, hi, Mistress Charlotte," said Jenny, more than a bit wary.

Mistress Charlotte had chubby cheeks and a face made for smiling. She wore pink slacks and a bright pink blouse, along with a pink scarf around her neck. She also wore a pearl necklace and a white hat with a large daisy on it. "How are you today, my darling?"

"Good."

"My, my, my, you seem so *tense*. Relax, dear, it's only Mistress Charlotte." She gave Jenny a reassuring pat on the shoulder. "We're certainly not going to hurt you this lesson."

Jenny considered that comment and decided that her initial thought of "Who the living fuck is this woman and what the living fuck is she doing at my door?" was apt.

Brian got up off the couch and walked over to the doorway. "Can we help you?" he asked.

"Oh, no, no, *I'm* here to help *you*," Mistress Charlotte insisted. She gave Brian a playful poke in the belly. "You're cute though. Thanks for asking. May I come in?"

"I don't think so," said Jenny.

"Oh now, don't be silly, of course I may. You're Jenny and Brian, right?"

"Yeah," said Brian.

"Then I'm at the right place. I may be a daffy old scatterbrain sometimes, but I can find my way to an appointment."

"What appointment?"

"To teach you young pups the fine art of bondage."

"I'm pretty sure we didn't hire you to teach any young pups the fine art of bondage," said Brian. Then he looked over at Jenny. "We didn't, right?"

"Of course not!"

"I think there's been a misunderstanding," Brian told Mistress Charlotte. "Sorry."

"I understand that you two made a not-so-successful attempt at the art of furry handcuff restraint last weekend."

"Hey!" Brian said, offended. "She came three times!"

"Brian!" Jenny exclaimed, shocked.

"Well, you did," Brian insisted.

"Yeah, but don't tell *her* that!"

"Jenny, Jenny, Jenny, you don't need to worry about what you say in front of dear old Mistress Charlotte." Mistress Charlotte gave her another reassuring pat on the shoulder. "I'm not one to spill secrets, heavens no."

"Listen, Charlotte—" said Brian.

"*Mistress* Charlotte, please."

"Mistress Charlotte, I need to speak with my wife in private for a minute. Would you excuse us?"

"Of course I will, sweetie. I need to go get my things anyway."

"No. Don't get any things. Just...we'll be back, okay?"

"Take your time. If there's one thing you should know about bondage, it's that nothing is gained from rushing. But of course there are lots of things you should know about bondage, not just one."

"Uh-huh," said Brian. "I'm going to shut the door. Is that okay?"

"Will I be inside or outside?" Mistress Charlotte asked.

"Outside."

She shrugged. "It does seem a bit impolite, but bondage has its own set of manners. You two go right ahead."

"Thanks." Brian shut the door, took Jenny by the hand, and led her into the kitchen. "Who the hell is that?"

"I don't know!" Jenny insisted.

"You didn't set this up?"

"No, of course not!"

"Well, I sure as hell didn't set it up. Did you tell anybody about last Sunday?"

Jenny was silent.

"You did! Oh my God! Who did you tell?"

"Just Carol."

"Who's Carol?"

"A friend at work. We have lunch together sometimes. She's got a wild social life, and she's always telling me stories, so I mentioned that you tried to tie me up, but I didn't give her any details!"

"Who else did you tell?"

"Nobody!"

"You didn't give an interview to *Freaky S&M Weekly* or anything?"

"Brian, I didn't tell anybody else. And I only mentioned it casually. She was too busy talking about her own threesome to even pay attention."

"A threesome? Really?"

"Yeah."

"Two guys or two girls?"

"Three girls."

"Oh wow. Cool." Brian shook his head to clear his mind. "So is Carol a lunatic? Would she do this?"

"I can't imagine that she would!"

"Well, *somebody* did. It sure wasn't me. We're not in an apartment anymore, so it's not like anybody could've heard us through the thin walls." An idea occurred to him. "Our house is bugged!"

"Our house is *not* bugged."

"That's it! Our house is bugged and somebody is listening to everything we say and hearing every sexual act that goes wrong and now they've sent a...okay, I'm not even going to finish this thought because it's so patently ridiculous, but Jenny, why the hell is Mistress Charlotte at our door?"

"I don't know!"

"Call Carol."

"Now?"

"Yes, now! If she's having girl-girl-girl threesomes she might be the kind of person who would send a professional bondage guidance counselor to somebody's house."

"Okay. I'll see what I can find out." Jenny took the phone book out of the kitchen drawer where they kept it and began to flip through the pages. "Should we leave Charlotte standing outside like that?"

"Charlotte will be okay. She seems like a very understanding individual." Brian wiped his sweaty hands off on his jeans.

Jenny dialed Carol's number and then watched Brian closely. He seemed genuinely frantic about the whole thing, but *she* certainly hadn't made any appointment with Mistress Charlotte. Her husband was a good actor. He could've arranged this whole thing.

"Hello?" a female voice answered.

"Is Carol there? This is her friend Jenny from work."

"One sec." There was giggling on the other end. "She's kinda busy. Can she call you back?"

"It's really important and it'll only take a moment."

"Just a sec." More giggling. "She says to give her a sec."

"Okay."

It was more like a minute before she heard Carol's voice. "Jenny?"

"Hi."

"What's up?"

"Do you remember me telling you about last Sunday?"

"Ummmmm...yeah, you got your hair done, right?"

"No, Brian used handcuffs on me."

"Oh yeah. Oh wait, don't tell me, I know what this is about."

"You do?"

"You lost the keys, didn't you? Yeah, that can be a bitch. Look, I know a really good locksmith, and he's very discreet, and he's also pretty cute so—"

"No, that's not it. Did you...did you tell anyone about this?"

"About the handcuffs? No."

"Are you sure?"

"Jenny, no offense, but you and your hubby playing with handcuffs is not the kind of shocking news I'd be spreading around."

"You're absolutely sure you didn't tell anybody. You didn't call anybody, arrange any appointments...?"

"You've been smoking a bit of weed, haven't you?"

"No!" Jenny decided that full disclosure was the only way to get the truth. "This lady just showed up at our door, and she calls herself Mistress Charlotte, and she knew all about last Sunday, and she wants to give us bondage lessons or something!"

"You've been smoking a *lot* of weed, haven't you?"

"Carol, I'm serious! Did you call her?"

"No, Jenny, I did not call the mysterious woman who showed up at your home to give you handcuff lessons. Maybe...and this is just a guess, mind you...but maybe your husband invited her."

"He swears he didn't."

"Okay. So you think it's more likely that *I* called her, based on a conversation that I barely even remember, no offense?"

"I know it sounds ridiculous."

"Less ridiculous through a cloud of marijuana smoke, probably."

"I just...look, we're freaking out here! This lady is at our door and we don't know how she found out about us!"

"Well, it sure wasn't me. Just relax and take some deep breaths. When your head clears, I'm sure you'll discover that this mysterious mistress lady was just your cat."

Jenny hung up.

"It wasn't her," she told Brian.

"Then it was you."

"It *wasn't* me."

"It wasn't me either."

"You didn't tell anybody at work?" Jenny asked.

"Sweetie, guys don't share true tales of sexual dysfunction. If I *had* told anybody, they wouldn't have sent somebody to help us out, they would've sent a camera crew to capture my legendary performance!"

"Well, then what do we do?"

"We get rid of her."

"Sounds good."

They left the kitchen and returned to the front door. When Brian opened it, Mistress Charlotte was still standing there.

"Did you two lovebirds have a nice chat?" she asked.

"Mistress Charlotte, we really appreciate you coming," said Brian. "Unfortunately, there's been some kind of mix-up somewhere, and we're going to have to ask you to leave."

Mistress Charlotte nodded. "That's very disappointing. I have to admit, I was really looking forward to teaching you."

"Yeah, well, shit happens."

"There's no reason to be rude, young man. I may not appear to have feelings when I'm administering punishment to one of my submissives, but I'm as sensitive as anybody."

"Bye-bye," said Brian.

Mistress Charlotte nodded and turned to leave. Brian shut the door.

"You swear you didn't invite her?" he asked Jenny.

"I swear."

"Swear on something...swear on that phone book!"

"Brian, I didn't invite her."

"Okay, I believe you. I didn't invite her either. I wonder if we should call the police? She could be an escaped psychopath."

"Let's not call the police."

"Yeah, you're right, I don't want to show up in the newspaper as Mr. Bondage Dork. But that was really freakin' weird, wasn't it?"

"And scary."

Brian sighed. "Oh well. No harm done, I guess."

"Except my co-worker thinks I'm a pothead."

"At least that's better than being a bisexual slut. Oh no, wait, actually it's much worse. Sorry."

"What do you think she wanted?"

"She probably wanted to look at my ass. Those kinky old ladies are like that, you know."

"Are you going to be okay?"

"Yeah, I'm fine. I'm going to go online and see if I can find out anything about her." He gave her a kiss. "Do you absolutely *swear* that—"

"Brian, I didn't call her."

"Okay."

They spent most of the evening searching for information on Mistress Charlotte but came up empty.

They didn't have sex that night.

The following Sunday, the doorbell rang again.

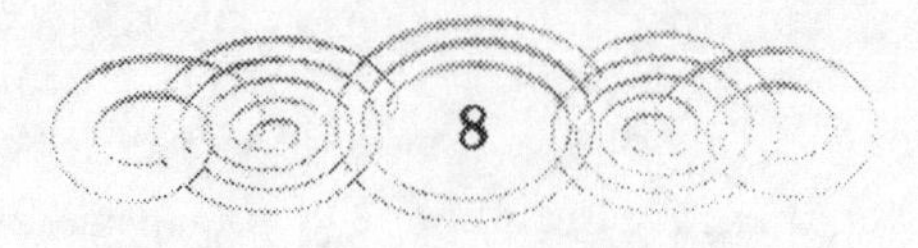

8

Jenny was alone in the house. Brian had gone to the library to do some heavy studying for one of his classes and wouldn't be back for a couple of hours.

When she answered the door, Mistress Charlotte stood there. She was still dressed in pink and still wore the daisy hat.

"Hello, darling," said Mistress Charlotte, a broad grin on her face. "How are you doing on this fine day?"

"What the fuck are you doing here?"

"Now, now, Jenny, let's watch the potty mouth, shall we? Naturally, in my line of business I use language that could burn your ears off, but there's a big difference between the way one should talk in the bedroom and the way one should talk to a guest at your front door."

"What are you doing here?"

"I realize that you asked me to leave last time, and I accepted that decision even if heaven knows I didn't agree with it. But the lessons have already been paid for, and it just wouldn't be right if I didn't show up and at least offer to conduct them. Many people in these sad times try to get away with doing as little work as possible, but not Mistress Charlotte. An honest day's work for an honest day's pay, that's what I say. May I come in?"

"No."

"Where's Brian?"

"He's at the...he's in the bathroom. Right now. Polishing his shotgun."

Mistress Charlotte chuckled. "Dear, you don't have to worry about your safety! Mercy, no. I'm perfectly harmless."

"You still can't come in."

"Then I won't push the issue. But perhaps we could sit and talk somewhere. Somewhere public. I'll use part of last week's fee to buy you lunch."

"Sorry, but no."

"Surely you don't think I'll knife you in a public restaurant, do you? Darling, a major component of bondage is trust. If you don't trust your partner, it will be an unpleasant experience for both of you."

"I trust my partner. I just don't trust *you*."

"I understand. But you do seem to have an overall lack of trust that may protect you but also keeps you from truly living, if I may be so bold."

"I'm living fine."

Mistress Charlotte nodded. "I'm sure you are, dear. I'll go now. But before I do, I want you to understand something that's very, very important."

"What's that?"

"I would have let you order appetizers *and* dessert at the restaurant."

Jenny smiled but then forced herself to scowl.

"Too late, dear, I already saw the smile," said Mistress Charlotte.

Jenny thought about it. Really, what could it hurt to sit down and talk with the poor woman for a while? It wasn't like Jenny didn't have a ton of questions about the whole situation. At the very least, she might be able to find out who hired her.

"Can I pick the restaurant?" Jenny asked.

"Of course."

"Okay. Let's go. We'll drive separately."

They sat across from each other at Bob's Deli. Jenny had ordered half of a turkey sandwich since she hadn't eaten lunch all that long ago, while Mistress Charlotte got a light salad with wine vinaigrette on the side.

"Did my husband hire you?" Jenny asked.

"Now, now, now, I've already told you that I can't disclose that kind of information."

"Please. I have to know."

"Did he say that he hired me?"

"He said that he didn't."

"And do you trust him?"

"Yes."

"Well, there you go then." Mistress Charlotte dipped a forkful of lettuce into her dressing and popped it into her mouth.

"I just don't get it. You showed up to give us sex lessons. That's the kind of thing that usually involves, you know, *permission*. And advance notice!"

Mistress Charlotte nodded. "I do agree with you."

"So you understand why we asked you to leave? I mean, you can't possibly think that we were going to let you into our house. Nobody could think that."

"*Somebody* did."

"Okay, nobody who isn't completely insane could think that."

"Sanity can be overrated."

"No, actually, sanity is a pretty cool thing. I like it."

"Well, I wouldn't know. I'm just a crazy old lady."

Jenny smiled. She had to admit that, though this was a completely fucked-up situation, she did like the woman. If she'd met her under circumstances that didn't involve her showing up unexpectedly to give bondage lessons, she would have really enjoyed Mistress Charlotte's company.

"Let me explain how I teach," Mistress Charlotte said. "First and most important, I will not be naked. You won't have to look at my saggy old bosoms."

"They're not saggy," Jenny insisted.

"Oh I know. They're actually quite wonderful. I've been very pleased with how they've held up. I was just kidding."

"Okay."

"That said, you won't be seeing me naked, nor will I be mounting your husband. Acceptable?"

"It doesn't matter, because we're not doing this."

"You might. Just keep an open mind. So is the no-nudity, no-mounting-of-your-husband rule acceptable?"

"Sure."

"Second, all of the lessons are optional. Though we're of course dealing with roles of dominance and submission, anything you do at my command will be your own choice. Acceptable?"

"Yep."

"So the lessons are optional and there's no need to see me stark naked. What have you and Brian got to lose?"

"Our dignity."

"Dignity, shmignity. You'll have fun. I promise."

Jenny shook her head. "It's not gonna happen. I mean, if nothing else, the whole tying-me-up idea wasn't even a big deal. It was just something we decided to try out. Definitely not something important enough to take lessons on."

"How important does something have to be for you to want to do it better?" Mistress Charlotte asked. "My grandson has a video game that wasn't very important to me, but I took a bit of time to learn to play it, and I beat him silly. It was well worth it."

"That's not the same thing."

"Why not?"

"Because it's not about sex!"

Mistress Charlotte patted Jenny's hand. "Well, just think about it, okay? Discuss it with your dear husband. I think you two will have much more fun than you expect."

"I'll bring it up," Jenny said.

"Good girl. And if you do change your mind, you know how to contact me."

"Actually, I don't."

"Well, you'll know when the time is right."

"Okay, now *that's* a creepy thing to say."

Mistress Charlotte winked at her. "But it's the truth. I think you'll find that you're a remarkable young woman, Jenny."

"Uh, okay."

Mistress Charlotte reached into her pink purse and handed Jenny a business card. "When the time is right, call me. I'll see you then." And with another wink, she got up and left.

Jenny drove home, trying to make sense of everything.

Well, actually, it wasn't so difficult to figure it out: Mistress Charlotte was crazy.

The business card said only "Mistress Charlotte" and a phone number. The lettering was pink.

What kind of dominatrix wore pink? Weren't they supposed to wear rubber gimp suits or something?

Maybe she hadn't changed into her work clothes yet.

Jenny got home, went inside and sat down on the couch. What a day. She wondered if she might have to get a restraining order. ("Really, officer, this woman wants to give us bondage lessons and we can't get rid of her!")

She also wondered why she hadn't thrown away the business card.

Y'know, it might be fun...

No. It would not be fun. Decent people did not have strange ladies come into their home and teach them lessons on that type of subject.

Why be decent?

The handcuffs *had* been kind of nice.

But even if she wanted better bondage in their life, they didn't need lessons. They just needed a different bed.

Mistress Charlotte was a crazy woman. There was nothing else to be said.

And she hadn't thrown away the card so that she could show it to Brian and share a good laugh.

That was it.

Brian returned home, looking amazingly upbeat. He set his books down on the dining room table and gave Jenny a big kiss.

"How'd it go?" she asked.

"Ask me how I did on the sample test."

"How'd you do on the sample test?"

"One hundred percent! I knew every question. I've got this material down pat." He flexed his muscles.

"How close is the sample test to the real test?"

"Same format, same basic material, and from what I understand they even repeat some of the questions. It clicked really well." He kissed her again.

"I'm so happy for you!"

"And it's sex night! Woo-hoo!"

"Oh speaking of that, guess who showed up again?"

Brian's face fell. "Are you serious?"

Jenny nodded.

"What did she want?"

"She's still insistent that she give us lessons. They're paid for and everything."

Brian pulled out a chair and sat down. "So what did you tell her?"

"I told her no. She even took me out for a sandwich."

"You got a sandwich with her?"

"Yeah."

"Why?"

"Because she asked me to. She wanted to talk about it."

"So you didn't just slam the door in her face?"

"No. She's actually a very nice lady, in a kooky sort of way."

Brian looked confused. "So, what, you want her to come back and teach me how to tie you up?"

"No, of course not. I just listened to what she had to say and told her no."

"What *did* she have to say?"

"That she wouldn't be getting naked, and that all of the lessons were optional. She gave me her card."

"She has a card?"

"Yep."

"Is it made out of black leather?"

"No, just regular card stock. Black leather would probably be too expensive in bulk."

"Yeah, I guess you're right. Are you *sure* you didn't contact her?"

"Brian..."

"Sorry. Just thought I'd ask. I bet it was Carol."

Jenny shrugged.

Brian scratched at his chin thoughtfully. "It *would* be pretty kinky. Getting lessons like that."

"Yeah, it would."

"I mean, I didn't know that service was even offered, not that I've really researched it."

"I didn't either," said Jenny.

"All the lessons are optional?"

"Yes. And paid for."

"Wow."

"You're almost sounding like you want me to call her."

Brian shook his head. "No, just saying wow. But, I mean, what kind of stuff is she going to teach? Knot-tying lessons?"

"I have no idea."

"If she turned out to be a dangerous lunatic, I'm pretty sure I could bring her down. She's not very tall. What do you think?"

"I think that a strange woman showed up on our doorstep uninvited and offered to give us bondage lessons, and we seem to be actually considering her offer."

"I'm not considering it," Brian insisted. "Well, okay, maybe I am."

"What changed your mind?"

"Nothing, really. I mean...I don't know, it might be fun."

"It might," Jenny agreed.

"What's the worst thing that could happen?"

"She could murder us both."

"What's the second worst?"

"She could smuggle in a camera and we could find ourselves all over the Internet."

"Third worst?"

"She could wreck our furniture."

"So, really, there are lots of excellent reasons why we should definitely not contact this woman."

"Yes."

"Ah fuck it," said Brian. "Let's call her."

9

They'd called her.

Brian couldn't fucking believe they'd called her.

They'd actually picked up the phone, dialed the number on the business card, spoken to some receptionist with an alarmingly squeaky voice and told her that it was okay for Mistress Charlotte to pay them a visit.

Holy fucking shit.

What madness had they unleashed?

What kind of kinky perverts had they become?

When would she get here?

The doorbell rang.

Brian and Jenny hurried over to the door. Brian opened it, revealing Mistress Charlotte, again in pink.

"I knew you darlings would change your mind," she said with a smile.

"We haven't completely changed our mind," Brian told her. "This is on a trial basis."

"Believe me, I understand," said Mistress Charlotte. She clapped her hands together. "May I come in?"

Brian moved out of the way. "Sure."

"Thank you, dear." She stepped through the doorway and surveyed the living room. "Very nice. Did you decorate this yourself?"

"Yes," said Jenny.

Mistress Charlotte nodded her approval. "Fine work. Which way to the bedroom?"

"Here, I'll show you," said Brian, leading her down the hallway. They usually kept a very tidy house, but they'd still done a quick emergency clean-up for her arrival.

Mistress Charlotte looked at their queen-sized bed and clucked her tongue. "Oh no, no, no, this won't do. There's nothing to attach anything to."

"I know," said Brian. "That was the whole problem."

"Well, perhaps not the *whole* problem, but it was certainly a starting point. No, this won't do at all." She reached into her purse, took out a pink cell phone and dialed. "Bruce? Bed swap. Queen. Thanks." She shut off the phone and replaced it in her purse.

"Bed swap?" asked Jenny.

"Yes, dear." She looked around the rest of the bedroom. "Brian, the temperature needs to be about three degrees warmer. Could you adjust that for me?"

Brian nodded and left the room.

"Let's see, everything else appears to be suitable. Do you have a favorite scent, darling?"

"Vanilla."

"Vanilla's a bit too sweet. How about something earthy?"

"Ummmm...pine?"

"Pine is a wonderful choice. In the top ten of what I would have picked myself." As Brian returned to the bedroom, Mistress Charlotte handed him a key. "Brian, be a dear and get my bags out of my trunk. There should be two pink ones. No fair peeking."

Brian nodded and left again.

"You seem nervous," Mistress Charlotte said to Jenny. "Just let that work for you instead of against you and you'll be fine." She reached back into her purse and took out a folded piece of paper, which she handed to Jenny. "This is a confidentiality agreement. It states that I will not discuss anything that happens during our sessions with anybody but you and your husband. There will be no audio or video taping, no transcripts, nor any artist renditions."

"Oh excellent." Jenny unfolded the paper. "We were going to ask about that."

"It also states that you may not discuss my services in a public forum, that being television, radio, the Internet or things like that. Agreed?"

Jenny looked at the contract. "Your legal name is Mistress Charlotte?"

"That's right."

"That's what's on your driver's license?"

Mistress Charlotte took her license out of her purse and held it up for Jenny's inspection. Next to a very flattering picture was the name "Mistress Charlotte."

"I can't believe they let you do that," Jenny said.

"My mother had very good foresight, it appears."

"Your *mother* named you Mistress Charlotte?"

"No, I changed it. I was only kidding. Don't be silly."

Brian returned with the duffel bags. Mistress Charlotte took them from him and set them on the floor. Brian and Jenny both took a second to look over the contract, which, bearing no resemblance to any contract that Brian had ever seen, was clear and easy to follow and then signed it.

"Now, I understand that both of you are beginners to this and are not looking for the intense stuff. So rest assured that we will be practicing what I like to call 'loving restraint' and not any of the more extreme forms of bondage, discipline and sadomasochism."

"How extreme do your lessons get?" Brian asked.

"You don't want to know, dear. With the exception of minors and animals, I'm pretty sure that I've taught every fetish on the planet." The doorbell rang. "Ah, that must be Bruce and Warren."

Brian went back into the living room and opened the door. There stood two young, shirtless, muscular, incredibly handsome men. They both carried several pieces of polished wood that Brian assumed was a disassembled bed frame.

Jenny emerged from the bedroom, followed by Mistress Charlotte, who was carrying one of the duffel bags. "Ah," said Mistress Charlotte, "there are the two young studs I was waiting for. It's right in here, boys."

The men strode into the bedroom. Mistress Charlotte watched their asses as they walked. "Yummy," she said. "Oh this job does have its fringe benefits. My, my, my."

She sat down on the couch, rested the duffel bag on her lap and unzipped it. She took out a black bag and extended it toward Jenny. "Take this, dear. It's your outfit for today."

Jenny took the bag from her, a bit wary. "We have to wear outfits?"

"Of course. What else would you expect?"

"To not wear outfits."

"Oh hush. It'll be fun. Go put them on. Separately. You have two bathrooms, right?"

"Yes," said Jenny.

"Then go get changed."

Brian looked at himself in the full-length mirror, as he'd been doing for the past couple of minutes. The same three words kept racing through his mind: *No fucking way.*

He was sure that some men could pull off the whole black leather fetish gear thing and not look completely ridiculous, but he wasn't one of them. The pants were way too tight, except for the crotch, which had a removable codpiece.

He was shirtless. No shirt had been included, and he was pretty sure that the green polo shirt he'd been wearing wasn't supposed to go with the black leather pants.

There was a light knock on the bathroom door. "Brian?" asked Mistress Charlotte. "Come on out."

"I think these pants are going to be too hot," he said.

"Oh now, don't be difficult. I'm sure you look sexy. Come on out."

Brian sighed and reluctantly opened the bathroom door. Mistress Charlotte nodded her approval. "Very nice."

"Thanks. I think."

"Come see your new bed," said Mistress Charlotte, taking him by the hand. He followed her, half-expecting to see something with spikes, sandpaper and a vat of boiling oil resting on the end.

But, instead, they'd replaced the frame. It was now a four-poster bed.

"Hey, cool," said Brian. The men had left. Brian wondered if he should have tipped them.

Mistress Charlotte knocked on the door to the bathroom in the bedroom. "Dear, are you almost ready?"

Jenny opened the door and walked out. She was wearing tight black leather as well. She appeared very uncomfortable and was nervously biting her lip, but Brian had to admit that she looked *damn* sexy.

Why hadn't he urged her to wear tight black leather before?

"Don't just gape, Brian," said Mistress Charlotte. "Tell her what you think."

"You look amazing!"

Jenny broke into a relieved smile. "Really? You think so?"

"Oh hell yeah."

"You look amazing too."

Brian shook his head. "No, I look ridiculous. But you look amazing."

"Okay, you two, sit down on the bed," said Mistress Charlotte. They complied. "First things first. Do you know what a safe word is?"

"Yeah," said Brian. "We had one last time."

"What was it?"

"Uh, Lysol."

"Lysol?"

"Yeah. It was an inside joke."

"Let's avoid silliness with our safe word," Mistress Charlotte suggested. "The safe word will be 'mercy'. If, at any point, either of you feels uncomfortable with what's going on, use that word and everything will stop immediately. Understand?"

Jenny and Brian nodded.

"Now, the roles are already defined. Brian will be the dominant, and Jenny will be the submissive. If we wish to switch these around, we can do so, but for now we'll stick to this arrangement. Acceptable?"

"How do you know that I want to be the sub?" Jenny asked.

"Because, dear, at your day job you're in a position of responsibility, one where you are expected to make quick decisions that have great impact. This is why you get sexual excitement from the idea of letting your partner have all the power and make all the decisions."

"Oh."

"And Brian is frustrated by his own lack of control over his work situation. He feels that his creativity is being stifled, and he's taking pains to fix this, but he also gets sexual excitement over the idea of being the one in charge."

"Should I even bother asking how the hell you know that?" asked Brian.

"No, you should not."

"I didn't think so."

"Okay, we're just about ready to begin the lesson," said Mistress Charlotte. She took a book of matches out of the second duffel bag and began to light the eight candles she'd placed around the bedroom. Once that was done, she shut the door and turned out the lights.

"Ah, this is much better, isn't it?" she asked. "What do you two think? Nice sexy atmosphere?"

"Very nice," said Brian.

"So, Brian, first things first. Remove the codpiece."

"I beg your pardon?"

Mistress Charlotte gestured. "The codpiece. Remove it. It's that thing in front of your crotch."

"I know what it is," said Brian. "I'm just not completely sure that I should be removing it."

Mistress Charlotte giggled. "Darling, do you honestly think I'll be shocked by the sight of your penis?"

"No but—"

"I have seen more penises than I can count. I've seen penises in every size, shape, color and state of arousal, with every accessory you can imagine. I've even seen one unfortunate penis that got slammed in a car door. There is nothing behind that codpiece that I haven't seen before."

Brian looked to Jenny for help. Jenny kind of wanted to see what was behind the codpiece, but she could also understand her husband's hesitation. She gave him a light nod, urging him to go ahead.

"This is humiliating," Brian said.

Mistress Charlotte shook her head. "No, no, no, no, no, no, it's liberating, young man. Haven't you ever just torn off all of your clothes and run free through the rain?"

"No," Brian admitted.

"You should. But make sure that you warm up afterward so that you don't catch pneumonia."

"I'll remember that."

"Anyway, I can't force you to remove the codpiece," said Mistress Charlotte. "Well, I *could*, and quite easily, but that's not the training you're interested in. So, if you want to keep your penis protected from the elements, that's fine, but it's going to be rather uncomfortable at erection time."

Ah screw it, Brian decided. He ripped off the codpiece, which had been attached with Velcro.

"Oh darling, that's a most superb penis indeed," said Mistress Charlotte. "You're a lucky woman, Jenny."

"I know," Jenny said.

Brian fought the urge to cover his equipment with his hands, but he had to admit that it did feel better.

Mistress Charlotte clapped her hands together. "Okay, let's begin!"

10

Now, I'm going to give you instructions," Mistress Charlotte told Brian, "but of course you're actually the one in charge. So when I give you instructions to give her, give her the instructions. Jenny, listen to the instructions he gives you and not the ones I give him to give you. Understand?"

Brian nodded. He figured that Mistress Charlotte would correct him if he did it wrong.

Jenny nodded as well.

"Brian, darling, tell Jenny to lie down."

"Do I have to say darling?"

"No."

"Jenny, lie on the bed," said Brian.

Jenny started to lie down, but Mistress Charlotte shook her head. "No, no, a command delivered in that tone of voice wouldn't encourage even the most willpower-lacking sub to do your bidding. You must be firm. But loving."

"Firm but loving," Brian repeated.

"So tell Jenny to lie down, in a firm tone of voice that lets her know that she must obey your command, but in such a way that she knows that you love her and would never hurt her."

Brian took a deep breath. "Jenny, lie down," he said, firmly but lovingly.

"That was whiny," said Mistress Charlotte.

"It was not! It was firm and loving!"

"It sounded whiny. Concentrate more on the firm, less on the loving."

"Jenny, lie down," Brian said.

"That's better."

"Should I lie down?" Jenny asked.

"Would his tone of voice convince you to do so?" Mistress Charlotte asked.

"Yeah."

"Then do it."

Jenny lay down on her back.

"Now, see, this was a trick," said Mistress Charlotte. "Brian, you need to be more in charge than that. Why should she get to make the decision about whether she lies on her back or on her tummy? Be much more specific. Keep in mind that you're going to be cuffing her to the bed."

Brian cleared his throat. "Jenny, I want you to lie on your back, spread-eagle. Immediately."

"Excellent," said Mistress Charlotte.

Jenny obligingly lay on her back as instructed.

"Now, Brian, you must bind her to the bed. You may do this quickly and efficiently, or slowly and methodically to draw out the suspense, but the important thing is that you don't want to bumble around."

"Well, duh."

"What I mean is that you want to be prepared. Know where the handcuffs are in advance. Do you know where the handcuffs are?"

"Top dresser drawer."

"Very good. Go retrieve them."

Brian got the fur-lined handcuffs out of the dresser drawer, still very much aware of his exposed penis. It just wasn't something he went around showing people. However, despite the awkward nature of the situation, he was definitely feeling a slight stirring in his groin.

Jenny was feeling her own stirring in the same general area, which surprised her. After all, there was a kooky woman in the bedroom with them. Kooky women in the bedroom should have been something of a turn-off, but it was as if Mistress Charlotte had some weird erotic power that made it okay that Jenny was lying on her bed in black leather while a strange kooky woman stood there giving her husband instructions.

"Now, cuff her to the bed," said Mistress Charlotte. "Jenny, are you right-handed or left-handed?"

"Right-handed."

"Then Brian, start with the right hand."

"How can that possibly make a difference?" Brian asked.

"It increases your sense of control over her," Mistress Charlotte explained. "She has more control over her right arm than her left, so by first taking away the power she has to move her right arm where she wants to, you're increasing the subconscious feeling of giving her willpower over to you."

"Are you sure you're not just talking out of your ass on that one?" Brian inquired.

"Brian!" Jenny exclaimed.

"I'm sorry, but c'mon, right hand first? I appreciate the four-poster bed and the leather suit you've got my wife in, but I just can't help but wonder if some parts of this lesson are, forgive my use of the word 'bullshit', bullshit."

Mistress Charlotte stared at him. "Brian, which one of us has the word 'Mistress' in front of her name?"

"That would be you."

"Then don't question the things I'm teaching you. The art of bondage is infinitely more complicated than you can ever imagine. *Saurrus trumuna ransorum.*"

Brian blinked. "What did you just say?"

"Nothing, dear."

"That last part. What was that?"

"I've no idea what you're referring to." Mistress Charlotte glanced down. "Oh my, darling, you seem to have become much friendlier."

Brian suddenly realized that he had an erection. As big of one as he'd ever achieved. How the hell did that happen?

Jenny looked at that delicious penis, suddenly realizing that she was incredibly wet. She wanted nothing more than for Brian to tie her up and just fuck her senseless with that thing.

"Right hand first," said Mistress Charlotte gently.

Brian unlatched one of the furry handcuff bracelets and then took Jenny's right hand. Staring into her eyes, he slowly but firmly placed her wrist inside the bracelet and then locked it shut.

Jenny shivered.

Not taking his eyes off his wife, Brian walked around to the other side of the bed and did the same to her left hand.

She tugged against her restraints.

She wasn't going anywhere.

"I don't need to tell you what to do next," said Mistress Charlotte, stepping away from the bed.

She sure as hell didn't. Brian took Jenny's right foot by the ankle and slid it toward the corner of the bed. Without an instant of awkwardness, he cuffed it to the bedpost. Then he did the same to her left leg.

Jenny lay there, legs spread, arms over her head, feeling vulnerable and more excited than she'd ever felt in her life.

"Blindfold next?" Brian asked Mistress Charlotte.

"You tell me."

"Yes. Blindfold next."

He knew exactly where the silk handkerchief they'd used before was, but Mistress Charlotte stopped him. "Try this one," she said, handing him a black leather blindfold.

Yeah, that would work.

"Raise your head," Brian told Jenny. She obliged immediately, and he slipped the blindfold over her head and over her eyes. It covered much of the top of her head, and there was no way in hell she could see a thing.

He stepped back and just looked at her. God, she looked amazing. He wanted to just lick her all over. Eat her right up.

Brian walked around the bed, getting different viewing angles. He'd seen his wife lying on their bed thousands of times, but never like this. She writhed gently as she lay there, pulling on the handcuffs but making no real attempt to escape.

He reached for her breast.

Like his codpiece, the leather covering her breast appeared to be attached only by Velcro. He slipped his fingers underneath it, gripped it tightly, and then prepared himself to just *yank* it off as hard as he could.

Then he decided against it. After all, he didn't know for sure how that thing was attached. He didn't want a nipple coming along with it. That would be bad.

He gently tore off the piece of leather, exposing her right breast.

Jenny smiled.

He leaned down toward it, mouth watering as if about to enjoy a five-star meal, and then took the nipple into his mouth, rolling it between his lips. He pressed them together tightly, but not *too* tightly, and she let out a pleasured cry.

He flecked his tongue across her nipple, keeping it between his lips.

Jenny couldn't believe the sensations. It hurt, but it was a *good* kind of hurt, and nothing that she could explain. She was so wet that she was worried about ruining that fine leather and being charged for it.

She wanted Brian to use his teeth.

But he was in charge of this encounter, and that's exactly the way that Jenny wanted it. She kept her eyes closed, not that it mattered beneath the blindfold, and just prepared herself to let him do anything he wanted to her.

And apparently he wanted to use his teeth.

It felt so, *so* good as he bit down on her nipple. It wasn't a hard bite by any means, certainly nothing that would break the skin or even leave a mark, but it was also more than a love nibble. Again, it hurt in a good way. How was such a thing even possible?

Now he began to suck on her nipple, hard, making her squirm with joy. She tugged further on her restraints as if to escape, but not really wanting to escape, wanting to stay exactly where she was for a good long while. It felt good to test the handcuffs. Felt good to know that she wasn't going anywhere.

Brian sucked on that wonderful breast with as much passion as he could muster, which was a hell of a lot. He was only barely aware that Mistress Charlotte was still in the room. She wasn't giving any more instructions, and he didn't even know if she was still watching. It didn't matter. She could be videotaping this for all he cared. All that mattered was pleasing his gorgeous wife.

He tore off another piece of leather, exposing her left breast.

He leaned down toward it but didn't lick, suck or bite. He just hovered there, making her wait for it.

Nothing wrong with a little suspense.

Brian breathed on her, making sure she knew exactly where his mouth was, making her anticipate the moment when he finally decided to savor her breast, thinking about how she would squeal when he finally—

He gently pinched her right nipple between his thumb and index finger.

She squealed nicely.

Then he dove in, sucking on her left nipple with even more vigor than the right. Jenny continued to tug on the restraints as she whipped her head back and forth, moaning.

"Does this feel good?" he asked, removing his mouth only long enough to say the words.

"Oh yes, *yes*! Don't stop!"

Brian grinned. *He* would be the one to decide whether or not he stopped.

But of course he didn't want to stop.

He sucked on her breasts, switching back and forth between them, until he noticed that Mistress Charlotte was standing next to him. For a split second he became embarrassed as he realized that his hand was on his erection, but the feeling passed immediately. It was a perfectly good place for his hand.

"Try these," said Mistress Charlotte, extending her palm. In it rested two silver items.

Nipple clamps.

Brian took them from her without a word. They were long clamps that sort of looked like tweezers, with a rubber pad where the nipple was supposed to go. He hesitated for a moment...this was sure not something he'd want affixed to *his* nipple.

Maybe he should ask permission first.

No, no, he was in charge here. That's what the safe word was for. And he'd also take "Ow!" as an acceptable substitute.

He placed the tweezer-thingie over her left nipple and began to tighten the screw, very, very slowly.

Jenny had no idea what her husband had just put on her breast, but she had a feeling that it was something wonderful.

He'd give her advance warning if there was piercing involved, right?

Of course he would. Don't be stupid.

What *was* it? She was incredibly curious, but she was also a bit scared. But like the pain, it was a *good* kind of fear, like the delicious excitement she felt watching a good horror movie. The kind where the fear was real but the danger was not.

Now there was some pressure on her nipple. Brian continued to tighten whatever it was, and she began to sense the first hint of pain.

"Your job is to let me know when this becomes uncomfortable," Brian told her. There was something odd about his voice, something controlling and sexy.

"It's already uncomfortable," said Jenny. "But don't stop."

"Then tell me when you want me to stop."

"I will." She almost added "master", but that would've been taking things too far, and she wasn't sure she could say it without giggling or doing an Igor voice.

The pressure and pain increased as Brian continued tightening whatever was on her nipple. She was getting even wetter.

Just before it reached the point where she could no longer stand it, she invoked the rights she'd been given as a submissive: "Okay, stop."

He stopped immediately and turned his attention to the other breast, leaving the first breast locked in a state of glorious pain.

He did the same thing to her right nipple. First pressure, then pain. This time she let him tighten it two more notches before asking him to stop.

Oh this felt good!

And how wonderfully *naughty*. They weren't generally a kinky couple, but this certainly was a step in that direction.

Lick my pussy, she silently begged, hoping that she'd developed psychic abilities since being handcuffed to the bed. *I want your tongue there. I want you to bury your face between my legs. C'mon, lick my pussy, big boy.*

She trembled as she felt his tongue on her.

But it wasn't on her pussy, it was on her left breast. That was okay. It still felt fantastic.

He licked her breast all over, including the clamped nipple. He nibbled the underside.

Then he tenderly kissed her on the lips.

The pressure on her nipple lessened as he unscrewed the torture device. Relief flowed through her, as did further pleasurable sensations. It felt as good to have this thing removed as it did to have it put on.

Soon her breast was back to its normal, unadorned self. He kissed and licked and sucked it gently.

He removed the other clamp and did the same to her right breast.

Then he unfastened the handcuff binding her left wrist. No! They couldn't be done already, could they?

She whimpered in disappointment as he freed both of her hands, followed by both of her feet, but she didn't say anything.

Then he rolled her over onto her stomach, and snapped the handcuff back onto her ankle.

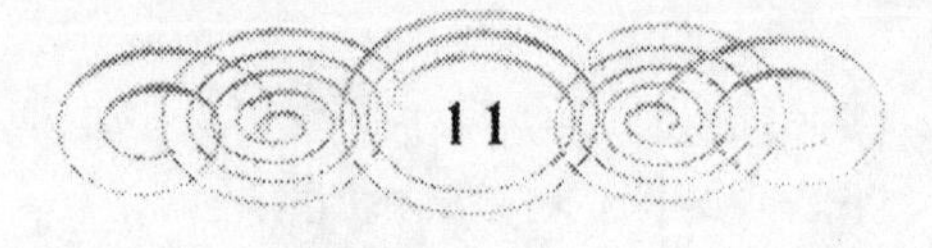

11

Within moments, she was restrained again. Brian stared at her, almost drooling. What a fantastic sight. His wife in black leather, face down on their bed. Well, their *mattress*, anyway.

"You want to spank her, don't you?" asked Mistress Charlotte in a whisper. He'd almost forgotten that she was there.

Brian nodded.

"It's okay, she wants to be spanked. Ask her."

"Have you been naughty?" he asked Jenny. It should have felt ridiculous to say that kind of thing, but it didn't. It felt like a perfectly normal thing to ask at this particular moment.

"Oh yes," she whispered.

"*Really* naughty?"

"Naughtier than you can imagine."

"Good girl."

Brian tore off the Velcro, exposing her beautiful ass. He wanted to grab it, knead the flesh, probe it.

"You two definitely aren't ready for a riding crop," said Mistress Charlotte. "I want you to use your hand on her. Spank her hard. Don't linger...pull your hand away immediately after each strike."

Brian hadn't known that there was an art to spanking, but apparently there were a lot of things he didn't know.

He gently ran his fingers over her ass. She flinched a bit at his touch.

He moved his hand away.

He could see her buttocks tighten, anticipating the first slap.

He waited.

Then gently let his fingers glide over her again.

Jenny whimpered as he moved his hand again.

He waited.

Then he spanked her ass, hard, on the left cheek. She let out a squeal that sounded like a mix of pain and sexual excitement.

He spanked her again, once more on the left cheek.

There was already a red hand mark forming.

"Do you like that?" he asked. Again, another statement that should have felt silly but didn't.

"Mmmm-hmmm..." she replied.

He spanked her right ass cheek.

Then the left.

With each strike of his palm, Jenny thought that she was getting closer to an orgasm. How the hell could you come from somebody spanking you? Why was she *enjoying* getting spanked? Really, she'd always thought that the whole spanking fetish thing was a joke, not something that real people enjoyed, but here she was, tied to the bed getting spanked, and loving every—

His hand struck her ass.

—second of it.

She wanted him to fuck her. She wanted him to crawl right up there on the bed and fuck her from behind. Not even unlock the handcuffs, just grab her by the hips, lift her up and thrust into her.

She wondered if his erection was still as hard. She wanted to see it. But she wanted to feel it even more.

He spanked her again. This time it made her wince, but she still didn't want it to stop.

And then his mouth was on her, soothing kisses on her stinging flesh, his warm tongue acting as a salve for her pain.

She felt herself relax. But not *too* much, because the love-pain could return at any moment.

His tongue slid all over her ass cheeks, warming her. She wanted him to probe deeper.

This time her desired psychic abilities seemed to work. His tongue slid between her ass cheeks, sending a shiver of pleasure through her that was so intense that for a moment she felt like she could rip the handcuffs right off the bedposts.

She didn't try though.

Had Mistress Charlotte left? Was she watching? Was this turning her on?

Jenny sighed. "That's so nice..." she said.

Brian caressed her buttocks while he licked. His gentle touch felt so good after the pain. If she weren't so incredibly fucking horny, his touch might even be enough to soothe her to sleep.

His tongue probed lower, and she lifted her ass, giving him better access to her pussy.

He slid a finger over her. "God, you're so wet," he said. "You're dripping."

Brian wasn't kidding. He had never seen his wife so wet before, nor even imagined that it was physically possible for her to *get* this wet. He slid his index finger into her and it was like sliding into warm oil.

He got to make the decisions.

He decided that he was going to lick her pussy until she came.

It wasn't the best position as far as neck comfort went, but he didn't want to have to switch her around in the handcuffs again, so he figured he could deal with it. He reached underneath her and carefully removed the piece of leather that was covering her pussy. This leather strip was definitely going to need a thorough cleaning. He lay sideways on the bed, pressed his face to her, and ran his tongue over her soaked pussy.

She cried out with joy.

Jenny's wetness covered his tongue. He licked her pussy all over, quick strokes, left and right. Her taste, her smell...all of it was wonderful.

"Oh God..." said Jenny, tightening.

"Don't let her come," Mistress Charlotte whispered.

Brian flinched as if somebody had set off a hand grenade next to his ear. He pulled his face away from Jenny's pussy and looked at Mistress Charlotte.

"Sorry to startle you, dear," she said. "But don't let her come. It's not time yet."

"It's *always* time to come!" Jenny insisted.

"Oh no, no, no. Patience, darlings. We still have more toys for this evening."

Brian grinned. Toys were good.

It briefly occurred to him that maybe it should bother him that this strange lady had just watched him go down on his wife, but it didn't, so screw it.

"How do you want her?" Mistress Charlotte asked, her voice still a whisper.

"On her back."

"Then make it happen."

Quickly and efficiently, Brian removed the cuffs, rolled Jenny onto her back again, and then cuffed her up. He looked at her glistening pussy and desperately wanted to put his mouth back there.

But Mistress Charlotte was right. It wasn't time for her to come. Her orgasm would be much more intense if he made her wait for it.

"Make her please you," said Mistress Charlotte.

That sounded like a perfectly good idea. Brian's cock was so hard that it almost hurt, and maybe Jenny's tongue could ease some of the tension.

He positioned himself directly over her head, his knees pressed against the undersides of her arms, and then slowly lowered his cock down toward her face, hesitating inches above her mouth.

She knew where he was and what he wanted. Her tongue protruded from her mouth, but it couldn't reach.

She whimpered in disappointment.

He lowered himself a bit more, just barely meeting her tongue. She licked with great passion, even though only the tip of her tongue could touch his cock.

After a moment, Brian took pity on both of them and lowered his cock into her open mouth. She sucked on it as if she'd been waiting to do this for years, head bobbing up and down, lips forming a tight seal, tongue swirling vigorously. Her mouth was so warm, so tight.

Brian closed his eyes and just let her suck on him, making his legs tremble.

She made happy moaning sounds as she sucked.

Brian felt like he could stay like this forever, but no, it was time to do the work himself. "Stop," he told her.

Jenny gave one last defiant swirl of her tongue and then stopped.

Brian slowly began to fuck her mouth. Her lips were still wrapped tightly around his cock, and he thrust as deeply as he knew she could handle.

Of course, with her mouth full like this, she couldn't exactly use the safe word or even push him away, so he made sure to stick with slow thrusts, nothing that could get out of hand.

He kept fucking her mouth until he felt like he was going to come. He was tempted to enjoy the release, to explode into her warm mouth, but no. She would come first. That was his official decision. No negotiation.

He pulled out of her mouth and scooted back on the bed. Mistress Charlotte appeared (not appeared, moved, but it sure *felt* like she appeared) next to him, a pair of golden ball bearings in her hand, about as big as regulation-size marbles.

"Put these in her," Mistress Charlotte said.

"Is that safe?"

Mistress Charlotte chuckled. "Yes, dear, of course. They won't get lost. And it will make her feel really good when you fuck her."

Brian took the golden balls from her, although now he could see that they were brass. He slid the first one inside of her, and Jenny gasped. She was so wet that it vanished immediately. The second one disappeared with equal ease.

Brian slipped his finger inside of her, pushing the brass balls farther inside, and then he began to rub his fingers against her vaginal wall, causing the balls to clack together with each motion.

"How does that feel?" he asked.

"Interesting."

"Interesting in a good way?"

"Oh yeah."

"Put them in deeper," said Mistress Charlotte. "You'll need more than your fingers."

Brian understood exactly what she meant. He mounted Jenny and effortlessly slid his cock all the way into her, pushing the balls as far in as they could go. He pulled out, his cock glistening. He wanted to fuck her some more, but wasn't sure he could maintain enough control at this point.

"Do you have other toys?" he asked Mistress Charlotte.

"Oh, of course. But how about a little liquid pleasure, hmm?" Mistress Charlotte handed him a very small bottle, no larger than his pinky, which contained a red liquid. "Put this on her. And then blow on it."

Brian removed the cork from the top of the bottle and poured a bit on his index finger. He gently blew on it, and the liquid warmed up immediately. Excellent.

He rubbed the liquid on Jenny's clitoris. She purred happily. He recorked the bottle and handed it back to Mistress Charlotte then placed one hand on each of Jenny's spread thighs. He leaned his face toward her pussy and exhaled a warm, slow breath on her clitoris.

Jenny reacted instantly. "Ohhhhh..."

Brian blew again, just as slowly.

"Oh it's so warm...so good..."

He continued to blow on it, sometimes making her wait for his breath, sometimes exhaling until there was absolutely no air remaining in his lungs. Jenny squirmed and gasped.

Then he licked her clitoris. Cinnamon.

"Oh!" Jenny cried out. "Oh God, yes!"

Brian went down on her, tongue lapping all over the surface of her pussy. He didn't care if there were more toys available or if he was supposed to be stretching this out further...he wanted her to come. He wanted to hear her scream with pleasure.

"It's not time yet," said Mistress Charlotte.

Fuck off, Mistress Charlotte, he thought as he kept licking.

"Oh fuck, I'm almost there!" Jenny announced.

Brian licked with even more enthusiasm. He reached up and

pinched her nipples as he licked, moving his entire face back and forth over her sweet pussy.

Then he felt a hand on his shoulder. He reluctantly pulled away and glanced at Mistress Charlotte.

"Brian...?" she began.

"Yeah?"

"I'll give you a freebie. Make her come."

Brian happily buried his face in Jenny's pussy, licking and kissing and sucking and completely immersing himself in her. Her juices covered his entire face and he absolutely loved it.

He licked and licked, finally giving his full attention to her swollen clitoris. He spiraled his tongue around it and then flicked his tongue across it, each flick causing Jenny's legs to twitch.

And when he knew she couldn't take it anymore, he licked it as rapidly as he could.

"I'm gonna come!" Jenny cried.

Seconds later, she did.

She screamed...literally screamed...and her entire body tightened. As she raised herself up, Brian reached beneath her and cupped her buttocks, lifting her to him.

"OH SHIT!!!" she screamed, twisting in his hands. And then there was a *snap*.

Brian looked up in shock.

She'd broken the chain on the handcuff that bound her right hand to the bedpost.

"How the fuck did you do that?" asked Mistress Charlotte, genuinely amazed. "My goodness! I haven't seen adrenaline like that in weeks!"

Jenny continued to flail around in orgasmic ecstasy. Brian quickly moved away from her, worried that he was going to get hurt.

It took her a long time to coast down from it. When she finally did, Jenny lifted up her wrist and shook it, jiggling the broken handcuff.

"Wow," she said.

"Wow is a good word," Brian agreed.

"Where did you get these handcuffs?" Mistress Charlotte asked.

"Paula's Pleasure Palace."

Mistress Charlotte nodded her approval. "They only sell top-notch merchandise there."

Brian looked at Jenny. "See if you can break the other ones." Mistress Charlotte slapped him on the shoulder.

"Everyone focus," she said. "Let's not allow Jenny's freakish burst of strength to take us out of the moment. Brian, fuck your wife. You know you want to."

Yes, he did indeed. Jenny happily spread her legs wider as he climbed between them and thrust into her.

Being fucked by Brian was always a fun experience, but doing it after such an intense orgasm and without being able to see a thing made the experience even more pleasurable. He thrust into her over and over. This wasn't romantic lovemaking, this was raw, bondage-style fucking, and it was good.

"Fuck me," she whispered. "Fuck me hard."

Brian kissed her lips as he thrust into her. She could hear and feel the brass balls knocking together inside her, and if he adjusted his position just a smidgen to the left she knew she'd be on her way to another handcuff-breaking orgasm.

"Move a bit to the left, darling," said Mistress Charlotte.

Whoa. How did she know to tell him to do that?

Brian moved a little bit to the left, hitting the absolute *perfect* spot and sending Jenny into yet another spiral of ecstasy. "Fuck me!" she shouted. "Impale me with that thing! Fuck me like your life depended on it!"

Brian thought that it would be pretty cool to be in a situation where his life depended on doing some really serious fucking. He slammed into her harder, loving the gasps that each thrust elicited, wanting to fuck her so hard that their bodies could never be pried apart.

His feeling of not having control over his own orgasm had passed. As far as he was concerned, he could fuck her like this all day and all night.

The bedsprings creaked. Brian wondered if this bed frame was used to such rough treatment.

He fucked and fucked, as hard as he could. He couldn't believe his endurance. Was this what Viagra was like?

Jenny screamed as another orgasm hit. Brian braced himself for her hand to break free of the restraints and accidentally club him over the head, but the handcuffs held firm. He continued to fuck her as she nearly wept in her bliss.

"Now, give her back some of the control," said Mistress Charlotte.

I still can't believe this woman is standing here giving me advice on how to fuck, thought Brian, but he didn't argue. While he continued thrusting into Jenny, he carefully removed her blindfold. Her wide-open eyes were wild with happiness. He tossed the blindfold aside, thrust into her a few more times and then pulled out. Mistress Charlotte handed him the key, and he quickly unlocked the remaining three cuffs.

As her last appendage was set free, Jenny shoved him onto his back. She mounted him and impaled herself on his cock. There was nothing gentle about the process...she began to fuck him every bit as hard as he'd fucked her, bouncing rapidly. He took her breasts in his hands and pinched the nipples once again.

"I love you..." Brian moaned.

Jenny smiled at him and didn't slow her frantic pace. They fucked like that for five minutes, maybe ten, before she lifted herself up off his cock, turned around and then started fucking him while facing the opposite direction, giving him a spectacular view of her ass.

He clutched her butt cheeks while she fucked him, squeezing them tight. Her ass slapped against him, over and over.

Okay, *now* he was starting to lose his sense of control.

This one was going to be a gusher.

Suddenly he had a desire, and he knew that he was treading on potentially dangerous territory by asking her to oblige it.

Maybe he should just come in her pussy.

No, he wanted to come on her, porn star style. Not in her face, but perhaps on her tits.

"I want to come," he gasped.

"Yes!"

"I want to come on your tits," he said, hoping she wouldn't be completely grossed out by his request.

She quickly dismounted his cock and then turned around to face him. She pressed her large breasts together, offering them to his cock.

Brian stood up and began to stroke himself. He was just about to come, so he pointed his penis at her breasts and gave it three or four quick, hard strokes.

He sprayed all over her, covering not just her breasts but her neck and leather-protected belly as well. He kept stroking himself, wondering how much he possibly could've stored up, practically drenching his wife in his seed.

None got on her face, though, which was good.

Finally he was done, and he collapsed on top of the bed.

Mistress Charlotte applauded.

"Good show, darlings!" she said. "Very good show!"

"Uh, thanks," said Brian, suddenly quite uncomfortable having her in the room.

"I'll go get you a warm wet towel," said Mistress Charlotte. "However, though you're welcome to ignore this observation if you wish, I do feel that as the person who is covered in ejaculate, it is entirely up to Jenny as to whether or not you two snuggle."

Jenny grinned and lay on top of Brian, covering him with his own stickiness. He let out a mock cry of disgust, and then they lay there together, laughing.

The warm, wet towel was much appreciated.

12

Minutes later, they'd changed out of their in-dire-need-of-cleaning black leather outfits and lay naked on the bed. Mistress Charlotte began to put her things in the duffel bags.

"Very good for your first lesson," she noted. "Brian, I hope that you'll learn to follow directions better, but still, you've done well. As I think I mentioned, the four-poster bed will stay until our lessons are complete."

"Thanks," said Brian. "I think we may go bed-shopping in the near future."

"An excellent idea." Mistress Charlotte glanced around the room. "Jenny, dear, I don't mean to be uncouth, but I'll need those pleasure balls back."

"Oh right. Be right back." Jenny got off the bed and hurried naked into the bathroom.

She shut the door behind her and looked at herself in the mirror. Wow, that blindfold had really fucked up her hair.

But that was okay. Nobody had perfect hair after those kinds of orgasms.

She spread her legs apart and squatted, waiting for the brass pleasure balls to drop out. Not the most dignified position she'd ever been in, but hey, neither was having sex with Mistress Charlotte in the room.

Oh my God. I had sex with Mistress Charlotte in the room!

She'd seen everything! Heard everything! She knew what kind of face Jenny made when she came!

She and Brian had become the kind of people who would have sex with somebody like Mistress Charlotte in the bedroom, giving instructions!

How had that happened?

And why didn't it bother her more?

She should be crawling under the toilet, her face burning with shame, but actually, she didn't feel all that bad. Yeah, it made her a little uncomfortable, but not *that* uncomfortable, and Mistress Charlotte had watched Brian lick her ass.

What kind of weird supernatural powers did this woman have? What variety of mind control did she exert over them? What the hell did *saurrus trumuna ransorum* mean?

And, what did it matter? She'd just had some of the best sex of her life. If Mistress Charlotte was the catalyst, then hell, she could grab Brian's cock and help guide it in!

Well, not literally.

She bounced up and down a few times, and the first pleasure ball dropped out onto the tile floor. She scooped it up before it could roll away, and then bounced the second one out as well. She decided that it was only polite to wash them off in the sink first.

"So..." said Brian.

"Yes?" asked Mistress Charlotte.

"Uh, nothing. Just thought I'd say 'so'."

"There's absolutely nothing to be embarrassed about, darling," said Mistress Charlotte. "I thought your first lesson went remarkably well. And believe me, I've seen infinitely more shocking things than what you did with your tongue."

"Well, that's good. I guess."

She sat down on the bed next to him. "Brian, you and Jenny are two of the most sexually compatible people I've ever known. I foresee that you two will be going at it hot and heavy when you're 98, pardon the visual. You just needed a gentle nudge, that's all. And that's what I was here for."

"To be perfectly honest, I think we just needed a different bed."

"No, you needed a nudge. Deal with it, dear."

"Okay."

Jenny emerged from the bathroom. She handed the two brass balls to Mistress Charlotte, who put them away in her duffel bag. "Thank you."

"No, thank *you*."

Mistress Charlotte stood up. "Well, I suppose I'll be going now. You two can discuss what happened, or have some more sex, or whatever strikes your fancy. And I'll see you next week, okay?"

"We're not sure yet," Brian admitted.

"Oh I think you will be." Mistress Charlotte reached into her pocket and handed Jenny a small card. "Don't be late."

Brian and Jenny looked at the card. In pink writing it said: *"You are invited to Mistress Charlotte's Bondage Ball. This Saturday night. Food, fun and kinky sex galore."* An address that Brian didn't recognize was on the back.

"This is for a very select group," said Mistress Charlotte. "It'll be fun. See you then."

Mistress Charlotte winked, picked up her duffel bags and left the bedroom.

"So, is it just me, or was this whole experience really bizarre?" Brian asked.

"It wasn't just you."

"Was that even us doing that? I mean, I *felt* like I was completely there, but would I really do that?"

"I don't know."

Brian took the card from her and looked it over. "We're not going to this Bondage Ball, are we?"

"Of course not."

"Good."

The following Saturday, they were in their car and on their way.

"We've gone mad," said Brian.

"Yes, we have."

"I guess there's nothing wrong with some good old-fashioned insanity," said Brian with a shrug. "Lots of historical figures have been insane. Like Edgar Allen Poe."

"Was he insane?"

"He looked insane. Creepy, anyway. And didn't we have an insane president?"

"Which one?"

"I'm not sure. One of the middle ones. Ah, it doesn't matter. I can't believe we're doing this."

Not only were they doing this, but they'd decided to do it with a minimum of discussion. On Saturday afternoon they'd simply looked at each other, nodded and went to the bedroom to change.

They weren't wearing black leather or anything like it. Jenny figured that if there were required uniforms they'd be provided at the door. Instead, she and Brian were dressed nicely but casually, as if going to a dinner party.

"I think I'm supposed to turn at the next light," said Brian, glancing down at the printout of the driving instructions they'd gotten off the Internet.

Jenny picked them up. "Yep."

"We can still turn back."

"We sure can."

"But we're not going to, are we?"

"I doubt it."

"We're sick."

"Yeah."

"Oh well."

There were a lot of twists and turns in the road, and for a long moment both of them thought they might be completely lost and miss the Bondage Ball altogether. But the driving instructions were ultimately correct, and they found themselves pulling into the driveway of a...

...run-down old shack.

"This can't be it," said Brian. "What was the address again?"

"29 Mistlette Road."

"Well, that's it, but...but that place sucks."

"Maybe being a bondage instructor doesn't pay as well as we thought."

"Yeah, but, I mean, if we tried to cuff somebody to the wall they'd pull the whole place down!"

There was one other car in the driveway. It was much like Brian and Jenny's...affordable but nothing fancy.

Brian pulled up behind the second one and shut off the engine. They sat there for a long moment.

"I guess we should go in. Maybe this is the wrong place. There might have been a typo on the card."

"Maybe."

"I guess we'll find out."

Brian and Jenny got out of the car and walked up to the shack. The door looked like Brian's hand might break through it if he knocked too hard, so he settled for a gentle little rap.

"Welcome, darling!" said a familiar voice on the other side.

The door opened, revealing a smiling Mistress Charlotte. To Brian and Jenny's complete lack of surprise, she was dressed in pink.

"Hi," said Brian. "We thought we might be at the wrong place."

"Oh no, no, no, you're exactly where you're supposed to be. Please come in!"

"It's not quite what we were expecting," Jenny admitted.

"Of course not, dear," said Mistress Charlotte. "That's because you were expecting a place that didn't look like complete crap. Come in, come in!"

They walked inside and froze.

The place was *much* nicer on the inside.

So much nicer, in fact, that it couldn't possibly be the same place. There were luxurious sofas, fine oak paneling, exquisite artwork and it was *way* too roomy.

"What the—?"

"Ask 'what the hell' later, darlings," said Mistress Charlotte, ushering them inside. "All will be explained."

Brian and Jenny walked inside. Another couple about their age sat on one of the sofas, looking a bit uncomfortable. "Brian and Jenny, this is Markus and Nancy," said Mistress Charlotte. "Markus and Nancy, Brian and Jenny."

"Pleased to meet you," said Brian, shaking Markus' hand. Markus was an attractive, well-built guy with a dark complexion, and Nancy was a petite woman with a short haircut and adorable blue eyes.

"Same here," said Markus. The four of them exchanged greetings and then Brian and Jenny sat down on the opposite sofa.

"Can I get you anything to drink?" Mistress Charlotte asked. "Water, fruit juice, soda, excessive amounts of alcohol?"

"Excessive amounts of alcohol is a good start," said Brian.

Mistress Charlotte nodded and walked over to the well-stocked bar. She returned moments later with a rum and Coke for Jenny and a gin and tonic for Brian.

"How did you...?" Jenny began.

"Save the how-did-you-know-what-kind-of-drinks-we-liked for later, darling," said Mistress Charlotte. She clapped her hands together. "So is everybody comfy?"

The four of them nodded.

"Good. Welcome to The Bondage Ball, a lovely affair so exclusive that only you four were invited. I'm so pleased that you showed up."

The four of them were silent.

"So, Jenny, how have things been since your lesson last week?"

"Uh, good, actually. Very good."

"How many times have you had sex since then?"

Jenny glanced over at the other couple. "I don't remember."

"Oh now, don't worry about Markus and Nancy. I've recently watched them engage in sexual intercourse as well, so we can all be open with each other. How many times?"

"Sixteen," said Jenny.

"Sixteen! That's an admirable number of sexual encounters. How many of them involved you being strapped to the bed?"

"Three."

"Three. Excellent. So you're using bondage as seasoning for your sex life but not the main course."

Brian raised his hand. "May I ask a question?"

"Certainly."

"Why is it so much bigger in here than this place looks from the outside? I don't mind admitting that I find it more than a little scary."

Mistress Charlotte chuckled. "Oh very well, let me explain things. First of all, nobody hired me. I arrived at your doorstep of my own doing."

"Oh," said Brian.

"I am, in fact, a sexual demon. My real name cannot be pronounced in your human tongue, and if you were to gaze upon my true form the flesh would melt off your skulls."

"Oh," Brian repeated.

"But that's neither here nor there. Suffice it to say that I have limited mind-reading and mind-control abilities, although I can use them only to influence your actions, not control them."

"Oh," said Markus.

"So anyway, darlings, my job on this silly ol' plane of existence is to help you reach your true sexual potential. In both of your cases, you were truly meant for the sexual partner you selected, but there was an element missing from your sex play: bondage. So my job was to teach you, encourage you, unleash your true sexual prowess. Is everything making sense so far?"

Jenny raised her hand.

"Yes, dear?"

"What was that part about you being a demon again?"

"Oh now don't think of me as a demon. Think of me as your own personal supernatural sexual assistant. Now, it's actually quite a bit more complicated than that. There are prophecies involved, cause-effect relationships that echo through the very fabric of time and a lot of that kind of stuff, but it's nothing that any of you need to concern yourselves with. Just pretend that I'm here to help you fuck better."

Nancy raised her hand.

"Let's not have any more questions quite yet," said Mistress Charlotte.

Nancy lowered her hand.

"Anyway, you all did exceptionally well in your first lesson, and in fact there is only one more lesson to go, after which I can release you to lives of unrestrained sexual bliss."

"Group sex?" asked Brian, glancing over at the other couple and blanching slightly.

Mistress Charlotte chuckled. "Oh no, no, though that would be a sight to see, I'm sure. No, all four of you were virgins until you met, and you will be happily boinking that one person until the end of your days. You're just going to have sex in the same room."

"Excuse me?" asked Jenny.

"Admit it or not, all four of you have always wanted to try having sex while watching another couple do the same. And so I'm here to make that happen. Once you've done that and had a splendid time, I will be removing myself from your life and memory and moving on to the next realm. Got it?"

"So your driver's license is fake?" asked Brian.

"Yes, dear."

"Oh."

The four of them sat there, somewhat uncomfortable. Mistress Charlotte clapped her hands. "All right, everybody on your feet. There's a great deal of fun to be had at this Bondage Ball!"

Nobody got up. Mistress Charlotte sighed. "You're going to make me use the spell again, aren't you? I hate using the spell."

"What spell?" asked Jenny.

"*Saurrus trumuna ransorum.*"

Suddenly Jenny felt extremely relaxed and more than a little horny. So what if Mistress Charlotte was some kind of supernatural creature? Who was Jenny to judge her based on whether or not she was human?

The four of them got to their feet. Jenny had to admit that she was more than a little excited. She never, ever would have said this to Brian, but she *was* very much intrigued by the idea of watching another couple have sex. It would be fun, like watching porn with really, really, really good reception.

"Let the Bondage Ball begin," said Mistress Charlotte, or whatever her real name was.

13

Nancy was the first to strip out of her clothes. She removed her blouse and handed it to her husband, revealing her lacy black bra. Then she removed that as well, showing off her small but firm breasts.

Don't get hard, don't get hard, don't get hard, Brian told himself. You only have erections for Jenny, you only have erections for Jenny, you only have erections for Jenny...

Markus got into the act as well, removing his own shirt.

Wow. Those two were actually going to get naked in front of them. They were actually going to *fuck*.

How freakin' cool!

Brian and Jenny looked at each other, shrugged and then began to remove their own clothes as well. Before too long, all four of them stood there, completely naked. Nancy had a nice, hairy pussy that was a nice contrast to Jenny's well-trimmed one.

"Oh don't we all look sexy?" asked Mistress Charlotte. "Well now, this is called the Bondage Ball, so we couldn't very well do it without some bondage, don't you think?" She clapped her hands loudly, and then Bruce and Warren stepped into the room.

"So are they, like, lesser demons or something?" Brian asked.

"No. They're from a temp agency." Mistress Charlotte addressed her servants. "Bring out The Racks!"

"Racks?" Jenny asked. "Are you sure that racks have to be involved?"

"No need to worry, dear," Mistress Charlotte assured her. "That's just a pet name." Within moments, Bruce and Warren returned, wheeling in a pair of upright padded doors. There were clamps at the top and bottom that looked suspiciously as if they might be there to bind one's hands and feet.

"Thank you, dears," said Mistress Charlotte, and the men left. "So those are The Racks. I think you'll quickly get the idea of what they're to be used for. Rest assured that they're perfectly steady and there's no chance of one of them toppling forward, which would, of course, diminish the sensual mood."

Brian wondered if she had earlier clients (could they still be considered clients if she was a sexual demon thing?) who got off on having The Rack topple over while they were attached to it. Probably. Lots of weirdos in the world.

"So, gentlemen, it's time to strap in your ladies."

Brian hesitated for a moment, but then took Jenny's hand and led her to the rack on the right, while Markus and Nancy took the left. Jenny obligingly raised her arms in the air, and Brian clamped them both into place.

"Give it a tug," he said.

Jenny did. She was held tight.

"Does it feel like this thing is going to topple over?"

"Nope."

"Good. Let's do your feet then." Brian crouched down and fastened Jenny's feet in place, then stood back up. "Are you comfortable?"

Jenny nodded.

"All right, gentlemen, step back and admire your handiwork," said Mistress Charlotte. Brian and Markus did as they were told. Brian had to admit that Jenny looked pretty damn good strapped to that thing, even if she wasn't wearing black leather.

"Don't feel that you have to avert your eyes," said Mistress Charlotte. "Brian, look at Nancy. Markus, look at Jenny. Admire their bodies. You won't be touching, but you can certainly gaze upon them. Markus, doesn't Jenny have lovely breasts?"

Markus looked at Jenny's breasts. Brian was surprised to find that he wasn't the least bit jealous. Markus nodded almost imperceptibly.

"Oh now, you don't have to be silent about it. Tell Jenny she has lovely breasts."

"I don't want him to kick my ass."

"He won't kick your ass," Mistress Charlotte insisted. "Will you, Brian?"

"No."

"See? Feel free to compliment her. Even if Brian *were* compelled to kick your ass, realize that both of you are completely naked, and the odds of him wanting to engage in physical contact are very remote indeed."

She had a point.

"Yes, she has lovely breasts," said Markus.

"Thank you," said Jenny, smiling.

"Now, Brian, return the favor. Compliment Nancy's breasts. I know you like them."

"Very nice breasts," said Brian with a polite nod. "You have my admiration."

"A little less of a wise-ass tone would be appreciated in the future, but that was otherwise fine," said Mistress Charlotte. "Okay, gentlemen, your wives are now affixed to The Rack and unable to resist your advances. The safe words remain the same. Have at it!"

Without hesitation, Brian walked up to Jenny and gave her a great big kiss. She responded passionately. When they finally broke the kiss, Brian stepped away and scratched his head.

"My, my, my. What to do, what to do?"

Jenny giggled. She'd never been so exposed in her life, and she knew that she should feel humiliated. But she wasn't. She didn't even *know* Markus or Nancy, hadn't even seen them until a few minutes ago, but she felt like she could trust them. She felt like everything would be okay.

And she really felt like watching Markus suck on his wife's breast, which is exactly what he was doing. Nancy, eyes closed, moaned with pure enjoyment.

"I'll have what he's having," said Brian, moving forward again and taking Jenny's breast into his mouth. He gently sucked on the nipple, feeling it stiffen under his tongue. He'd tasted her breast more times than he could possibly count, but it was always exciting, like having filet mignon for the very first time.

Both men switched breasts in unison.

The angle of the racks were perfect, allowing Jenny to watch what her dear husband was doing while seeing everything that the other couple was doing as well. She absolutely loved how he could make her breasts feel, and it was clear that Nancy was getting the same amount of enjoyment from her own attention.

Both of them moaned and sighed and savored the experience.

Jenny glanced around to look for Mistress Charlotte, but the woman seemed to have left. Oh well. No instructions were necessary, apparently.

The men simultaneously went back to the first breast.

Jenny felt herself getting wet. She wondered if Nancy was getting equally wet. She looked down and saw that Brian was fully erect. Markus' back was to her (nice ass on him) but she suspected that when he turned around she'd be greeted by the sight of a nice, firm erection.

One of the finest sights in the world, in her humble opinion.

Brian began to kiss a trail down her belly, running his hands along her sides as he did so. This time, Markus looked over to see what Brian was doing and then proceeded to do the same to Nancy.

As Brian kissed her navel, Jenny wanted to run her hands through his hair, but unfortunately her hands were clamped above her head. Oh well.

He kissed down past her navel, down, down, down, until he reached the top of her pubic patch. Then he kissed his way back up.

Markus, on the other hand, seemed perfectly happy with his projected destination and kissed his wife's pussy. Again, she seemed to be really enjoying it.

Jenny loved this sensation, which was quite a bit different from the lesson in their bedroom. She was certainly more exposed here, but she also liked being able to see what was going on, especially when she had a nice-looking naked couple to view. And though she had to admit that she enjoyed the feeling of being helpless, she liked that the attention she was receiving now was all tender and loving.

Not that she would necessarily *object* to a spanking later, but she did enjoy the tender/loving elements.

Jenny could only see the back of Markus' head, but it was clear from his movements and Nancy's reaction that there was some licking going on. *Good* licking, from all outward appearances.

Brian glanced over his shoulder at them then looked up at Jenny and smiled. "That looks like fun."

"Do you want to go join them? I bet two tongues would raise her fun level a few notches."

"I don't think there's enough room," Brian noted.

"Oh. What a pity. You'd better lick my pussy instead then."

"That sounds like a perfectly worthy substitute."

Brian kissed his way back down her belly, down, down, down... and this time he didn't stop at the top of her pubic patch. He kissed down to her vulva and then, yes, began to lick.

As usual, it felt great.

But somehow it felt even better getting licked while watching somebody else get licked, and also while being unable to move her arms and legs. Two very nice additions to the whole licking experience.

Brian licked her slowly, running his tongue all the way up and all the way down. Then he used his fingers to open her up further to him, so he could probe more deeply with his tongue.

She closed her eyes and sighed.

Then she opened them back up. What was she doing? There was a show to watch!

Markus was clearly doing an exemplary job with his own licking because Nancy looked like she was about ready to lose her mind. She wasn't even paying attention to what Brian and Jenny were doing, which Jenny thought was a trifle rude. She writhed and moaned and struggled against her own bonds, breasts heaving the entire time.

I've got better tits, Jenny thought, but then she immediately felt bad about her competitive nature.

Both women stood there, reacting noisily to the delightful oral sex that they were receiving. Jenny wondered if she should suggest that they race to see who got to reach orgasm first, but then decided that would be silly. And besides, Nancy had received a head start.

"Doing fine, doing fine," said Mistress Charlotte, appearing out of nowhere. Well, not *literally* nowhere, just appearing when Jenny hadn't realized that she'd re-entered the room. Of course, with Mistress Charlotte being a sexual demon creature, she very well may have appeared out of nowhere, but ultimately it didn't make any difference either way.

Jenny wondered why she wasn't absolutely terrified to be in the same room as the woman/creature. Helplessly strapped to The Rack, even.

Ah, she'd wondered about a lot of her own feelings lately. Best to just go with what felt right. And at the moment, what felt right was standing there letting her husband continue to do a marvelous job licking her pussy.

"Toys, anyone?" asked Mistress Charlotte. "I've got toys!"

Brian pulled his mouth away. "What kind of toys?"

"Fun toys, of course. I do have those brass balls from before, although since your wife is in a vertical position it's unlikely that they'll work as well. Actually, I was thinking of something more along the lines of nipple clamps and a riding crop."

Oh shit, thought Jenny.

"I know, I know, that seems a bit extreme, but you'd be surprised at how good a couple of nice whacks on the ass with a riding crop can feel. We won't do more than a couple, heavens no, you're not ready for that, but I think that two or three will suit you most nicely. Any objections?"

Jenny looked over at Nancy to see if she had any objections. Nancy shrugged. Jenny shrugged as well. "No, I guess not."

"Good." Mistress Charlotte stepped forward. "Gentlemen, clamp those nipples!"

Jenny let Brian tighten the screws even more this time. It was almost scarier having them applied when she could see what was happening, because it just didn't *look* like something that she should enjoy. But she did enjoy it. A lot. She couldn't see how tight Nancy's nipple clamps were, but Jenny suspected that her own threshold of pain was quite a bit higher than that of the other woman. Not that she was competitive, of course.

After the nipple clamps were affixed, Jenny and Nancy were released from their respective racks, given a couple of seconds to turn around and then bound back into place.

Jenny took a deep breath. "What if this hurts too much?" she asked.

"Don't worry, dear," said Mistress Charlotte. "I wouldn't make this happen if you weren't ready."

Mistress Charlotte handed Brian and Markus each a riding crop. Brian slapped his in the palm of his hand, testing it out. "Maybe this is too much," he said. "Maybe we should stick with just me using my hand."

Mistress Charlotte shook her head. "You're ready. Trust me."

"Are you sure?" He smacked his hand again and flinched. "It seems kind of painful."

"It's going to be okay, I promise," said Mistress Charlotte. "Just think about how horny she's going to be when you crack that across her ass."

Brian wasn't sure. He certainly wouldn't want that thing cracking against his own ass. Maybe this wasn't a good idea.

Markus took the riding crop and walked up behind Nancy (who, Brian noted, had an exquisite butt). "Are you ready for this?" he asked.

"Yes," Nancy said.

"Are you sure?"

"Yes."

"Good."

Markus smacked the riding crop against her bare ass. Nancy's wince of pain quickly turned into a giggle of pleasure.

Markus smacked her ass again. The same reaction.

Maybe it wasn't so bad.

Brian turned his attention to Jenny. "I know I'm supposed to be in charge here, but I'm gonna leave this decision up to you. Do you really want me to spank you with this thing?"

Jenny wasn't completely sure that she did. But she also had to admit that Nancy sounded like she was having a pretty good time.

"Yeah," Jenny said. "Yeah I do."

"Okay."

Jenny closed her eyes and waited for the impact.

She heard the *swish*.

And then a sharp pain as the riding crop connected. The pain quickly spread through her buttocks, and it was the best fucking pain she'd ever felt.

She wiggled her ass and practically gurgled with pleasure. "Do it again!" she begged. "Please!"

Another smack followed, this one harder than the first. Her pussy was instantly twice as wet.

Oh they were *definitely* going to have to get one of these rack things for their bedroom. Or maybe they'd go all-out and install their own dungeon.

"Again!" she demanded.

Another smack on the ass. Her eyes widened and she cried out.

"Excellent job, both of you," she heard Mistress Charlotte say, although her words seemed as if they were being spoken from a great distance away. "That's enough."

"It most fucking well is *not* enough!" said Jenny. "I want more! Spank my ass!"

"I believe you should continue to spank her ass," Mistress Charlotte suggested.

Another smack with the riding crop. Then another. Then another.

I'm gonna come. Holy shit I'm gonna come!

Another smack.

Jenny threw her head back and howled as the orgasm rushed through her. Though not as intense as the orgasms she'd experienced yesterday, this one was plenty sufficient. She came with a gasp that almost hurt her throat.

"Do you want another one?" asked Brian.

She shook her head. "No, no. I'm good. That was good."

"Did you...did you just come?"

She looked over her shoulder at him and nodded. "Uh-huh."

"Wow," said Brian, amazed. "That's...that's just...wow."

Jenny glanced over her other shoulder and saw that both Markus and Nancy were staring at her. *I won the race*, she thought with no small sense of pride.

Then Nancy looked at Markus. "Give me some more."

Nancy did not come from the riding crop activity, although they had a fun time trying to make it happen. Jenny's ass was now more than a little sore and she wasn't looking forward to sitting all day at work on Monday, but the orgasm had been more than worth it. The whole experience had been worth it.

"Again, my compliments to all of you," said Mistress Charlotte. "Gentlemen, you may set your wives free."

"Is that it?" Jenny asked.

Mistress Charlotte shook her head. "Almost. There's one small matter to take care of before I release you to the world."

"What's that?"

"There's still some fucking to be done, of course!"

Jenny and Nancy crouched side by side on their hands and knees, on a remarkably comfy mattress. Their respective husbands were behind them, thrusting into them.

Oh yeah. Nothing like good doggy-style sex after a nice ass-whipping. This is the life.

Brian had his hands tightly on her waist, which she always liked. Normally she would've liked him to squeeze her ass cheeks as well, but they'd do that some other time.

Jenny glanced over, enjoying Nancy's expression of ecstasy. That Markus could sure fuck. His rhythm, the power behind each pelvic motion, all of it top-notch. In fact, she almost felt compelled to compliment him on his excellent performance.

Oh hell, why not?

"Your husband has excellent technique," said Jenny to Nancy.

Nancy grinned as she continued being pushed back and forth by his vigorous thrusts. "Why, thank you. Your husband seems like he knows what he's doing too."

"Oh yes. I certainly have no complaints."

"Nor should you."

"I can't *believe* I'm having my performance critiqued like this," said Brian, without losing his rhythm.

"It's not being critiqued, it's being complimented," said Jenny, although one particularly nice thrust almost made it difficult for her to speak.

"That's right," Nancy agreed. "We weren't ridiculing or making suggestions for improvement, but rather focusing entirely on the positive."

"Which is all there is to focus on," said Jenny.

"Can you believe this?" asked Brian, turning to look at Markus.

Markus shrugged. "I'm just trying to stay focused."

The women giggled.

"I think we're not doing our job right if they can carry on a conversation like this," said Brian. "What say we make them forget how to even talk?"

"Sounds good to me."

"On three. One...two...three!"

Jenny squealed as Brian suddenly began to *slam* his cock into her, pulling her back by the waist to meet him. She heard the loud slapping sounds and moans as Markus did the same to Nancy.

Jenny wanted to make a witty comment using a really big word, just to mess with the guys, but they'd done their job. She couldn't speak. All she could do is moan. Loudly.

She accepted her lack of coherent verbal communication skills as Brian fucked her within an inch of her life.

When Markus admitted that he couldn't keep up the pace much longer, they switched positions. The men lay on their backs on the mattress, side by side, and the women mounted their respective spouses.

Brian's cock slid deep into Jenny and she settled into a slow rocking motion, a nice intermission from the frantic fucking. She watched Nancy ride Markus at an equally slow pace. She couldn't quite see her pussy sliding up and down on his cock, but Jenny was at least getting a softcore show, and it was exciting as hell.

Nancy glanced at her and winked.

Brian could clearly see everything, although he was being a good boy and alternating between watching Nancy getting fucked and Jenny getting fucked. Markus wasn't doing quite so well, keeping his eyes fixed on Jenny's body. Nancy didn't seem to mind, and Jenny *certainly* didn't.

The two couples had slow, relaxed sex for several minutes, speaking only in soft murmurs.

Then they switched positions again, this time with the women on their sides, facing each other, and the men doing them from behind. Markus held Nancy's left leg in the air, and Jenny could clearly see his large cock as it slid in and out of her pussy. It was quite a sight to see.

Brian threw his arm over Jenny's breasts as he thrust into her. Moments later, he changed his mind and moved his hand down to her pussy, stroking her wet clitoris while he fucked her.

Markus did the same thing to Nancy.

Jenny had to admit that there was great temptation to reach over and touch the other couple. Not in a tit-grabbing bisexual way, but she had an urge to put her fingers on Markus' cock, feel it as it slid in and out of his wife. It would be slick and wet, and feel just great.

She didn't act on it, of course. *Keep your hands to yourself, young lady.*

Nancy came first, her breasts swinging back and forth as she cried out. Markus, who had clearly been struggling to hold out until this moment as evidenced by his agonized expression, followed her immediately, and together they made serious contributions to the problem of noise pollution.

Jenny came a second time shortly after that. By now her ass was feeling good enough that she could lie flat on it, so she got on her back and let Brian do her in the missionary position. They kissed passionately as he came.

The two couples snuggled for several minutes until Mistress Charlotte entered the room.

"And that's it," she said. "There's nothing more I can teach you. Well, that's not accurate at all. There's plenty I can teach you. There's just nothing more I'm *going* to teach you."

"Will we ever see you again?" asked Nancy.

Mistress Charlotte shook her head. "I'm afraid not, darling. But you'll go back to your lives with a heightened sense of sexual awareness, an increased sense of adventure, a boost in your horniness. And thus the prophecy will indirectly be fulfilled, but like I said, you won't need to worry about that."

"How can we thank you?" Jenny asked.

"You can't, because once you leave here, you won't remember anything that happened. The lessons will stick with you, but you'll forget that dear old Mistress Charlotte ever existed."

"That sucks," said Markus.

"Yes it does, but though it does suck, it's part of the plan. Now get dressed. It's time to go home."

The four of them nodded, got up off the comfy mattress and put on their clothes.

"Nice meeting you, Markus," said Brian, shaking the other man's hand.

"Same here."

"I'd like to say that I hope we run into each other again sometime in the future, but I think we can both agree that it would be awkward and uncomfortable."

"Yes, I think it would."

"But have a nice life."

"You too."

Brian took Jenny's hand, and they walked toward the exit. Mistress Charlotte watched them, a subtle grin on her face.

"Thanks for everything," said Brian. "I won't lie and say that you weren't kind of creepy, but I really do appreciate everything you did for us."

"No problem," she said. "And I won't lie either. You really do have a nice cock."

"Thanks."

Brian and Jenny smiled and then walked out of the shack.

Epilogue

"Man, that party sucked," said Brian as they drove away. "That was probably the crappiest fruit salad I've ever had in my life. Why did we even bother to drive all this way?"

Jenny shrugged. "I don't even remember who invited us." She shifted uncomfortably in her seat.

"What's wrong?"

"Nothing. For some reason, my rear is kind of sore."

"Were you sitting on it funny?"

"No, I was not sitting on it funny. Must've been the couch cushion or something."

"My rear is fine."

"Yeah, well, I probably have a more delicate tushie." Jenny leaned over and gave him a kiss on the cheek. "Do you want to hear something really weird?"

"Oh yeah. I always want to hear something really weird."

"My butt is sore, but it feels really good too."

"Say what?"

"I don't know how to explain it."

"I think you've gone nutty."

"No, I've always been nutty."

Brian nodded. "Oh yeah, that's right."

"Maybe tonight you can give me a nice spanking."

"Oooooooh yeah," said Brian with a chuckle. Then he glanced over at her. "Are you serious?"

"Yep."

"You want me to spank you?"

"That's right. Maybe we'll even pick up a riding crop on the way home."

"That's just demented."

"But it sounds like fun, right?"

"Actually, yeah."

"And I also think we need to get rid of our old bed. We need a four-poster one."

Brian frowned. "I thought we already had a four-poster bed."

"No."

"Didn't we get one last week?"

"Uh, no, honey."

"I'm sure we did. I remember having it."

"I think your memory is screwy."

"That's strange. I really do remember us having a four-poster bed, and me using it to...actually, I can't remember now. I guess you're right."

"I'm always right."

"Yeah, sure, that old bed was getting kind of creaky anyway. It's time for a change."

"It's time for a lot of changes."

"Cool."

Brian and Jenny maintained their sex schedule for another month. Then they decided that the sex schedule seemed rather pointless, considering that they were having sex almost every night.

Their new four-poster bed cost way too much but resulted in countless hours of playtime. After Jenny snapped three pairs of furry handcuffs, they upgraded to a much better brand, which also cost way too much.

The riding crop earned a place of honor on the wall above their headboard.

And, yes, they lived happily ever after.

The End

P.S.: The prophecy ended up being completely fucked up by a moth being in the wrong place at the wrong time, but Jenny and Brian never found out about it.

DIANA HUNTER is the author of *Secret Submission.* She lives in St. Phelps, New York. Visit her website at www.dianahunter.net.

S. L. CARPENTER, a born and raised Californian, is a writer and cover artist. Visit the author's website at www.slcarpenter.net.

CHRIS TANGLEN writes sexy comedies for Ellora's Cave. Chris is a fan of energy drinks, red licorice, Gummi bears, and short walks on the beach.

9 781416 536185